Son of a Snitch

To Desiree
Thanks a lot
Stay Positive
Stay Strong
One Love
Michael
Em

Son of a Snitch

Michael Evans

MonteME Publishing

ISBN 10: 0-97427751-7
ISBN 13: 978-0-97427751-6
Library of Congress Control Number: 2005906730

Book production: Tabby House
Cover design: OspreyDesign
Cover art: Ariel Medel

A glossary of street terms is found at the end of the book.

MonteMe Publishing
Brooklyn, New York

Contents

Acknowledgments

First and foremost, I would like to thank God for giving me a chance to change my life.

To my mother who passed away January 28, 2004: I love you with all my heart and I know in heaven that you are watching over me and your children.

To my father: I love you and miss you so much. Keep watching over me with your wife up there in heaven.

To my sister, Carolyn: You are a positive and strong woman, so keep your head up.

To my brother, Kevin: You are responsible for your own life and one day when you are truly ready to make a change for the better, you will. Love always.

To my ex-wife, Susan: I thank you wholeheartedly for helping me with my transition from a boy to a man. I would not be a real man if I did not give props where props are due.

To my sons, Curtis and Michael: I love you both more than words can ever say. It always brings me a pleasant rush to my heart when you, Curtis, call me "Pops," and when you, Mikie, call me "Daddy." I think, *Man I'm a father.*

To Doug (who looks like Puffy to me): Sorry to hear about your losses. If you ever need to talk with someone who can identify with the feelings you are going through, just call. One love.

To all my friends and co-workers at the job: Thanks a million for supporting a fellow officer. When he was putting in work at the sally port, thanks for never blocking the writer. To Sergeant Watkins: Thanks for giving me all that jazz.

To the Boys Club on Hoe Avenue: Thanks for helping to save the children. Peace and love.

To Sidi, the man to see on the streets: You are a good person and I have so much fun working with you and your co-workers on 125th Street. Like you always say, "That's uh good."

I would like to thank my excellent editor, Linda, and her husband, Jim, for their support in making my second book a reality. Thanks for answering all my questions concerning writing, publishing and promoting. No nervous, no nervous.

To the bookstores, street vendors, radio stations, cable shows and printed press: Thanks for all your support.

To my 169th Street and Midtown family: The memories we share will last a lifetime.

To the Evans family: I love you all just because. Without your love, help and guidance, there would be no me.

To Bud: Some people say birds of a feather flock together, and in our case, they are right because we both are doers, not just talkers. You are my first cousin, my best friend and my confidant. I love you, man!

And last, but not least, to my fiancée, Tara: Thank you for all your love, support and patience. Whenever I asked you to do something pertaining to this book, you never said no. One day I hope to reciprocate all the things you have done. Love always.

My son said, "Yo, Pops, they ain't ready for this one!"

Introduction

When I started writing *Son of a Snitch*, my mother was in a nursing home, dying of numerous illnesses. I was trying to figure out a way not to let her spend her last days there.

Her doctor told me that the only way I would be able to sign her out of the nursing home was if I paid for a team of nurses and home health aides to provide twenty-four-hour care on the outside.

I knew that would take a lot of money because there was no time frame for when she might die; it could be months or years. I knew that coming up with the needed money was not going to be easy. But, even though I was just a working stiff and not rich like some professional sports figures or entertainers, I had to find a way.

One day my mother looked at me and said, "Mike, when are you going to get me out of here? I want to go home."

Looking into her sad eyes, I vowed to her that the book I was writing would provide the money to get her home. She believed me one hundred percent. My first book, an autobiography titled *It was all in the Cards: The Life and Times of Midtown Mike*, was written to purge all the garbage out of my system and possibly help someone avoid my mistakes. This, my second, attempts to get the attention of readers so they will listen to me in my third book.

1

One Dollar Don't Holla

"Tonesha, here's a dollar for you. Little Jimmy, here's a dollar for you—and I betta not catch you buying those fake cigarettes or no toy gun. Yo, Chauncey, ain't this little yellow nigga right here Lorenzo's son?" said Howie Tee, the local drug dealer.

"Yeah, Howie, that's his seed," said Chauncey.

Howie Tee motioned for eleven-year-old Jessie to come closer. Jessie smiled from ear to ear because he was expecting to get a dollar just like the other kids, so he stepped to the front.

Slap, slap, slap.

Howie Tee slapped him so hard that he left a big hand print on the side of Jessie's face; his light-skinned complexion made it more noticeable.

"Now, shorty, get your little beggin' ass outta my face and go get some money from your snitch-ass father in prison," said Howie Tee.

Howie Tee and everybody standing by the corner grocery store busted out laughing hysterically as Jessie ran off crying and rubbing his bruised face.

He ran without stopping to the town house on Strivers Row on West 138th Street, and feverishly pounded on the lacquered wooden front door shouting, "Ma, let me in, let me in."

His sister, Crystal, rushed out of her room and quickly opened the door, wondering why Jessie was yelling.

A flustered and sweaty Jessie, with tears in his eyes, hurried inside and screamed, "Where's Ma, where's Ma? That nigga Howie Tee just slapped me and called Pops a snitch."

Crystal identified with her brother's pain and anguish. Ever since their father dropped a dime on his drug crew a few months earlier, she had to suffer snide remarks and dirty looks from people on the streets.

Recently the situation had escalated. Jessie was physically abused on the streets, and their father, who used to protect his family from harm, was in prison doing twenty-five years. Lorenzo had refused to let the children visit him there. It was hard on Crystal so she acted like her father was dead.

After asking Jessie the details of what had transpired, she felt his spirits needed to be lifted.

"Jessie, let's play house," said Crystal, smiling.

Jessie, surprised, said, "Didn't you tell me just last week that we were too old to be playing house?"

At the time Crystal said no ten-year-old girl and eleven-year-old brother should be playing such a game at these ages. Every time the two of them did, it always turned into a humping session, which made her feel funny afterwards.

"Yeah, Jessie, I said it but I don't see nothing wrong with playing the game one last time."

While she was talking, a little more than Jessie's spirits started lifting in his pants. The big grin on Jessie's face that showed all his pearly white teeth told Crystal all she needed to know. He wanted to do the damn thing.

"But, Crystal, where's Ma at?"

"Oh, she went to see Pops at the jail; she won't be back for a few hours," said his sister.

When Jessie and Crystal's eyes met, they knew immediately what the other was thinking.

That this time they could play house and have the whole town house to themselves. So they went to the kitchen, where Crystal faked cooking dinner for her "husband."

Crystal, trying to sound grown said, "I been cooking this delicious steak dinner for you all day."

Then she passed Jessie a big bowl of Frosted Flakes. Jessie played along, "Thanks, baby. I have had a hard day at the office, and I'm real hungry, sweet cheeks," said Jessie.

Then with a smirk on his face, he looked at her nice butt that seemed to be getting bigger every day. Crystal just smiled as they ate their "big dinner."

After they finished, Jessie rubbed his stomach and said, "Boy, that sure was good, honey. You really did your thing. That was good. Now all we have to do is take a shower and go to bed," said Jessie, grinning as he got up from the table.

This caught Crystal by surprise, because they had never taken a shower together. Then she thought, *What the heck*, being that this was going to be the last time they played house. They went to the bathroom, where they took off their clothes and got into the shower.

As soon as they stepped in the bathtub, Jessie put soap all over Crystal's body. She became aroused from the way he was touching her. Next thing they knew, they were kissing and humping on the bathroom floor, which led to both of them losing their virginity.

Afterwards, Crystal felt kind of funny and ashamed. She reminded her brother that this was the last time they would play house. For real, for real.

But when Crystal got a taste of real sex, she wanted more. And little did Jessie know that this would be something that they would continue to do for many years to come!

It would be their little secret.

2

Little Devil

While sitting in the town house on Strivers Row, Jessie's mother's best friend, Sheila, said, "Kathy girl, that boy of yours is a little terror on the streets. He was out there fighting the other day and like ta killed a little kid for just talking to his sister."

"Well, the kid must have been messing with Crystal," said Kathy as she reached in the kitchen cabinet for instant coffee.

"Nah, the kid was just talking to her," said Sheila.

"Maybe so, girl, but the question then is, what was the kid saying to my child? Let me hip you to something a lot of people on the streets been messing with my children and calling their imprisoned father a snitch," said Kathy, tapping her fingers on the table.

"Yeah, I heard that poor-excuse-of-a-man Howie Tee slapped Jessie around and all the kids were laughing at him," said Sheila.

Kathy said, "And I had Red pay his stupid ass a visit and put the fear of God in him. Sheila, I am so worried about Jessie because he has not been the same person since the day I got arrested and all that feds' drama started. Jessie used to be an honor student. Now his grades are down and he's getting into fights, talking back to me and being very disrespectful."

Sheila, noticing Kathy's eyes tearing up, got up from a chair at the kitchen table, walked over to her best friend and placed a comforting hand on her shoulder. She said, "Don't worry, girl. Everything's gonna be all right 'cause your kids got a strong momma."

Kathy hugged her friend and smiled as she got up to pour the boiling water in their cups.

3

Payback is a Bitch

A few months earlier . . .

"Sad to say, but once uh-gain we are gathered here ta-day in the house of the Lord to pay our hum-ba respects to a good man, a working man, and a true fam-lee man," said Pastor Lee, commencing a funeral service for Mohammed at Abyssinian Church.

"Hey, Mary, I been looking all around the church since we got here and I haven't seen Lorenzo. All the other SSJ Crew members are here—Dee Boy, Country, Reno, and everybody else. If he don't pay his respects that would be real foul," said Pat.

"You sho is right, girl. Lorenzo should be here. Mohammed been running with that damn SSJ Crew for a long time. Word on the streets is whoever ran up in Mohammed's house and killed him tortured and molested his wife, Diane, and young daughter. They still in St. Luke's Hospital," whispered Mary.

While the two gossips talked in church as Pastor Lee droned on, on the other side of town Lorenzo and Red were at a jam-packed DJ Funkmaster Flex Car Show at the Jacob Javits Center. The latest and top-of-the-line vehicles—Bentleys, F430 Ferraris, Cadillac Escalades—were being showcased. Lorenzo and Red stood next to a 755 BMW watching their plan to rid the world of the two guys who killed Mohammed being put into motion.

"Whoa, that's real nice, real nice," said Tony, one of the murderers.

"Yeah, buddy, that Maybach is looking real proper and it cost major paper," said Chip, the other, as he eyed the expensive automobile.

"Nigga, I ain't talking 'bout no damn car. You must be blind if you don't see that beautiful honey wit' that fat ass and those big ta-tas," said Tony, looking fly in an Akademiks spanking white shirt and new tan Timberland boots.

"Tony, you right, and I must really be slipping. I should have figured out yo horny ass wasn't talking about no cars," said Chip.

"Forget all that, nigga, I bet you five hundred dollars I could bag home girl," said Tony. He was in the mood to trick some of the money from their robbery on a beautiful young lady.

"I'll fade that bet and you ain't said nothing, you bag shorty and I'll even give you a thousand dollars," said Chip, rocking a dead man's $25,000 Jacob diamond pendant and trying to sound like a big baller.

Lighting a big Cuban cigar, Tony looked at his partner in crime, nodded, then headed in the direction of the object of his desire.

Unbeknownst to the two sheisty guys was that they had just entered the twilight zone of a sinister plan set up by Lorenzo and Red for them violating and killing a loved and trusted SSJ Crew member.

A year earlier Mohammed had gotten out of the drug game on his own terms, money right, mind right and family life right. Even the SSJ Crew members were really happy for him.

But just when Mohammed thought he was out, the nasty side of the drug game showed its ugly head. A beautician who worked in Mohammed's wife's beauty parlor was jealous of her because she was not business-oriented enough to

21

own one herself. The beautician's jealousy had a close companion called Murda.

Murda Tony, who had a teardrop tattoo on the right side of his face, and his mentally challenged partner Chip, were stickup artists whose specialty was robbing drug dealers, rappers and rich homosexuals. At first, when the beautician broached the subject of them robbing Diane, they wanted nothing to do with it because the intended target were connected to the notorious and vicious SSJ Crew. But through the beautician's unrelenting determination, she prevailed and convinced the stickup artists to put their fear aside. The sheisty trio then decided that since they were going to do the damn thing, why not go all the way and rob Mohammed, too.

After kidnapping Diane from her beauty parlor on a Friday night, they proceeded to her house in the Riverdale section of the Bronx. During the robbery things got out of hand when Tony and Chip humiliated Mohammed and his family by stripping them naked. Then Chip molested Mohammed's young daughter.

Chip's sick actions put Mohammed over the edge because he had been complying with their demands by giving them $226,000 dollars from a safe. Mohammed's failed attempt at grabbing Tony's gun cost him big time. Tony shot him dead and then helped Chip finish molesting and torturing Mohammed's family.

In Lorenzo and Red's book, the only proper punishment for such despicable and violent behavior was cruel murder. The beautiful female whom Tony and Chip had their eyes on had been recruited by Lorenzo and Red to use as bait to lure the two fiendish individuals.

Her name was Shelly, but people in the hood called her Shells because of her propensity to bust her guns. Any man who came in contact with Shells was mesmerized by her pretty face, ample breasts, bodacious ass, and superior intellect. Shells was more than happy to be of assistance in helping two friends she highly respected, get some serious payback.

As Red and Lorenzo stood by the dark burgundy 755 BMW, they watched Tony head over to Shells who was faking like she was checking out a money green Maybach.

Tony tapped her on the shoulder and said, "Hey, lovely lady, I just put in an order for this same car you're admiring, and how would you like it if I gave you the first ride around the big city when I pick it up?"

Shells almost laughed at his weak game, but she smiled and said, "That would be real nice, I'd love to ride shotgun with a handsome guy like you."

"Okay girl, but for now if it's all right with you, would you mind having a drink at the bar, 'cause me and my boy over there are going to get a drink on."

When they looked over at Chip, he smiled with a devilish grin.

"Sounds like a plan. I'm kind of thirsty myself. But I must warn you, alcohol makes me freaky," said Shells as she added some extra swish to her step. Tony acted like he just hit the lottery.

From afar Lorenzo and Red watched as Tony and Chip tried to get Shells drunk by buying bottles of champagne and Bacardi Limon. Shells let them do most of the drinking, but acted like she was drunk and down for everything, even a threesome.

After about an hour of drinking, Shells convinced them to finish their party at her house in Yonkers. On the way there in her Lincoln Aviator, Chip and Tony were so preoccupied with touching and feeling her that they never noticed Red's Jaguar following two cars behind.

Lorenzo fiddling with a silver Glock on the passenger side said, "Red, I still can't believe Mohammed is dead. He would give the shirt off his back if asked. I cringe at the thought of what he endured the last day of his life, and at what those two slimy bastards did to his family. But be rest assured the repercussions for their serious violations won't be minimal. It's gonna be slow and painful."

While gripping the wood-grain steering wheel and with a mean look on his face, Red nodded and said, "Patience is a virtue."

Whenever Lorenzo and Red had to resort to violence their gangster mentality and rhythmic ebb and flow were so in sync, fools never stood a chance when it came down to them putting the finishing touch on a death sentence.

"Welcome to Shells's hot and steamy pleasure trove, where things get hot and sticky," said Shells as they entered her beautiful home.

Chip laughed hard when Tony slapped Shells on her bodacious ass that jiggled like Jello in her tight red spandex.

Tony had slapped her hard because Shells had squeezed his ass on the way to the bar at the car show. It reminded him of the time a woman stuck her finger up his ass during sex and he gave her a vicious beat down.

"Pretty Tony, with big hands like that you must be packing something long and strong in them baggy jeans you got on, big boy," said Shells, flipping on a high-tech Bose stereo and taking off all her clothes while doing a freaky dance. She exposed a banging body to die for.

Shells' big tits and ass blinded Tony and Chip to the big drama Red and Lorenzo had in store for them. This party had an open door policy and the SSJ Crew members were definitely invited. And being such nice guys, they were bringing a brown bag packed with extra goodies.

Naked Shells slithered like a snake over to Tony feverishly gyrating to Tupac's "How Do You Want It" blasting through the speakers.

Shells whispered to Tony while doing her dance, "Let's play a game called stop and frisk." Then she quickly tapped Tony's jean pockets and grabbed his crotch.

This took Tony by surprise, making him blush like a little boy, and Chip, who was sitting on a plush velour green couch smoking a blunt laughed his head off.

"Pretty Tony, I think I made a big mistake," said Shells.

Tony said nervously, "What do you mean?"

"Pretty Tony, tell me something, because I don't feel a thing. Where's the beef at, honey?" said Shells, looking dead serious as she felt around his crotch area.

Chip laughed so hard he almost pissed on himself.

Tony, at a loss for words and really not knowing what to say to Shells said, "Stop playin', boo, stop playing." His small ego was so depleted that he headed straight to a mini bar in the living room to get a stiff drink. Before he could make it there, Red and Lorenzo were standing in the room holding silver Glocks and a small brown leather satchel containing acid, razor blades, nails, hammer, a sharp knife, molasses and oranges. During a prison bid, a Russian inmate had told Red about the many household products that could be used for torture. Red, having knowledge of this sort of information, had always been real helpful when he needed special treats for special occasions. This was one of them.

Tony's and Chip's screams did nothing to stop Red and Lorenzo from giving them their just desserts. In the "rip the toes and fingernails off" part of the session, Red was truly amazed by Lorenzo's unique skills and thought he had all the makings of being a good pedicurist and manicurist. The only thing that threw Lorenzo off a bit was when Chip started screaming, "Oh my God, dear weezy, please help me!"

The "weezy" part sounded real familiar to Red and Lorenzo because it came from the old television series *The Jeffersons* that they used to watch. The two fiendish individuals were asking to be put out of their misery by the time it was all said and done. Red and Lorenzo granted their wishes.

4

Cops' (ER) Fund

Red spotted an old lady while he and Lorenzo stood on 149th Street.

"Mrs. Daisy, how are you feeling today? Every time I see you, you look prettier than ever. That husband of yours must be one happy fella," said Red to the old lady who looked every bit of her eighty-plus years.

"Oh, I'm all right, Robert. You sure know how to butter up a sista," said the gray-haired Mrs. Daisy. She smiled as she admired his cream-colored Panama hat with a red band. She always called Red by his government name.

"Nah, gal, I ain't shucking and jiving, Mr. Harris betta hope I don't start acting like I'm Harry Belafonte and snatch you off your feet. By the way, let me help you across the street with those bags," said Red, reaching for the straps.

As Red helped the old lady, Lorenzo just smiled, thinking about how his best friend treated everybody, especially the elderly, with kindness and respect.

Red could be the nicest person in the world until someone tried to take his kindness for weakness and disrespect him. Then they would see a whole different side of the person, whose facial expressions would never reveal what he was really thinking. If someone got it twisted, their mistake could possibly turn into the last one he made.

Lorenzo admired the fact that Red had the ability to

transform himself, like a mild-mannered David Banner turning into the Incredible Hulk. And the punishment he was capable of inflicting could be more devastating than the other comic book hero, The Punisher. Red could be the judge, jury, and executioner at the drop of a dime.

Lorenzo thought it sure felt good to have a brother like that in his corner, because the street corners that they had on lock had to be held down and watched over like a money vault on Wall Street, due to the keys that the SSJ Crew moved.

On the mean streets, there are always coldhearted thugs looking to take the place of the head niggers in charge.

As Lorenzo watched Red talk to the old lady, his mind drifted to the time some stupid nigga on 112th Street tried to extort the SSJ Crew. Looking back, it all seemed kind of funny to Lorenzo because the guy had tried to extort the extorters. What was even more pathetic was the guy's ignorance in thinking that a ten-year bid in prison for murdering a drug dealer translated into the streets owing him something. He got paid in full: a bullet in his head for every year he spent in prison. Lorenzo thought killing the guy was not his rude awakening. Nobody wakes up after the murder game has been laid down. Lorenzo knew that dead men tell no tales and that chump would never get a chance to tell the streets that he took anything from the SSJ Crew.

Lorenzo always got a big adrenaline rush after the fresh kill of some fool. That feeling made him think something was seriously mentally wrong with him. He always wondered why he got such a thrill from taking another person's life. He thought maybe it had something to do with not caring about his own life—hating himself. But that crazy feeling changed when Kathy had their two kids.

Lorenzo looked at life differently. Now, whenever the murder game had to be laid down he later had disturbing thoughts of making some poor kid grow up fatherless. It tore him up thinking that because of him, another kid would

27

endure the same pain and suffering that he did. Even so, he still was not going to let fools take advantage of him or anything he held dear.

Holding on to the SSJ drug empire fell into that category. God help the person that even looked at his best friend, Red, wrong. Since the day they became friends, they have had each other's back to the fullest.

The SSJ Crew had a ten-year strong run with just a few minor problems that were handled quickly.

They already had the nice clothes, jewelry, expensive cars, houses, beautiful females, and loads of money but chose to stay in the game because of all the worshiping and adulation from other people.

Years ago, Lorenzo realized that he would never leave the drug game.

While Lorenzo smoked a blunt and Red talked to the old lady, a black Crown Victoria pulled up next to him.

Detective Kennedy and his partner, O'Grady, both got out the vehicle with stupid grins on their faces.

"Lorenzo, don't be shy. Come over here and have a nice chat with your friendly neighborhood po-po," said a laughing Detective Kennedy.

Lorenzo faked like he did not hear him and tried to walk off but the other detective, O'Grady, stepped in his way.

"Hey, my man, you must be deaf or in a rush. You heard my partner," said O'Grady.

Lorenzo stopped dead in his tracks and said, "What y'all niggas want? 'Cause I'm on my way to church and, yes, I'm in a rush."

Detective Kennedy laughed so hard that Red heard him across the street where he stood watching the action.

"Damn, Lorenzo, you sure are one funny dude. Maybe you and I can make one of those good cop and funny criminal movies. We can make a killing. But first we got to work on your acting," said Detective Kennedy.

Then he got serious. "Now, cut the crap and put out the smoke. I could take you in and run you through the system, but I'm gonna cut you a break due to the fact the Police Department has a new protocol called CPR—Courtesy, Professionalism, Respect. This means we have to be nice to the public," said Detective Kennedy, sarcastically, making his muscle-bound, red-faced partner laugh.

"Hey, O'Grady, you think we should tell our good pal, Lorenzo, about our own little secret protocol for rich drug dealers," said Detective Kennedy, after he finished laughing at his partner's CPR nonsense.

Lorenzo angrily stood there waiting for their next round of gibberish.

"Yeah, Harry, let me school our good friend 'cause the sorry look on his face tells me he can't wait to hear our proposal. Lorenzo, you and the SSJ Crew been having a nice long run with all the product *y'all* been selling with *y'all* illegal neighborhood drug program. Now, don't you think it's about time that *y'all* share some of the wealth with New York's finest two detectives?" said Detective O'Grady, mocking Lorenzo, not waiting for a reply.

"Starting next week, my partner and I will be expecting a 10,000 dollar-a-week donation to, let's call it our ER Fund, meaning our early retirement fund. Man, ain't that something? The department wants us to do CPR and this poor guy winds up dealing with the ER. Both detectives laughed.

Lorenzo wanted to tell them both to kiss his black ass, but he sternly kept his mouth shut and listened to their stupid comments.

"Mr. Resident Drug Dealer, you can stand here and play dumb, if you want to, but even a stupid guy like you can figure out that our little proposition is in the SSJ Crew's best interest. And besides, you help us out, and we'll make sure that you'll stay in business. Get my drift?" said Detective O'Grady, as he and his partner got in their dirty vehicle and sped off.

As they pulled off, Lorenzo yelled, "Suck a fat dick," as he grabbed the crotch area of his blue linen pants.

Red walked up to him and said, "Man, what those two chumps want? Something tells me it can't be nothing good."

Lorenzo relit his blunt, took a long pull, then passed it to his homeboy and said, "Well, man, if we don't start paying New York's finest 10,000 a week, they said they gonna make things a little difficult to conduct our business out here."

"Maybe we need to entertain their offer, 'cause they could jam us up big times, and you know those two stupid crackers play for keeps," said Red.

"Man, fuck those pussies, I ain't giving them a dime, and if they keep fuckin' with the kid, them motherfuckers will be getting a real retirement," said Lorenzo, as he looked at the time on his diamond-bezeled Presidential Rolex watch.

"Lorenzo, I'm just saying maybe we need to seriously think about this and not just brush it off," said Red, with a concerned look on his face.

Lorenzo, took a pull of the potent chocolate weed, blew zeroes with the smoke, and said, "Fuck them niggas."

5

Slip, Slap, Jammy

Red was totally pissed off at his partner in crime and decided to give him a piece of his mind.

He found Lorenzo standing on 155th Street by a new car, the same model and color they had been next to at the car show. "Lorenzo, you must think it's sweet out here. How many cars can you drive? So what it's a 755 BMW, when our assess wind up in prison because of all the attention it's gonna bring? That damn car won't be able to fly us out of there."

"Man, Red, why you always messing with me? Can't a brother live some time?" said Lorenzo, wiping the shiny dark burgundy hood of the BMW even though it was spotless. Red was always trying to correct Lorenzo when he thought he was doing something wrong, but he did it with good intentions because of his genuine love for him.

"You know why? Because this here black man's wish ain't about getting out of prison when some futuristic Jetson shit has become a reality. Do you feel me on that?"

"Yeah, homey, but like I said, can't a nigga live some time?" said Lorenzo, smiling as a pretty female stared at them as she passed by.

As partners, they had both made millions in the drug business. The difference was that Lorenzo spent money as fast as he got it, while Red saved and invested.

"You see that's the problem. You been living too good lately and you've forgotten how much shit we been through to make it this far. I just don't want us to get too relaxed and blow it all on some ignorant bullshit," said Red, staring hard at his best friend, as the sparkle from Lorenzo's champagne-colored two-karat diamond earring nearly blinded him.

"Man, can we talk about something else, said Lorenzo.

"Renzo, you still my nigga, even if you don't get no bigga," said Red, playfully punching Lorenzo on the shoulder.

Red's old school sayings always broke the tension whenever they would start getting too deep, and what he just said had them laughing.

Lorenzo loved the times when he saw a smile on his best friend's face, because Red's personality and demeanor was mostly serious, like that of actors Morgan Freeman or Ving Rhames. Red was a very light-skinned guy with strong features. He sported a Caesar haircut and would be considered handsome in any person's book, but his menacing eyes said: "Come in peace or leave in pieces."

"By the way, Renzo, how's that pretty wife of yours, and those two beautiful kids?" said Red, digging in the pockets of his cream-colored linen pants as he searched for a piece of chewing gum.

"Well, everybody is doing fine. Jessie is knocking out all the other kids in his weight division up at Gleason's Boxing Gym. He said Mike Tyson was by there the other day and seen him in action. Kathy and Crystal, well they're all right, and if I can help it, my kids ain't 'gon get caught up in this thing of ours. That's why I keep them focused on going to Catholic school and getting their educations. Ain't nothing good on these here streets. One of the reasons I made sure I moved my family out of the PJs, like the Polo Grounds across the street, is because they're breeding grounds for drama."

Lorenzo thought the projects was some fool politician's

idea of keeping a whole bunch of struggling minorities confined to specific ghetto areas where they could be watched and kept away from all the Caucasians and big power brokers. And when the security cameras were put up, the saying about big man is watching became a reality, for real, for real.

Although his family now lived on Strivers Row, a prestigious section of Harlem on West 138th Street, where doctors, stockbrokers, and entertainers also resided, he still could not keep his kids away from the PJs. To them, that was where all the fun and excitement went down all day, every day.

Lorenzo tried hard to keep his street business away from them, but the streets talk and his name happened to be ringing bells throughout the hood. Word traveled fast when somebody got a little something and everybody else got nothing.

Ever since Kathy became his wife, and they started having children, Lorenzo wanted better for his family. Drugs, extortion, kidnappings, murder and other ghetto drama can do that to a person.

Lorenzo could have easily moved his family out of Harlem years ago when the SSJ Crew blew up. But no other place made him feel like he belonged more than Harlem. Harlem was becoming prime real estate, and even white people were moving in. Regentrification, some say good, some say bad.

Sometimes Lorenzo liked to reminisce about "back in the days"—how Lorenzo met the love of his life happened in the most peculiar set of circumstances. He had gotten into a fight over a dice game and knocked a guy out cold.

Instead of walking off diddy bop in a brawler's ego, Lorenzo had to add a finishing touch to something that was already finished by stomping out the guy then waking him up with a vicious elbow thrust to the throat. He looked up and thought he saw an angel.

Looking right at him with pure disgust was the prettiest girl he had ever laid eyes on. At that moment, he felt real sorry, not for the guy, but for the female who bore witness to his horrendous act.

For some strange reason, he had the urge to apologize to her because he felt like a kid who had gotten caught by his mother with his hands in the cookie jar.

While everybody who observed the fight looked on, he walked up to her and apologized for his actions. After that day, they were inseparable.

Lorenzo liked Kathy so much because she was the only girl who did not act like he was an evil monster.

But, ever since the time he had disfigured a guy's face with a broken beer bottle, people looked at him funny. Lorenzo's propensity to resort to acts of extreme violence in fights scared them. Any girl he tried to talk with trembled with fear in his presence, even though his extremely handsome looks could have him easily mistaken for actor Terrence Howard.

Acting on all the negative aggression that went on in his head gave him a feeling of pure ecstasy, tantamount only to sex. Every time Lorenzo experienced the feeling after bashing some guy's head in, it scared the shit out of him. But talking to Kathy afterwards always calmed him down. She was his calming elixir and had the ability to temporarily make him see the error of his ways. Just looking at her pretty, brown skin, long black wavy hair and bedroom eyes, and hearing her soothing voice took Lorenzo away from the clutches of the devil.

Lorenzo respected Kathy's opinions because he had witnessed her transformation from a wild, down-ass chick to a classy young lady. When Kathy, at twelve, first moved on the block, girls tried to start trouble because she looked better than them. But after she started laying the smack down, those bitches stopped hating.

Lorenzo thought if she could change, he could at least

try. For a little while, everything in their relationship was going well. Lorenzo spent more time with his woman and less time running the streets. They went to the movies, out to eat, amusement parks and zoo—just enjoying one another's companionship. But while all this went on, a guy by the name of Red was causing havoc on the streets of Harlem. Just like Lorenzo, he had a propensity for acts of extreme violence.

His specialty was spitting razor blades out of his mouth and slicing people from ear to ear. At first people on the streets started to call him Bloody Valentine, then when he got older, they switched to calling him Red for the color of blood. Red did not like starting trouble, but he sure knew how to finish it.

On the other hand, Lorenzo sometimes instigated some of the drama he was involved in. Everybody on the streets knew that both men had inner rage that they tried their damndest to keep in control. Lorenzo's stemmed from being teased about his light-skinned complexion, so-called good hair, and hazel eyes.

People would make fun that his father must have been a white trick that his mother fucked when she was a prostitute. If someone got the nerve to play the dozens at Lorenzo's expense, his "Fist of Fury" ended it. Red's inner rage had much to do with growing up in foster homes because his family was killed in a car accident.

Any kid growing up in the foster system is bound to be mixed up. This was one of the reasons he resorted to using razor blades to cut through the bullshit. A lot of the older bucks and street hustlers wanted to see the two most violent shorties on the block go at it. So they got in the habit of making up stories telling them that the other one was going around saying he could kick his ass.

Some things are just destined to happen.

Take these events, for instance. Nothing in this world could have ever come between the battles of Ali vs. Forman,

Chicago Bulls basketball star Michael Jordan vs. Lakers' star Magic Johnson, or rapper Jay-Z battling rapper NAS. Nothing. When karma's destiny penetrates the atmosphere, nothing can stop it.

And the love Kathy had for her boyfriend, Lorenzo, would not be enough to stop Red and Lorenzo from getting it on—not even if people say love conquers all.

Lorenzo knew that a month before he met Kathy, she had a brief fling with Red, but they broke up because Red had beat up her cousin.

It all went down on a sunny Friday afternoon. They got into a nasty knockdown drag-out fight all because one of them looked a second too long into the other's eyes.

Lorenzo and Red's egos made them want to show Kathy who was the better man. Their animosity towards each other added fuel to the fire.

They fought until they were both bloody and bruised. Pastor Lee from the neighborhood church, who happened to be walking by, finally stopped it.

Later, Red and Lorenzo became the best of friends, causing drama up and down the streets of Harlem after learning to respect each other's gangster abilities and thuggery.

They were ruthless, don't-give-a-fuck thugs who thought nothing of just going on a drug block that they wanted to take over and beating the crap out of the head nigga.

Other thugs thought they were crazy due to their total lack of fear and how they didn't care about any drug crew's street reputation.

Growing up poor, fatherless, and hungry can do that to a person. To them, they had nothing to lose, they were already broke, busted and disgusted, and death was only a word.

First they got a tight stickup crew together. It consisted of a eighteen-year-old, big, muscle-bound, bald-headed dude named Bolo, who wasn't too smart, but he did everything they told him to do; Deeboy and Country, two cousins who were known to rob banks and also free-lance hit-men-for-hire; a Puerto Rican guy named Spanky, who Red met while doing a bid at Rikers Island and who ran the house gang: Rahiem; Reno, Jay-One, Black Jack, Jeff Left, plus their childhood friend, Mohammed.

Lorenzo and Red called their stickup crew the SSJ Crew, because they had mastered the art of doing their robberies by slipping quietly into some crowded gambling spots and before anybody knew what was happening, they would be getting slapped and hit over the head with jammies, their weapons. They called this method the slip, slap, and jammy jumpoff. That's how the SSJ Crew got its name.

The SSJ Crew was always professional, and when it came to putting in work, they were about their business.

They knew that the type of thugs and characters that they robbed would not hesitate to put them out of their misery if they made any mistakes. One time a wannabe badass tried to play super thug and grab Red's gun up in a gambling spot in the Sugar Hill section of Harlem on 146th Street. It was a badly lit and dirty gambling spot, with cartoon characters drawn on the formerly white walls.

Bolo, with a Tech Nine, covered the front door; Mohammed, in a kofi hat, waited outside in a black van for a quick getaway; the other SSJ Crew members proceeded to take all the money and valuables from everybody.

Meanwhile, as the vics lay on the floor, spread-eagled, with their hands behind their backs, Lorenzo aimed an Uzi submachine gun at their backs.

Red stood by a bathroom door with a 9 mm automatic in his hand. All of a sudden somebody busted out of the bathroom and lunged for his gun. But the Puerto Rican guy with braids was a split-second too slow and paid dearly for his last mistake in life. In one swift move, Red shifted the gun to his left hand and blew the top of the guy's head damn near off. Blood splattered everywhere. No more booty calls, chronic and snitching.

A bitch-ass chump squirming on the floor screamed like a little girl, making Lorenzo and the SSJ Crew laugh their heads off.

As Red yelled from the back, "When you slow, you blow," they proceeded to finish the task at hand.

Then the SSJ Crew graduated to extortion, kidnappings, and taking over drug spots.

In no time, they were the talk of the town, rolling in dough, buying fly clothes, cars, and jewelry, and fucking all the dime pieces.

The more money they made, the more guns they acquired, like Uzis, Tech Nines, 9 mm automatics, and all types of submachine guns—all for the purpose of protecting their interests against the other thugs who wanted to take their place.

Lorenzo and Red always kept in mind that not only thugs wanted to do them harm, they also had to worry about police looking to put them away for life.

6

Party Over Here

Lorenzo was in a festive mood as he glanced at the white paper with gold lettering in his hand. "Red, did you read the invitation that Bolo's girlfriend, Jody, sent everybody?" he asked. They were sitting at a table in the big reception hall at the Water Club by the FDR Drive eating and drinking with their wives.

"It says, 'You are cordially invited to attend a baby shower for Jody and Bolo . . .'"

"Man, if I didn't know any better by reading all this I would think I was being invited to a wedding instead of a baby shower," said Lorenzo, trying hard not to bust out laughing.

"And to top it off, look at Bolo over there at the table with a pregnant-ass Jody acting like he's a Mafia don collecting envelopes," said Lorenzo, making everybody at their table laugh hysterically.

"I think the slimy bastard invited the SSJ Crew and everybody and their mama living in Harlem just so he could get them fat envelopes and be on some Don Corleone godfather shit."

As they all continued to enjoy the evening festivities, a Kool-Aid smiling Bolo looked on in their direction seeming to confirm his SSJ Crew members' suspicions on what was taking place before their eyes.

Bolo had the personality of comedian Jamie Foxx. He could be funny as hell and cracking jokes for days, but in a instant he could switch and become a person's worst nightmare.

Everybody in attendance was having the time of their lives at the baby shower. Though it took on a tinge of a ghetto event and people were dressed up in their Sunday best: pimped-out diva-delicious and ghetto-fabulous, they had a good time. They all ate, drank, and danced up a storm.

One chick, dancing next to SSJ Crew member Rahiem on the Electric Slide line that Kathy and Nina started, was wearing a New Jersey Nets throwback dress.

Rahiem yelled to nobody in particular, "Tonight, I'm going home with the cheerleader and we're gonna make something happen for the home team."

Everybody including the DJ's laughter shook the mirrored walls of the elegant reception hall with its shiny marbled floors and chandeliers.

The Water Club was a place where the big power brokers of the city came to shake their asses. But this time, it was reserved for the big moneymakers of the underbelly of the city. The SSJ Crew's been rolling in major dough ever since their robberies became more lucrative and they branched off into the drug game. This is why Bolo was able to hold such an elaborate event that usually would be at someone's house or community center. All the eating and drinking made Red have to use the bathroom. A long line of people were waiting to use it when he got there.

A fat woman wearing a black mini skirt was frantically pacing back and forth like she was going to piss on herself at any moment.

"What's the damn hold up with the rest room?" yelled a pissed-off Red.

"Them guys in there won't let us in," said the fat lady, struggling to get the words out.

"Nigga, you heard me, I'll fade that 500. Now drop

those motherfuckers like it's hot."

That's all Red had to hear through the door as he barged to the front and busted through the yellow door that read REST ROOM.

"I should have known from the git-go that it was y'all ignorant asses, always gotta mess up a good thing. Put them damn dice away and let these nice people use the damn bathroom," he said.

SSJ Crew members Deeboy and Country, along with some other guys, had turned the bathroom into their own little money-smoke-Hennessy-and-dice-smoky gambling spot. The odor of marijuana permeated the air, giving the fat lady contact as she quickly ran to one of the bathroom stalls. The contents of her stomach exploded inside the toilet.

Poo. Pooh. Puh. She grunted, "Ahhh, yeah."

The first person Red spotted was Reno, who had his Avirex plaid shirt hanging on the sink. He had a fist full of money and dice in his hands. He pinched his nose. Sounding like a house nigga caught doing wrong on a plantation, he jokingly said, "Sorry, Red, I told these sorry bastards not to be disrespecting Bolo's shit like this, but they wouldn't listen."

"Stop the bullshit, Reno. You the one who suggested we start the damn game, now you trying to act like an innocent bystander," said Ziggy, from the Eastside Boys drug crew.

This made everybody in the smelly bathroom, including Red and people waiting to use it, laugh their heads off as they left.

As Red and the gamblers headed to the reception hall, SSJ Crew member Deeboy spotted Lorenzo hiding in a corner kicking it to this big-booty brown-skinned chick.

"I guess Lorenzo's up to his old tricks trying to hit some skins, but ain't his wife Kathy up in this piece?" said Deeboy.

Red shook his head, then headed in the direction of his best friend. "Nigga, is you crazy or is it that you just ain't

41

thinking straight?" asked Red, chastising Lorenzo.

"Excuse me gorgeous. I gotta go talk some business with my partner over here, but I'll catch you a little later," said Lorenzo, running his hand down her buttery soft arm.

"Red, man, I don't feel like hearing none of yo' shit today. Just let me do me," said Lorenzo, shooting Red a sharp look.

As soon as Lorenzo said it, he spotted Kathy from a distance, holding her long black mink in her hands and slyly checking out everything.

Lorenzo realizing Red had just saved his ass said, "Sorry, my brother, my bad. I betta go dance with my woman before I get myself into some trouble."

"Yeah, man, I think that's a good idea," said Red, as he headed over to Bolo and Jody's table to give them their money envelope for the baby. After all, what are friends for?

7

Chess Moves

Bare-chested and in his boxer shorts, Lorenzo stretched out on a leather couch in the living room of the town house. He was forty but looked ten years younger. Crystal sat on his stomach and playfully touched his ears as they watched TV. "Daddy, can you buy me a diamond tennis bracelet like you bought Mommy? I did real good in school."

Lorenzo smiled, tickled her and said, "I'll buy you anything you want as long as you keep up the good work."

Jessie, who was standing by a beige marble cabinet that held his boxing trophies was tired of Crystal's daddy's-little-girl routine, so he headed toward the front door. He was peeved that Crystal could do no wrong in his father's eyes, and she always got what she asked for. Lorenzo had never attended any of Jessie's boxing matches or award ceremonies at Gleason's Gym.

Many nights Jessie fantasied about turning professional and having a winning father-and-son boxing partnership like middleweight boxing champion Felix Trinidad and his pops. Jessie visualized going back to his corner in the ring after a good round. His father would yell, "You're doing good, boy. You're doing good!" But this was not to be. His father never had time for him. All his father seemed to think about was chasing the almighty dollar, women and running the streets.

Lorenzo spotted his son leaving and stopped him in his tracks. "Listen, Jessie, you been spending a little too much time running them damn streets and not enough time upstairs studying and doing your schoolwork. Ain't nothing outside but a gang of trouble. Yo mama and me want more for you and your sister than to see y'all wind up another statistic in jail or dead," he said. "I tell you this because I wish my father had said it to me."

Although Jessie knew where his father's waxing philosophical and preaching stemmed from, it still made him want to talk back. But he decided that he didn't want to risk getting slapped across the room, so he flipped the subject.

"Pops, the other day I saw Red sitting outside his bar playing chess with Spanky. Man, that brother's real good. He beat Spanky two times."

"Yeah, son, Red be putting heads to bed when it comes to playing chess," said Lorenzo. He moved his gun away from the edge of the coffee table. "Red said chess helps with his mental clarity," said Lorenzo as he flipped the channels on the sixty-inch color TV.

8

Roxanne-Roxanne

A million things went through Roxanne's head as she stared at her little brother, Biffy, sleeping on the queen-size bed in the small bedroom of the little tier-three apartment where the Department of Welfare had placed them. After their mother died of cirrhosis of the liver because of her addiction to alcohol and drugs, they quickly found out that all they had was each other.

When Roxanne and Biffy moved in with their uncle Buck after the funeral, instead of offering his sister's children a much-needed pleasant environment and a shoulder to lean on during their traumatic grieving period, he abused them.

Uncle Buck slapped Biffy around for no reason during the day time, and, at night, he would sneak in fifteen-year-old Roxanne's bedroom and force her to have sex. At first, Roxanne endured the sexual abuse by coaxing Uncle Buck into leaving Biffy alone by satisfying all of his sexual needs. She had to because they had nowhere else to stay.

For a little while Roxanne's plan worked until one day Uncle Buck beat the shit out of Biffy for drinking some Kool-Aid. That was the last straw because that night when Uncle Buck came home drunk and ready for some hot sex, he got exactly what he deserved, but not what he asked for. When the lights were off and while Uncle Buck oohed and aahed from Roxanne's oral stimulation, all of a sudden he felt a sharp, piercing pinch. Roxanne had sliced his little dick right off. The sweet, caring Uncle Buck woke up some of the neighbors when he screamed, "Oh my god! Help me. The ungrateful bitch dun sliced my dick off!"

Roxanne's culinary skills had put Lorena Bobbit to shame, and, as anybody with half a brain would know, that was Roxanne and Biffy's last night at the house of pain.

Afterwards they found themselves living on the streets then eventually winding up in a shelter, which led to the tier-three apartment.

The little money Welfare provided them was not enough to last through the month so Roxanne had to use her street smarts and her body in order to put food on the table.

That meant stripping, and sleeping with drug dealers and entertainers. Some people say beauty is in the eyes of the beholder, and Roxanne's Hershey chocolate complexion, looks of a young Diana Ross and banging body had men as well as women mesmerized. Sometimes having the ability to affect people in that way can work for a person, but it can also work against them. It cuts both ways.

Roxanne met a big-time drug dealer named Pepsi Diehard, who lavished her with gifts of cars, clothes, expensive jewelry and money. Whatever Roxanne wanted was given to her.

When Pepsi Diehard gave her money, half of it went to Biffy. This always put a big smile on his face. To Roxanne the genuine brotherly and sisterly love they shared made life worth living.

But all good things must come to an end, and Roxanne's came by way of getting caught in Pepsi Diehard's apartment in a big drug sting. When she had to do a few years in the Bedford Hills women's prison and little Biffy had to fend for himself, it made him despise Roxanne. He rebelled by selling drugs. Although his sister messed around with drug dealers, she secretly hated them.

Some of the drug dealers had put Roxanne through pure hell. In prison, Roxanne quickly found out that drug dealers were not the only ones capable of wreaking havoc in her life.

Inmates tested her because they thought pretty girls like her did not like to fight, for fear of messing up their pretty faces. Not.

The first bitch that tried to rape Roxanne got the surprise of her life. Roxanne sliced and diced the woman's face so badly that, in an odd way, the hideous act worked in Roxanne's favor. Because of Roxanne's slicing skills they gave her a good job in the cafeteria cutting meat, which enabled her to steal some and sell it to the other inmates who feared the butcher.

Although Roxanne's prison stint was better than a lot of the other prisoners', it still did not stop her from hating being incarcerated. But she made the best of it, knowing that one day she would get out and be with Biffy. Prison can harden the best of them, but it could also teach an inmate the skills needed to make it on the streets.

Roxanne, being a fast learner, adapted quickly and became good at using people to get what she wanted.

When she got out of prison, her superb skills of mind manipulation combined with street smarts and a gift of gab, made her a triple threat.

9

Vengeance is Mine

Lorenzo's worker, Jay-One, spotted a curly-haired, light-skinned kid who looked no older than twelve, staring at him in front of the corner store on 148th Street while he served a bunch of customers. When the fiends walked off, Jay-One said, "Yo, shorty, I seen you busting my moves, what's up with that? Why you sweatin' a nigga?"

The kid looked him up and down, then took off the headphones that were connected to a Walkman CD player. He was listening to rapper Nas' "Sweet Dreams." Then he stared at his new white Air Force Ones, black Sean John jeans and blinging big diamond-encrusted cross and said, "Jay-One, I want to be just like you when I grow up. Word to my dead mother."

"So what you telling me, shorty, is that you ready for prime time and you want some of this?" said Jay-One.

"Yo, son, my shit's so fucked I ain't gotta choice. My mama's dead and I don't even know who my father is, and besides if I did, I'd kill the son-of-a-bitch," said the little shorty.

Just by the little kid's statement about his pops told Jay-One that shorty had heart, and it made him want to take him under his wings and show shorty the ropes.

Jay-One's plan was to let shorty hold all the product and if po-po ever came, shorty would be the one to take the weight. Even though the SSJ Crew did not let young bucks sling, he went against the rules because he was tired of everybody looking up to Red and Lorenzo and treating him like a stepchild. Now he would have his own little admirer to worship him like a street legend.

As he stood there talking to shorty, Roxanne, one of the neighborhood dime pieces, stepped up into the mix. Jay-One thought she was jumping on his dick, and boy did she look good wearing a white Versace mini shirt, tight red spandex that showcased her voluptuous ass, and some nice red and white Jimmy Choo pumps.

Jay-One could tell she was not a bum bitch by the Cuban link gold chain and diamond-encrusted pendant on her neck.

She yelled, "Come here, Biffy. What did I tell you about hanging around these damn drug dealers? Don't you know these are the same guys that used to sell Ma crack? Can't you find something more constructive to do with your time? Matter fact, ain't yo ass supposed to be in school?" This was not the first time Roxanne had to run Biffy away from the drug dealers. But this time Biffy was not having it. He spoke to her like common street booty.

"Roxanne, mind your fucking business 'fore I stomp a mudhole in your ass. That drug nigga, Cisco, bought all that shit you got on now. If you stop fucking drug dealers, I'll stop hanging around them. Until then, mind your fucking business," said Biffy.

Roxanne was shocked. Her brother had never talked to her that way. Jay-One just smiled as little shorty told off his big sister.

This only made Jay-One like shorty even more, thinking shorty had all the makings of a good drug dealer.

"All right, Biffy, you go ahead and do what the fuck you want, but like Ma used to say, never try an' grow up too fast."

Then she walked off, giving Jay-One the finger.

* * *

Biffy's career as a drug dealer was short-lived because one night while he was out on the avenue alone, slinging dope for Jay-One, a fiend snuck up on Biffy and tried to rob him. Biffy resisted, and the dope fiend slit his throat, covering his green Nike sweatsuit and new white Air Force Ones with blood, as he bled to death.

When Roxanne was told, she ran on the block and spotted her little brother laying in blood on the dirty Harlem sidewalk. As the rain came down, she let out a loud, bloodcurdling scream that woke up the whole block.

After she buried her little brother, she secretly vowed to herself that the SSJ crew would pay for him being killed.

10

New York's Finest

As Detective Kennedy slapped Roxanne on the ass, he smiled and said, "Damn, Roxanne, you got enough ass to lend my flat-ass wife some. You make a guy want to go get his marriage annulled."

Detective Kennedy, tilting on his knees, strained to get leverage doggie-style, but was handicapped by a small penis. Roxanne just smiled as she proceeded to suck off his partner, O'Grady, in front of him.

"Yo, man, this bitch got betta head than a white chick in a porno movie," said Detective O'Grady as he pushed Roxanne's head up and down and at the same time trying his damndest not to bust off. Roxanne bucked her ass cheeks in a frenzied motion, making it hard for Detective Kennedy to keep up. Then she slyly said, "What's the matter cowboy, can't keep your pistol in my holster."

Detective Kennedy just grinned as he palmed Roxanne's big butt cheeks.

Roxanne loved the fact that her shapely ass had the power to drive men wild. Since the young age of ten she had known it. Even grown-ass men used to try to talk to her when they spotted her big ass, attributed to the genetics of her mother.

Like they say, shake what yo mama gave you, and Roxanne learned this rather quickly.

When Roxanne first spotted Detective Kennedy shaking down a local drug dealer in this bar on 155th Street and Broadway where she hung out, bells went off in her head.

Word was already out on the streets that Detective Kennedy and his crew of corrupt cops had major drug dealers paying them off for years to look the other way. So Roxanne figured, why not entertain Detective Kennedy's offer for a date and get some of his illegal cash flow. Their little sexual arrangement benefited all parties involved. Roxanne getting hit off lovely on the money side made it that much easier to deal with those two sorry bastards that much easier. And the detectives benefited from Roxanne setting up the drug dealers for extortion and drug busts. They always had their ménage à trois at the detective's plush secret apartment on 76th Street and Central Park West, paid for with drug dealers' proceeds. Roxanne felt, judging by how fly the apartment was laced, they had to have finagled it from a big drug dealer.

The leather couches, fancy artwork, Tiffany lamps and other nice furniture told her all she needed to know. The satin sheets on the king-sized mahogany bed, tossed on the plush beige carpet in their rush to get things started, combined with the smell of sweaty sex, thrilled her to the fullest. When Roxanne felt it was time to end their lusty sex session, she did two things in succession.

While Detective Kennedy and Roxanne had sex in a missionary position, she put a finger up his ass and sucked off his partner kneeling at the top of the bed. This made both of them bust off at the same time. Every time Roxanne put her finger up Detective Kennedy's ass, it always made him come. Secretly she thought maybe homeboy had a thing for his partner. If so, that was their business and getting at their cheddar was hers. All Roxanne cared about was loot given for services rendered.

Give me the loot, give me the loot! thought Roxanne.

As they all lay in their sweat, Detective Kennedy got up off of the bed and picked up a $100 bill with some cocaine in it off the night stand. Then he took a few hits of the Peruvian flake and passed it to his partner.

"Y'all silly bastards don't know nothing about ladies first, do y'all?" Roxanne said, making both partners laugh as Detective O'Grady passed her the bill.

"Girl, you betta be careful, this shit is so good it almost stopped my heart from beating," he replied, with a scrunched-up look on his face.

"Nigga, if how I just made you bust off didn't do that, nothing will," said Roxanne, laughing.

"Man, Harry, I love it when a black chick calls me nigga. Makes this Irish white guy feel a part of." Then he jokingly slapped his partner a pound and tried to sound like a black guy while saying, "What's up, my nigga?"

They were just two racist cops in a fly apartment gigging on a conniving tramp.

Roxanne felt a little saddened by their mockery because when she was a young girl she had aspirations of being a ballerina. Back then it never crossed her mind that that yearning would translate into her dancing on dicks.

Roxanne stared at both of them with deceit in her eyes, as Irish eyes looked, smiled and laughed at her.

As the cocaine penetrated their brains, it changed the mood of the room and they relaxed and got high as Mt. Everest. Every time they all got blasted, the detectives blabbed about all the drug dealers who were paying them off, all the money they were making and who was next on their list. When they mentioned trying to extort the SSJ Crew, Roxanne's eyes lit up like a Christmas tree, thinking maybe these two knuckleheads would play a big part in her taking down the SSJ Crew. She listened intently.

"That yellow prick, Lorenzo, thinks he's real hot shit. The way he looked at us when we propositioned him, made me want to put a bullet in those icy eyes of his," said Detective O'Grady.

"Yeah me, too. If that asshole doesn't pay up, we'll just

put the federal dick heads on their tails and nail their asses to the wall," said Detective Kennedy as he took a hit of white powder and clicked on the fifty-five-inch screen television. And by coincidence, Al Pacino's classic movie *Serpico* about corrupt rogue cops was playing, making everybody in the room bust out laughing as they realized the connection.

In a more serious tone, Detective Kennedy said, "My darling, Roxanne, I think we gonna need for you to do us a little favor that you already know you'll be paid handsomely for." He opened the mahogany night stand that was topped with tan marble by the bed and passed her two stacks of $100 bills. "If you bring us back some useful information on the SSJ Crew, there will be plenty more where that came from."

She nodded her head and smiled and said, "I got you," as she grabbed his penis and proceeded to suck him off lovely.

11

Love to Love You

As Lorenzo sat in the basement of Red's town house listening to some of his classic R&B and jazz tunes, the music and alcohol they drank made him introspective.

"Red, I know at times I can be a real knucklehead and the architect of most of the nonsense that I find myself in, but thanks for always having my back, and holding a nigga down. Remember that time when I tried to steal that wild pit bull from old man Cujo's yard and his dog was biting the shit out of me and you jumped over the fence and put 'em in a dope fiend yoke and saved my ass?" said Lorenzo.

"Yeah, man, that was a Kodak moment. You was crazy for even trying to steal that damn wild dog, and I was crazy for trying to save yo ass," said Red, taking a sip of Hennessy.

Lorenzo laughed and said, "True dat, but hear me out Red. You know how it's real hard for a man to tell another man their most inner feelings, let alone anything concerning love," said Lorenzo sipping his Hennessy and puffing on a big Cuban cigar.

"What are you trying to get at, Lorenzo? 'Cause every time you get that Hennessy in your system you wanna get all sensitive and deep and shit," said Red puffing on his Cuban cigar.

"Just hear me out, Red. What I'm trying to tell you is I love you man, and I'll die for you," said Lorenzo almost shedding tears.

"Renzo, stop yo' shit. I want you to live for a nigga, not die, and besides I love . . ."

"See, see, you can't even say it, Red. See how hard that shit is trying to tell me you love me. It's so hard for another man to tell his homeboy he loves him. Maybe if a lot of us brothers could, we'd stop killing each other. Know what I'm saying?" said Lorenzo.

"Yeah, that's some real deep stuff you kicking. Come to think of it, maybe if we could have just said we loved each other when we were younger, we would never have had to fight before becoming best friends," said Red, making them both bust out laughing at how he flipped their love conversation.

"Man, we was some ill little shorties. I tried to knock your ass into next week," said Red.

"Yeah, but my bob and weave threw yo' ass off, yo' game plan," said Lorenzo moving his head from side to side and weaving his shoulders making Red playfully throw punches in slow motion.

"Now look at us. Living the good life, not wanting for nothing. Big screen TVs, fancy cars. Like Don King says, 'Only in America'," said Lorenzo nodding his head to Miles Davis' "Freddie Freeloader."

"Renzo, you sound like Superfly's partner, Eddie, when he said, 'Eight-track stereo, color TV in every room. That's the American Dream, nigga.'"

"Well, ain't it. You betta come on in," said Red, helping Lorenzo finish the dialogue from the '70s black exploitation film *Superfly*, making them both laugh and hug each other.

Afterwards a strange thing happened to Lorenzo as he sat down. While Red went over to change the song on the phonograph, another scene in the movie came to mind. It was when Superfly, played by actor Ryan O'Neal, told his best friend and partner in crime that he was leaving the drug game and he drops dimes on him to corrupt cops.

Lorenzo wondered why that scene came to mind. As he sat there in Red's basement, an unsettling feeling came over him, so he took a long sip of the intoxicating liquid.

Then a glassy-eyed Lorenzo looked at his best friend standing by his 1930s phonograph and whispered, "I love you, man."

12

The Devil's Mistress

It was a beautiful night, and the mood was right as Red stood behind his packed bar. He was serving drinks and joking with Lorenzo.

"Lorenzo, a guy comes into a bar and orders drink after drink real fast and the experienced bartender, sensing the guy was going through something said, 'Are you all right, sir?'

"The guy says, 'Man, I just found out that my brother's a homo.'

"The bartender says, 'Listen, fella, that's no big deal. There's a homosexual in every family.'

"The guy smiles, says, 'Thanks,' and leaves the bar.

"Two weeks later, the guy comes back and drinks himself into oblivion and the bartender says, 'Weren't you here a few weeks ago stressing out about your brother being a homo?'

"The guy says, "Yeah, but I just found out that my other brother is a homo.'

"The bartender says, 'Damn, does anybody in your family like pussy?'

"The guy says, 'Yeah, my sister.'"

Lorenzo busted out laughing, as people turned to look at him. Lorenzo got off the stool and went to use the bathroom.

Red liked the fact that even though they sometimes had disagreements, it never stopped them from enjoying each other's company. Red's wife, Nina, and Lorenzo were the only people he trusted and had shared his innermost feelings with. He had told them the pain of losing his parents at a young age when they were in an accident. Then he was physically abused by foster parents who eventually kicked him out onto the mean streets of Harlem.

While Red washed glasses at the bar, Roxanne, who had been known to lean both ways—sometimes chicks, sometimes dicks, walked in. She looked like a Greek goddess in a pink Christian Dior pant suit that looked like it was tailormade for her voluptuous body. And that ass of hers had everybody messed up in the bar. Even the females were hating her as she sat down and ordered a Long Island Iced Tea.

Red smiled as he watched Lorenzo leave the bathroom and head right to her.

"Yo, Red, whatever this pretty young lady is having, it's on me. By the way, give me a glass of that Hen-dog," said Lorenzo. He winked at Red and gave him a nod.

"Girl, you got it going on," said Lorenzo, as he looked at the beautiful female that sat beside him. Roxanne's beautiful pedicured toes and diva-type Prada pumps got foot-fetished Lorenzo into trick mode. "Yo mama still got that big ole ass of hers?" Roxanne just smiled and took a sip of her drink.

"Girl, last time I seen you, you were such a little itty-bitty kid. Now look at you, all grown up."

"Yeah, Lorenzo, I had to grow up fast after my mother died," said Roxanne.

"Oh, I'm sorry to hear that," said Lorenzo.

"Thanks, but I'm all right. By the way Lorenzo, how's that beautiful wife of yours? I saw her the other day. We both shop at Bergdorf-Goodman on Fifth Avenue in Manhattan. That girl stays fly," said Roxanne.

Lorenzo saw right through what Roxanne was trying to do. By mentioning his wife, she was letting him know right off the bat that she was not a dumb chick who did not know what time it was.

He smiled and countered, "Oh, wifey. All right. Old girl holds a nigga down to the fullest."

The way he said it made Roxanne wonder in what capacity did his wife hold him down. It made Roxanne think about the suspicious behavior she witnessed at Bergdorf-Goodman. She once saw his wife coming out of the manager's office tightly holding a big bag that looked like it held more than clothes. Roxanne made a mental note that the next time she saw her at the store she would look more into it.

"Playboy, that makes you one lucky guy. So why you out here on a Thursday night looking for a mistress?" said Roxanne, smirking.

Lorenzo thought, *Damn, homegirl is good.* He figured she was wasting no time in establishing the rules. This meant her role had to be that of a mistress and not some dumb young hottie on the side.

Lorenzo was right because Roxanne knows a drug lord mistress always gets hit off lovely. "Roxanne, I can't lie, you got a brother open and I like your style," said Lorenzo, staring straight in her eyes.

"Maybe it's that Hennessy you drinking that's got you like that," said Roxanne as she playfully ran her pink-white painted manicured nails on his hand that held the drink.

The bling from his three-carat diamond pinky ring and diamond-encrusted Cuban bracelet almost blinded her.

"Nah, young lady it's something about you that separates you from the other females. You seem to know exactly what you want, and I like that. I like a sista that knows what she wants in life."

Roxanne smiled as she thought to herself, *Yeah, I want all you bastards dead or in jail in retaliation for my brother's death.* "You are so right, Lorenzo, I ain't got time for no games, so if we gon' do something, we got to do it right, feel me?"

"No problemo. Now all I want to know is, where do I sign now that we have worked out the contract," said Lorenzo.

Roxanne just smiled as she yelled to Red washing glasses at the end of the bar, "Give this brother another drink on me."

Lorenzo smiled as Red said, "I like that." But what Lorenzo failed to realize was he had just signed a deal with the devil's mistress.

13

Hit 'Em Up

Kathy decided to let her husband have it. "Lorenzo, I am sick and tired of your philandering and not coming home for days on end."

"What do you mean philandering?" said Lorenzo, immediately thinking of how Roxanne's sexual gymnastics rocked his world the other night. Caught off guard, he tried to buy time to think up quick lies.

"Stop acting stupid and being sarcastic. You know damn well what I'm talking about. And if you don't, I mean stop putting your dick inside those trifling hoes and scandalous bitches. Bad enough I got to deal with you buying them cars and things," said Kathy.

Lorenzo felt that even though his wife was telling the truth, it hit a little bit below the belt, so he resorted to playing the madman role by screaming and hollering a bunch of nonsense.

"What trifling bum bitch, crumb bitch, what da fuck, I ain't did nothing. You bugging . . . I'm a good provider. . . ."

A lot of guys resort to doing this when their women catch them lying and cheating. They play the madman role and usually their women get so angry listening to the gibberish that they walk off saying stuff like, "Let me leave this crazy nigga alone." This is what Kathy did.

After Lorenzo resorted to his usual mind games, Kathy

shot him a pitiful look, then shook her head and walked to their bedroom.

Kathy had always been a smart and mentally strong female, even before she first laid eyes on the man who would one day be her husband. She liked to think everything began to unfold in their relationship during what she called the "three rings phase." First came the engagement ring, then the wedding ring, and then the *suffer*-ring."

She learned rather quickly after getting married that a wife of a drug dealer has to take the bitter with the sweet. That meant knowing when to pick her battles.

She was pissed off at Lorenzo, but in the whole frame of things she knew boys will be boys.

Although Lorenzo knew he was wrong and should be spending more quality time with his wife, it did not stop him from leaving the town house angry. The truth hurts.

Lorenzo got in his 755 BMW and headed to 148th Street to drop off product and pick up money from the SSJ Crew members. When he reached 132nd Lenox Avenue, a black Crown Victoria with flashing red lights was right behind the BMW motioning for him to pull over. Lorenzo, pissed-off, sped down Lenox Avenue, intending to give the cops and his new 755 BMW a run for their money. He maneuvered the expensive automobile in and out of traffic, and laughed as the Crown Victoria tried to keep up.

Lorenzo made a quick right turn on 125th Street, slowed down halfway into the block, cut the car off and waited for the Crown Victoria. Thirty seconds later, he spotted the car pulling up and a red-faced Detective O'Grady and his partner, Kennedy, getting out.

"Hey, slime bucket, get the fuck out of the car nice and slow because I got a itchy trigger finger and I don't want to make a mistake shooting such a nice guy, who thinks he's a damn speed racer," said Detective Kennedy. His partner chuckled.

Lorenzo ignored him and rushed out of the BMW

because he was not in the mood to be dealing with their bullshit, especially after the argument at the town house.

"What the fuck y'all two silly assholes want 'cause I'm in a hurry. Plus it don't look good for me to be talking to no po-po," said Lorenzo, looking around at an almost empty 125th Street, Harlem's main shopping area. Normally it was bustling with people, but it was now 10:30 P.M.

Lorenzo was shocked at how he came out so harsh, knowing he should have shown more restraint.

In one swift move Detective Kennedy shattered the bubble glass of the BMW's front headlight while his partner O'Grady punched Lorenzo hard in the stomach, making him buckle and fall to the tarred street.

"Get up, you prick, before I crack that thick skull of yours," said Detective Kennedy, enraged.

As Lorenzo slowly lifted himself up, he was greeted by Detective Kennedy, spit-spraying his face. "Prick, we been looking for yo black ass concerning that $10,000 a week we talked about and you been ducking and hiding."

"Listen, chumps, I ain't never been hard to find, y'all just too stupid. Matter fact, check this out." Lorenzo reached in the pocket of his black jeans and pulled out two c-notes, tore them up into little pieces and said, "Now take that money and shove it up both your asses, because that's about all you'll be seeing from the kid."

Both officers commenced beating him senseless like his name was Rodney King.

After they finished, they got in their car. As they pulled off, Detective Kennedy yelled, "This ain't over my friend. This ain't over!"

Pop Swayze who was en route to cop a bag of heroin to get the serious monkey off his back, wiped his runny nose and stopped to help an old friend in need.

Lorenzo was awakened by a smelly and dirty Pop Swayze saying, "Renzo, baby wake up, wake up. It's gonna be okay."

Lorenzo dazed by what just transpired, swung at the first thing he saw, Pop Swayze.

Bam, bam, bam! Down went Pop Swayze from the flurry of Lorenzo's punches.

It took a second for Lorenzo to gather his thoughts and realize that he had lashed out at the wrong person. Pop Swayze was a dope fiend, but he was not always like that. Back in the days, he was a big-time drug dealer, a pimp, and part of the Harlem crime syndicate. Although Lorenzo and Pop Swayze were in different drug crews, they ran in the same circles and eventually became good friends. Pop Swayze was like an uncle to Lorenzo's kids.

As Pop Swayze rubbed his swollen lip dripping with blood, Lorenzo yelled, "Oh, man, what the fuck have I done? I'm sorry, Pop, I didn't mean to, I thought you was—"

"Yeah, you thought I was those two sheisty coppers who like you, take a hands-on approach," said Pop Swayze, making them both bust out in laughter.

As they got up off the dirty street and brushed each other off, people stared but kept it moving.

"Yo, Pop Swayze, sorry to be meeting in such strange conditions but you know how shit go."

"Yeah, Renzo, I can see the game still ain't safe no more, but troupers like you always stay on top, no matter what," said Pop Swayze.

"Thanks, Pop, but I learned a lot hanging around older bucks like you," said Lorenzo, staring at his shattered headlight as he got in the car. "Yo, Pop, those bastards need to get it in the worst way. If I could kill one of them jake motherfuckers and get away with it, I'd do it with quickness."

Before Lorenzo pulled off, he reached in is pocket and gave Pop Swayze a wad of money. Pop Swayze smiled then thanked him and off he went to the only place he still felt like a king. The dope den.

14

Knocked

Roxanne wanted to be flossing some new bling on her planned trip to Miami with Lorenzo. She spent most of her day on 47th Street, in the diamond district, but had no luck finding some iced-out jewelry to her particular liking, so she caught a yellow cab and went to Bergdorf-Goodman on Fifth Avenue to buy footwear.

"Let me see those shoes right there, the green Gucci half boots on the top shelf, and those blue-beige Coach shoes at the bottom," said Roxanne to the Asian clerk. While sitting in the red-cushioned comfortable chairs waiting to try on the shoes she selected, Roxanne spotted Lorenzo's wife coming into the store. Kathy looked like a top model on a runway.

Kathy's long, black wavy hair was nicely styled and she wore some tight black Pepe jeans, a brown and beige silk blouse, short black mink and black pointy Manolo Blahniks diva boots. She browsed around the store like she owned the place, making Roxanne green with envy.

For an instant, they made eye contact and Roxanne thought she detected a look of pure disgust. She felt Kathy gave her the look of royalty looking down on a mere peon.

Kathy turned the other way, then pranced toward the manager's office and went inside. Roxanne immediately got up from her seat and walked in the same direction.

When she got near the manager's office, Roxanne tried to tune into any sounds that might be coming out of the room but she heard nothing. Roxanne decided to try to peep inside, and if she got caught, her ploy would be she thought it was the bathroom.

So in slow motion she turned the door knob and slightly eased open the door.

What she saw blew her mind. On top of the manager's desk were multiple stacks of kilos of cocaine. A nervous-looking Kathy, with the help of the manager, was putting them in plastic Bergdorf-Goodman bags.

Roxanne slowly closed the door, quickly walked to the front entrance and left the store. When she got outside she placed a call on her pink Phat Farm cell phone.

"Harry, I think I got some useful information concerning your boy, Lorenzo."

Roxanne ran down everything she had just witnessed to Detective Kennedy.

In fifteen minutes flat police had flooded the area, then swooped down on Bergdorf-Goodman and busted Kathy and the store's manager as they put bags in the trunk of her Mercedes. Roxanne, smiling, watched it all go down from across the street as she sipped a cappuccino in Starbucks.

15

Caught Up

While sitting in Copeland's Restaurant on 145th Street and Broadway, Lorenzo ate a steak, potatoes and corn dinner. Two white guys wearing suits took a seat at his candlelit table.

One of them flashed a federal badge and picture ID, and then said, "Mr. Thompson, sir, I know you would not mind if we have a little talk while you enjoy your good southern cuisine."

Lorenzo, looking the agent dead in the eyes, said nothing.

"Mr. Thompson, we are here to inform you that earlier today we arrested your wife, Kathy Thompson, and another gentleman for drug possession with intent to distribute. As we speak, your wife is being held at the federal courthouse downtown on Centre Street. We, the Federal Bureau of Investigation, along with the NYPD, the state police and the district attorney's office have had our drug task force watching you and the SSJ Crew for quite some time. We know through wiretaps and surveillance that your wife is not an SSJ Crew member. If you are smart and provide us with some useful information, maybe you can save your wife, because you and the SSJ Crew are going down when we drop a federal indictment," said Agent Stewart, staring at Lorenzo, and then at his diamond-bezeled Presidential Rolex watch.

Lorenzo's mind was a blur. He thought it all was just a bad dream that he needed to wake up from. He wanted to get downtown and bail out his wife and then figure out everything else the federal agent was telling him. As Lorenzo sat there trying to keep his composure, his neck stiffened and his chest pounded from a rapid heartbeat as the other federal agent spoke. "Mr. Thompson, from what we have gathered, you and your wife have two beautiful children."

"Man, leave my kids out of this," said Lorenzo angrily, as he spoke to the agents for the first time. He had almost decided to get up and leave.

"Hear me out, sir. If you and the missus wind up doing hard time, your kids will have to go in foster care. And we both know what happens in the foster care system. So if you agree to testify about the SSJ Crew's activities, we can make sure that your wife, Kathy, does not take the fall with you."

Lorenzo listened to the agents, then clammed up again. "All right, Mr. Thompson, you can play this however you want to. We will give you a little time to make a decision, but do not wait too long," said Agent Bradley as he tried to pass Lorenzo his card.

Lorenzo took the fork in his hand and pretended to be eating even though he had lost his appetite. The agent saw right through it and placed the card on the table. Then he said, "We will be in touch," as he and his partner got up and walked away.

As soon as they stepped off, Lorenzo hurriedly paid the bill. As he made his way out towards the front door, he spotted Detective O'Grady and Detective Kennedy eating and grinning at him. Detective Kennedy nodded and said, "Lorenzo, have a good day, ya hear."

Lorenzo gave him the finger as he quickly left the restaurant. When he got to his car, he used the remote to open the door. He sat down in his dark burgundy 755 BMW, which he bought because the color reminded him of dried-up blood, started the ignition and headed to the court-house. As rain poured and slid off the car's front window, a million things flew through his brain.

Damn, when it rains it pours. Just when I have made up my mind to rethink my position of staying in this drug game, I find out the feds got their own plans of putting up some going-out-of-business signs. And they're tailormade for yours truly. Boy, have I got myself into a whole mess of trouble. All because of my stupid need to be on some Mr. Big trip with all my flossing. Deep down I know I am the cause of all this drama with the feds.

My main man, Red, since day one, told me when we first started raking in the dough, not to start acting like some stupid drug dealer that ain't used to nothing, then starts buying fly cars and jewelry to let everybody in the hood know that he's made it. Then wonders why those same people he's fronting on start hating him and telling shit to the cops. Why? Simple, you stupid asshole, you should have never put your business out in the street. Red always says that the gangster John Gotti was the dumbest criminal in the world for acting like a celebrity wannabe, when he knew damn well what type of shit he was involved in. That is why him and his crew are locked up doing crazy time.

Now I find myself facing the same predicament. I know Agent Stewart ain't lying about what's about to go down because they have already taken down the 116th Street Crew and the Dominican cartel up in Washington Heights. They busted everybody from the guys doing hand to hand to the ones calling the shots. Ending in them all receiving lengthy prison terms.

Them getting caught in the mix should not have surprised anyone of them due to the fact that all us drug dealers know that when the feds come for that ass, you better start shitting on yourself. Because the feds always come correct. Those bastards cross all the T's and dot all the I's when they bring a federal indictment against a chump. Now these agents got me trapped off in a cruel game of which door do you choose? Door number one—trick myself into thinking there is no indictment coming down! Door number two— say fuck the feds, wait for the indictment then go to trial and fight the case. Door number three—snitch on everybody, then make a deal to save the mother of my kids. Damn! I never even played along with that game on TV called "Let's Make A Deal." So what do I do now that the feds are telling me I got next? Damn!

16

So Sorry, So Sorry, Sorry Didn't Do It

It made Lorenzo feel real bad when he bailed Kathy out of jail and saw how being locked up had mentally beaten her down. Personal experiences told him that dirty cells, unsavory prisoners, nasty food and disrespectful correction officers made for an unpleasant environment.

That he had contributed to her being arrested and put in this predicament did not help matters. Even his kids were mad at him. Today, Lorenzo was going to tell Red the consequences of his stupid actions, something he had been putting off. Lorenzo having to admit to Red what he had done would confirm things his partner predicted.

He thought, *Yes, yours truly, Charlie Dick Head, who always does things without thinking, would one day get them in trouble. It would not take a rocket scientist to figure out that saying stuff like "Damn, you was right" and "Yo, I'm sorry, bruh," was just not going to cut it. The fact being that Red ain't never been no you're my ace boon coon, you're my pride and joy, whatever you do you're still my boy type of guy.*

Lorenzo knew he was just going to have to roll with the punches, as he made his way up the stairs of Red's beautiful reddish-brown town house, the same color as his on the same block. Homes were the first assets they purchased when the money started rolling in. That was a very smart move on both their parts, but now stupid decisions on Lorenzo's part made him a liability.

Although Lorenzo was nervous and fidgety he tried to act calm by popping the collar of his black three-quarter-length leather coat as he took a strong pull off a Newport cigarette and knocked.

Red, wearing a blue-and-white nylon Adidas sweat suit, was about to go jogging in Central Park. He was surprised to see Lorenzo because he usually called before coming. Red immediately noticed that Lorenzo looked stressed-out.

"Man you look like a brother whose world is ending. What you need is some of my wife's freshly squeezed orange juice and some of her tasty banana nut muffins that I was just going to sink my teeth into," said Red, stepping toward the kitchen.

Lorenzo cracked a fake smile and followed his friend into the spacious kitchen that was wider than some people's entire apartment.

As Red poured them both glasses of orange juice on a white marble countertop lined with gleaming appliances, and placed the muffins on some small Lenox dishes, a jittery Lorenzo stood by the counter by the silver Kitchen Aid refrigerator and said nothing.

"Okay, Lorenzo, tell me what's going on in that empty head of yours," said Red, as he passed him a cup of juice.

"Red, what I'm about to drop on you, I'm gonna need more than this juice. You got some Hennessy to go with it?"

"Renzo I ain't never seen you drink this early in the morning," said Red.

"Yeah, but shit done changed, I need a stiff drink."

Red left the kitchen then came back with a fifth of Hennessy. He watched Lorenzo as he poured out most of the orange juice, replaced it with the Hennessy, and swallowed most of the drink.

As the intoxicating liquid burned his throat, Lorenzo wiped his mouth and said, "Red, I want you to do something for me. But if you can't, I'll do it myself."

"My brother, what do you want me to do?" asked Red. Lorenzo reached in the waist of his grey linen pants and pulled out a silver 9 mm automatic and tried to pass it to Red.

Then he said, "I want you to kill me. Don't ask me why, all you need to know is I deserve to die, so end my misery."

Red backed away and said, "First of all, put that gun away and tell me what the fuck is going on."

Lorenzo nervously put the gun back in his waist as sweat trickled down his forehead. The tension in the kitchen cut like a knife. The thermostat on the wall read sixty-six degrees but it felt more like one hundred degrees.

"Man, uh, uh, I done messed up real bad. Kathy got busted picking up some product at the store and now shit's about to hit the fan," said Lorenzo.

Red was dumbfounded. "Nigga, what do you mean? Kathy don't even sell no drugs. Nigga, I know yo ass ain't been stupid enough to get your wife caught up in our shit, especially when I told you business and family don't mix," said Red.

As Red stared at Lorenzo, he remembered the argument that they had a few months earlier. Red told Lorenzo that if he continued doing ignorant and stupid things they would eventually wind up in prison for a long time. Lorenzo had replied, "Can a nigga live some time?" Now Red felt the urge to kill him. His muscles tensed under his jogging suit.

Lorenzo had not seen his best friend this mad since they were two little shorties fighting each other on the streets.

Before Lorenzo finished nodding and saying yes, Red pounced on him like a raging bull throwing punches and elbows from every angle. Lorenzo's eye swelled up like he had been hit by a devastating uppercut by Mike Tyson. It looked worse than the big lump that heavyweight boxer Rahman received by way of Evander Holyfield's hard head. Lorenzo did not try to defend himself, knowing he deserved every bit of the punishment. After Red finished beating him like he stole something, Lorenzo could tell by Red's pained look that he felt bad, but he was still pissed.

"Listen, Lorenzo, and you better listen real good. You are the one that got us into this mess and you better figure out a way to get us out of it. I'm sick and tired of you tearing down something that we took so long to build. Blood, sweat, and tears, nigga do you hear me? Blood, sweat and tears," yelled Red as he got up in Lorenzo's face.

The intensity in Red's voice told Lorenzo that he was a split-second from continuing his assault. But Red turned around and exited the kitchen. He was afraid that he might take Lorenzo up on his offer of killing him.

Lorenzo, feeling like a complete idiot and fully conscious that his stupidity could possibly take down the SSJ Crew, walked out of the town house with his head down. Red, sweaty and pissed off, totally worked out mentally and physically from dishing out the vicious beating, sat on a burgundy leather couch in the living room and drank Hennessy from the bottle.

17

Decisions

Lorenzo figured there was only one way to rectify the critical situation he had created. After going over different scenarios of how his wife's drug bust could possibly play out, it just did not look good. The only chance Lorenzo had of keeping Kathy and Red out of jail was for him to take the weight and to snitch on the SSJ Crew. He already knew the feds' case was weak in regards to Red because he and Red had agreed when they first got involved in the drug game that one of them would be a silent partner. This arrangement would give them a jump on anything that could transpire like street drama and arrests. Being that Red had proven himself to be the wiser of the two, that position fell to him.

Lorenzo's lawyers said that Red's voice was not on any of the feds' wiretaps, and they also did not have him doing anything illegal on their video surveillance. But in regards to the SSJ Crew and himself, the lawyers said a thirty count indictment that included six murders and the 848 Federal Kingpin Statute charging Mr. Lorenzo Thompson with running a continuing criminal enterprise was already written up.

Lorenzo felt strong that a case could be made of an unsuspecting wife thinking she was just picking up money from her husband's legitimate business. Deep down, Lorenzo knew it was his fault that Kathy had been arrested. She had never once sold drugs in her life. Days earlier he had persuaded her to pick up the drugs, when he lied and said he had to go out of town on other urgent business. The real reason was that he was taking his new chick, Roxanne, on a vacation to Miami. The only other time he had gotten Kathy mixed up in his drug business was when, against her wishes, he made her pick up money at the store.

There was not a doubt in Lorenzo's mind that Kathy, and possibly Red, did not deserve to be held accountable for his stupid actions. In his mind there was only one possible solution, but it would go against everything he stood for. Becoming a federal informant, a snitch. But still he could not sit back and chance letting his best friend and the mother of his children, who had always been nothing but good, take the weight. Especially not the two people who had saved his life when they were all young kids.

He remembered the day they were at a project picnic in Van Cortland Park and he had a seizure while running after a ball during a baseball game. As he lay on the dirty glass-covered field, foaming at the mouth and not able to breathe, Kathy and Red quickly went into action, performing CPR that they had learned in the PAL Community Center. Everybody else out there stood gawking and acting like Lorenzo had AIDS.

A lot of people in the hood felt like comedian Richard Pryor when he joked that if he ever saw somebody on the street having a seizure and foaming at the mouth, that person was one dead motherfucker because he was not going to help them. Good thing for Lorenzo that Red and Kathy did not feel the same way. The EMS crew told him their actions saved his life.

For years after that close encounter with death, Lorenzo had bad dreams of drowning in quicksand or offshore from Gilligan's Island, when Kathy and Red would save him just in time. People say payback is a bitch and Lorenzo knew how to make deserving enemies suffer for any wrongs that they did to him. By the same token, Lorenzo knew that you do not pay back people who helped save your life by putting them in a position to face twenty-five years or life in prison.

Lorenzo's mother would always tell him when he was a little boy, "A hard head makes a soft ass," and it was ironic that he was destined to be sitting in a courtroom as the feds star witness against the SSJ Crew.

18

Friend or Foe

As Red sat alone in his bedroom, staring at a picture of himself and Lorenzo, the phone rang. It was Lorenzo, sounding very nervous and antsy. Lorenzo was in a precinct, spilling his guts.

"Red, I ain't got too much time to talk, but I'm calling to tell you I've decided to become a federal informant against the SSJ Crew. Take care of my family."

After Red got off the phone he said, "Damn, my ride-or-die homey done turned into a snitch."

Red wanted to yell, scream, curse, then reach out and touch someone by strangling him with a phone cord.

His wife, Nina, who had just stepped into the room, noticed his angry face. "Red, honey, do you want some water? You look flushed."

Red could not answer because his vocal cords and jaw locked as his teeth chattered. He felt like he had lockjaw. Agua was not going to relieve his stress.

On the mean streets that Red and Lorenzo had roamed, traitors were dealt with swiftly. While Nina went to get water, he stared blindly at the picture of the two of them during happier times. It was taken when he and Lorenzo were in a library on Forty-third and Fifth Avenue. Lorenzo had accompanied Red there to get an autobiography of jazz legend Miles Davis. As Red looked at the picture, he thought about the library as a place where people do not talk out of respect for other people.

Red and Lorenzo had been through the bad and good together. Back in the days, both of their families were so poor that toast with syrup was their pancakes, and sugar water was considered Kool-Aid. Back then, Red thought there was nothing cool about not getting no aid from anywhere. Red felt that Lorenzo was like a brother from another mother, and through thick and thin they had always managed to find a way out of their messed-up circumstances.

Now in what could be considered the worst of times, Lorenzo was doing the exact opposite, snitching to the feds. Lorenzo was turning out to be a low-down, dirty, rotten scoundrel, and his true colors had come to light. Sometimes compassion and love for a friend made a person with twenty-twenty vision think that his eyes are deceiving him.

As Red sat on the bed, he blamed himself for letting a person with the mind-set of a Machiavellian, modern-day Judas tiptoe and betray his trust, respect, and loyalty with the feet of Sasquatch.

Checkmate. Yes, yes, yes, Red thought. Lorenzo, who he has seen knock guys out, stare death in the face and even kill for him, has turned into a snitch. *I smell pussy*, he thought. Long ago, Red had spotted cracks in Lorenzo's armor.

When they were just two little larceny-hearted shorties, Red and Lorenzo robbed Eddie Jughead, the slimy numbers runner who tried to have sex with everybody's mother. Eddie Jughead kept his pockets stuffed with money like an old Italian construction site foreman, while Lorenzo and Red were broke, busted and disgusted. They thought a perfect crime had been committed; no one would suspect that two scrawny thirteen-year-olds had the balls to try to rob the mob-backed Eddie Jughead, a known killer.

Lorenzo and Red caught Eddie Jughead slipping in a dark staircase in the Taft housing projects. They rocked his world with a rusty frying pan, and stole $2,700. Jackpot! They would have gotten away scot-free, but Lorenzo went around the block buying marijuana and tricking on all the pretty girls. The only reason Eddie Jughead and his goons did not kill them was because they were impressed that Lorenzo and Red had the audacity to do what they did.

Instead, Eddie Jughead had them tied up in an old warehouse. What happened there should have been a telltale sign for Red. Although Lorenzo did not squeal or confess to their crime, his scared look and big Mr. Magoo eyes told Eddie Jughead and his goons all they needed to know. Seeing eyes, seeing all things.

Now Red saw how dick-dastardly a so-called friend could be. The sip of the cold water his wife had handed him did nothing to soothe the dryness in his throat. He was still having a hard time dealing with the fact Lorenzo turned snitch.

19

Snitching

Crackhead Devon spotted Jessie coming out of the corner store with a twenty-five cent orange-flavored drink and said, "Hey, Jessie, I heard the feds busted the SSJ Crew, and your pops is snitching on everybody. What's up wit' that?"

Jessie figured this type of nonsense was bound to happen after his mother told him what his pops had done. It was not a doubt in his mind that there would be problems on the street. And now it was starting.

"What you talking about? You stupid crackhead," said Jessie, ready to spaz out.

"You heard me. Everybody says your pops is dropping dime."

Bam, bam, boom! Before Devon knew what was happening, Jessie hit him with a flurry of punches, making him hit the hard cement pavement. "Compliments of Gleason's gym," said Jessie.

Crackhead Devon's face swelled up and he started dripping blood. As he rubbed his swollen eye and busted mouth, he could not talk because his jaw was broken. For the next few months he would be swallowing soup through his crack pipes.

Jessie just smiled and walked off into the blistering cold winter day to see his best friend, Wayne.

Through the course of the day, Jessie had to endure

being asked if his pops snitched to the feds when the SSJ Crew got busted. Each time, his blood would boil, making him sweat profusely. It took a lot of restraint on his part not to lash out. He thought they were laughing inside. Meanwhile, the hate Jessie had for his father became extreme. The night before Jessie's mother had been arrested, Jessie heard his father on the phone in the kitchen setting up plans to get to Miami the next day with a woman he was fucking on the side. What little love he had had for his father was gone. He asked himself:

Are sons always destined to suffer the sins of their fathers or is that only true if they believe that? I am in no shape or form a snitch but yet everybody is messing with me. All because my father chose to rat on his so-called friends. Why do I have to eat my father's poisoned cheese when I really don't even like dairy products due to the fact that it makes me shit my guts out? But because my father is considered a piece of shit for having no guts and did not take the weight for the ton of bullshit him and the SSJ Crew did, I stand accused. Fuck my father and his stinking legacy. I'm a trouper, not a pooper-scooper who picks up shit after other motherfuckers.

Come to think of it, my mother always joked about my father's little beady eyes, and don't rats have the same thing. Mama, why you go ahead and fuck a chump with rat eyes? Man, I'm bugging out 'cause that's a stupid question, knowing that if she didn't I would never have been born.

But, Mama, why you go fuck a chump anyway? Didn't you know thoroughbreds always find a way to rise to the top and while I was floating around in your ovaries with the other million eggs, I would have still found a way to break through without you letting that rat chump bust off? Now I feel like I'm the one who's ready to bust off. And, Mama, the next chump who mentions anything about snitching is gonna feel it big time.

20

Fed Up

A million things went through Lorenzo's mind in the small, dreary cell of the federal courthouse as he waited to testify against the SSJ Crew. As he tried to make excuses for informing on his drug crew's illegal activities, not one justified his betrayal.

Lorenzo knew all eyes were going to be on him and, although he craved the spotlight, a courtroom was not where he pictured himself shining. For a person known to entertain people with a witty joke or two, being stricken with stage fright was not normal. But, because this was a totally different type of venue, fear was understandable. There would only be one person singing and dancing around certain parts that a wife and best friend played in a script written in blood—Lorenzo.

Wearing an orange, jail-issued jumpsuit, Lorenzo entered the federal courtroom. The sounds of people talking, papers rustling and the tapping of computer keys that filled the air, ceased. It was as if someone put his hand to his mouth and said hush.

This did not escape Lorenzo's attention as he sat in a witness chair under large letters that read: IN GOD WE TRUST. To his right sat a black judge in a black robe with a white shirt and tie visible at the collar. Lorenzo hoped his name was Cut 'em Loose Bruce, a judge known to do just that.

The first familiar face Lorenzo spotted, and who shot him a deadly menacing look capable of topping rapper Ice Cube's, was Bolo sitting at the defendant's table wearing an expensive, black, pin-striped suit. If looks could kill, Lorenzo would be dead. And, sitting at the same long defense table were SSJ members Deeboy and Country, who had to be told to stop pointing a black pen at Lorenzo, as if it was a gun, by one of their two white Jewish lawyers who wore expensive Armani suits. The other SSJ members, along with Spanky, Reno, Jeff to the Left, and Black Jack, had already copped out to lesser charges and time when they found out Lorenzo had become a federal informant.

The bespectacled prosecutor, Miles, who was on a mission to protect his 100 percent conviction rate, stood up in his blue Armani suit. The night before he promised his greedy wife with diva ambitions, that after taking down the SSJ Crew, they would be living on Easy Street. He planned to open up a law firm and get some of the money his lawyer friends received from defending the drug cartels. He had come to the conclusion long ago that trying to uphold and defend the laws of the court was a losing battle because, for every drug dealer they convicted, there was another ready to take his place. So, if you can't beat 'em, join 'em. But, for now he had a case to prosecute.

As the prosecutor made his way over to Lorenzo, all of a sudden, Bolo stood up from his chair, looked at the judge and made a weird hand signal. Earlier, while he and the other SSJ Crew members were in a cell in the back, Bolo told them not to worry because he had a brilliant plan that was going to solve all their problems in the courtroom once he acted out said plan. Everybody in the courtroom, including the judge, laughed their heads off when they made the connection that Bolo was trying to persuade the judge to let the SSJ Crew go by using some foolish Masonic signs.

What Bolo was attempting stemmed from a farfetched rumor that had circulated around courthouses for quite some time. Urban legend had it because that most judges were Masons, by displaying the secret hand signal to them you would beat your case. Pure nonsense.

As Lorenzo sat in the witness chair, he stared at Bolo for a moment and thought about how Bolo was always known more for brawn than brains.

After looking at Bolo like he was crazy and enjoying a good laugh, the judge told him to sit down.

Then in a loud and authoritative voice that Perry Mason would be proud of, Prosecutor Miles said, "Mr. Thompson, did you authorize and participate in the murders of Mr. Charles Wilson and Mr. Cleveland Harris with your fellow SSJ Crew members?"

In a loud and authoritative voice that thugs and other criminals that have been snitched on would kill him for if they heard it, Lorenzo said, "Yes, because they tried to extort and take over our thriving drug business."

"Mr. Thompson, were you and the SSJ Crew responsible for selling and distributing huge quantities of cocaine and heroin through the past ten years all up and down the streets of Harlem?"

Lorenzo, sounding like a student trying to please his teacher, said, "Yes, sir."

As Lorenzo honestly answered question after questions the prosecutors, families of the SSJ murder victims and the police smiled from ear to ear as he put on a performance worthy of landing him on *Court TV*. Strangely enough, in the mob world Lorenzo would have been considered a standup guy—that is, until he stood up and testified.

Detectives Kennedy and O'Grady, sitting in the front row, even gave Lorenzo a thumbs-up sign, and then they looked toward the SSJ Crew defendants' table and held their thumbs downward. Sorry for the SSJ Crew that the truth was not going to set them free.

As Prosecutor Miles continued the questioning, Lorenzo suddenly clammed up at the sight of Kathy and Red, watching him from the second row. Their looks penetrated his psyche and he felt as if he had a vice grip on his tongue, which is why he shut up and looked away. Even though Lorenzo had made a deal with the feds to drop Kathy's charges and Red had not been charged due to the fact that no incriminating evidence was found to warrant arresting him, they both still were having a hard time dealing with the whole turn of events. They knew the families and friends of those on trial might turn against them.

When Prosecutor Miles noticed Lorenzo was not concentrating, he said, "Mr. Thompson, Mr. Thompson. I'm asking you a question. I know you are tired from all of this, but you are doing very well under cross-examination and you have my word that it will all be over soon."

The voice of the prosecutor did not overcome Lorenzo's mental funk. He imagined Red and Kathy having sex as teenagers. As he continued on telling in detail all the SSJ Crew's criminal activities except for anything incriminating against Kathy and Red, he secretly wondered why a vision like that crossed his mind at a time like this. He knew Red and Kathy had had sex once before he hooked up with her. But he had never bore witness to their copulation. So, why was he thinking about it now? Lorenzo failed to realize that people facing long prison terms have a lot of time to think, and sometimes strange things cross their minds as they try to cope. He quickly got back to the business at hand. The words coming out of his mouth may have pleased and put smiles on some people's faces in the courtroom, but definitely not the SSJ Crew's. Because of Lorenzo's stellar performance, they all received twenty-five years to life.

21

Seven Years Later

Catholic high school teacher Mrs. Campbell noticed that her students were getting a little too rowdy and yelled, "Quiet down, class, and everybody take a seat while Jessie takes the attendance."

Jessie was tired of his boring task of doing the attendance check every morning, but he really liked his beautiful teacher with her big booty self. One day the little rascal in him was even tempted to bring her an apple. Jessie also liked the fact that she always gave him good grades when report card time came around.

"All right y'all. Class is in session so y'all can stop guessing. Okay, we got Christopher Reyes on the check in. We also got Brenda Buttaface who got everything but a face on the check in," said Jessie, cracking a joke that had a lot of his classmates laughing.

Brenda Butafuco yelled at the top of her lungs, "Jessie, don't call me that and I'm tired of you disrespecting me." She knew Jessie had a thing for her."

"Jessie Thompson, stop playing and finish taking the attendance," said Mrs. Campbell with a half-serious expression.

Jessie looked at her with a sly grin, then got serious and finished up.

Then Felix, whom Jessie had disliked since the time he

caught him trying to kick game to Crystal, started up some nonsense.

"Yo, homes, why you marked me absent the other day when we had that substitute teacher? I was here." Felix's lying through his teeth made Jessie so angry that his light-skinned complexion turned a light red. He prided himself in never making a mistake when taking attendance. This always pleased Mrs. Campbell.

"Nigga, shut up, and be quiet. Yo ass was absent so I marked you absent," yelled Jessie. His vulgarity angered Mrs. Campbell. She tried to bring order to the classroom by saying, "Please. Please, calm down. You both know that we do not talk like that in Catholic school."

For an instant, Mrs. Campbell thought the boys were listening to her because there was complete silence. Then Felix began to sing his own rendition of a familiar army jingle. "You're in the hood now / You're in the hood now / Daddy's no longer rich / You're the son of a snitch / You're in the hood. . . . '

Jessie jumped up and ran towards Felix screaming, "Nigga, I'm gonna kick yo ass."

Ever since Jessie's father Lorenzo dropped dime years ago, everybody, including Mrs. Campbell, knew that whenever someone called him a snitch, Jessie would go ballistic. The majority of his fights started because of it, but he was always the one to finish them. All the boxing and karate classes that his father enrolled him in were put to good use. *Stick and move. Stick and move.*

Jessie, with the rage of Mike Tyson and the swiftness of karate movie star Jackie Chan, grabbed Felix by the neck with his left hand and in one swift move jugged the pen in his right hand, into Felix's eyeball. Blood gushed everywhere as it splattered Mrs. Campbell's white ruffled shirt with a crimson red, making her, Brenda and the other students scream in pure panic as they ran out of the classroom that had turned into the devil's playpen.

Jessie, Mr. Calm, Cool and Collected, picked up his book bag and nonchalantly walked out of the room. Meanwhile Felix lay on the dirty floor with his bloody hand covering a perforated eye, shaking like he was having an epileptic attack.

22

Who's That Knocking at My Door?

Crystal heard knocking as she was reading in the living room by the fireplace. "Who's there?" she called, as she headed for the front door.

"Damn it, man, what took you so long?" said Jessie, huffing, sweating and covered in blood.

"Oh my god! Jessie, what happened to you?" asked Crystal, as she rushed him into the house.

Jessie took off his ruined shirt and flung it on the couch. "I showed that stupid nigga Felix and anybody else who thinks they can fuck with the Thompson family that I ain't having it," said Jessie, practically spitting out the words.

Crystal said nervously, "Jessie, what did you do? What did you do?"

"Well, I'll tell you one thing. From now on they gonna be calling Felix 'Deadeye' 'cause I took his eye out with a number two pencil.

Crystal screamed at the top of her lungs, "No. No, Jessie, no!" She flopped on the leather couch.

"Crystal, you should be happy that I made an example out of that scumbag. Ain't you tired of people messing with us because of something our pops did?"

"Jessie, that's not the point. Two wrongs don't make a

right. Bad enough we are growing up without a father, now me and Ma gotta deal with another family member going to jail," wailed Crystal.

"You bugging out. I ain't going no fucking where because that chump started it and I just finished it," snarled Jessie, not fully understanding the consequences of his actions.

They both heard knocking. Crystal nervously looked at Jessie, then walked slowly to the door.

Two policemen and a school safety officer, who spotted Jessie looking over Crystal's shoulder, were there. He said, "Put on your shirt, young man. You're coming with us."

Shortly after Jessie was arrested for first degree assault, he was kicked out of Catholic school.

Kathy, at her wits' end, called his godfather, Red. Red paid a high-priced lawyer who managed to get Jessie a one-year sentence to be served on Rikers Island. Red told him it could have been worse because the district attorney prosecuting the case wanted a longer sentence due to the severity of the crime. Red also secretly paid off Felix's family.

When Jessie arrived at Rikers Island, he was greeted by a mean-looking, burly, black corrections officer with a gray spotted beard.

The officer yelled, "Welcome to the place where everybody's innocent, so smile."

A few hours later, Jessie, nervous and depressed, noticed that nobody was smiling on Rikers Island.

His mind drifted off as he looked at the unfamiliar surroundings of the C-76 jail dorm that resembled a hospital ward except for barbed wire on the windows and its ice-grilled inmates. Jessie had heard many stories about Rikers Island, and none of them were good. Even though the stories were really violent and ran the gamut of beat-downs, stabbings, sexual assaults and riots, they were told in an excited and amped-up manner. He remembered hearing, "The gangs were wilding out and some nigga stepped on a red flag and all hell broke loose."

Two inmates grabbed his attention when they walked to a bunk bed next to him. "What did you say your name was again? Oh my bad. I remember. Corey. Like I been telling you, don't worry about nothing 'cause anybody fuck with you I got your back. And to make you feel right at home, I put those candy bars and cupcakes under your pillow right there. Me and you can handle that nut later," said the Puerto Rican with shifty eyes to a tall black guy.

Jessie wondered what the guy meant by "handle that nut later."

While the Puerto Rican walked behind the other inmate, staring at his ass as they left the area, he shot Jessie a nasty look. Meanwhile, in the gym in another part of C-76, another inmate had some serious payback on his mind.

"Yo, Stan. I just heard from one of my homeboys that Jessie is in the building. That nigga Pops Lorenzo snitched on my pops, Deeboy. So you know what time it is," said cock-diesel Big Dee, as he mopped the gym floor.

"Yeah, Dee, a lot of niggas heard how that nigga Lorenzo went out like a sucker. I'm down for whatever 'cause I never liked that yellow nigga anyway," said the black-as-night inmate.

After they finished their work detail, they headed to the jail yard. A few minutes later, while lifting weights, they spotted Jessie reading a *Source* magazine. Big Dee, and the guy named Nugget, walked over to Jessie.

"Yo, homeboy, ain't you from Harlem?" asked Big Dee.

Jessie looked up and said, "Yeah, and what's it to you?"

Big Dee, with a Kool-Aid smile, said, "Oh, 'cause I'm from there, too, and us Harlem niggas got to stick together."

Before Jessie grasped what was happening, Big Dee tried to stick him with a sharp, jail-made weapon as Nugget, and other inmates who had run over, joined in the fracas. They punched and kicked Jessie.

A corrections officer watched from afar, pretending he

did not see what was happening as the inmates under his charge beat Jessie to a pulp. The last thing Jessie heard before being knocked unconscious was Big Dee saying, "This is the beating your father should have got for snitching on my pops, Deeboy."

Jessie awoke a few hours later in the Rikers Island infirmary with a throbbing headache, a swollen eye, a few minor puncture wounds in his arm, and multiple bruises. A fat white nurse, with a name tag that read BETTY, told him it would take a few days to heal, but that he would be okay. The way she said it made Jessie think the nurse wished he was in critical condition.

What the nurse failed to take into consideration was the unstable mental condition caused by the vicious beating, especially when he was beaten because of what his father had done.

Jessie's emotions flipflopped. He was torn between retaliation and thinking that perhaps he deserved the beating. But Crystal's words that "two wrongs don't make a right" rang in his ears.

When Jessie, battered, defenseless and handcuffed looked to the other side of the room he saw Big Dee, mopping the floor and talking to Nurse Betty. His heart beat real fast as Big Dee headed toward his bed.

He knelt beside Jessie and whispered, "Nigga, I hope you ain't a rat like your old man because if you tell that we beat you up, there's nowhere to hide."

Then Big Dee bit Jessie hard on his earlobe, making him scream.

"What's going on over there?" yelled Nurse Betty.

"Oh, it's nothing, nurse," said Big Dee. "I'm sorry. I just tried to massage my cousin's sore shoulder."

* * *

A few days later, Jessie was discharged from the infirmary and returned to the jail population. He did not know that the doctors—just interns—had misdiagnosed the serious head trauma that would cause him serious problems later. Every day Jessie had to endure the taunts of inmates who made fun of him for being the son of a snitch. Jessie even let Big Dee punch him in the face every time they ran into each other because he felt guilty that his father had snitched on Big Dee's pop.

In fact, throughout most of the year, he let the other inmates punk him, even though he still had superior boxing skills. He was seen as weak. But Big Dee picked the wrong time and the wrong place when he tried to punch Jessie in front of his mother and Crystal during their jail visit. The fight ended quickly when Jessie caught Big Dee with a vicious right uppercut that put him to sleep.

Jessie smiled as the corrections officers in the visiting room tackled him and took him away. When he made it back to the dorm, the other inmates stared in disbelief. Jessie laughed like a crazy man, thinking about the perfect right uppercut he had landed.

* * *

Once his time was up, Jessie wanted to forget the experience in jail. From time to time, Wayne asked Jessie about what went on at Rikers Island. All Jessie would say was, "Jail ain't no place to be, mentally or physically, so please, let's just forget about it." Wayne stopped bringing up the subject.

The two friends tried out for a basketball team, and both were picked.

"Hey, Wayne, what time is our game at Rucker?" asked Jessie.

"Yo, Jess, we play the Gladiators at one o'clock. I'm gonna hit thirty points on them bitches," said Wayne.

Wayne's prediction was dead on the money because he was so good that a bunch of top college recruiters were already checking him out. And being blessed with NBA pro league dimensions of six feet, four inches, a nice jump shot and a crossover dribble that could put Allen Iverson to shame, nothing could stop him.

Jessie and Wayne had been best friends after going through a lot of drama together on the mean streets of Harlem. The two were so close that they made a pact by pricking their fingers with a pin, drawing blood, and touching them together. Official blood brothers—just like in an old gangster movie they had seen.

Since they were blood brothers, they vowed to always have each other's back, no matter what.

One time, a crazy dude named Jimmy, who lived around their block, disrespected Wayne by spitting in his face. Jimmy was jealous because all the girls, including his girlfriend, sweated Wayne.

When Jessie saw what Jimmy did, he grabbed a Pepsi bottle and clobbered him over the head.

Ever since the Felix incident, and his jail time, Jessie had an even shorter fuse and was more violent. Some people wondered if he had a screw loose. But everyone knew that if you messed with Wayne, you were messing with Jessie.

People joked that they hung out so much, and because nobody ever saw Jessie with a girlfriend, that maybe they were homosexuals. None of them, not even Wayne, knew that Jessie did have a girl he hung around with—his sister.

"Yo, Wayne, whenever you make the pros, I want to be your agent. We are gonna make so much dough together."

"Nah, Jess, you won't have to be my agent, because me and you are going to be playing on the same team. We gon' be smashing niggas like Shaq and Kobe," said Wayne, faking like he was getting a pass from Jessie and then slam-dunking.

"Nah, son, you know my skills are too weak. I ain't got no jumpshot or no handle. A nigga like me couldn't even make the Harlem Globetrotters as a mascot."

They laughed.

As they stood by Wayne's building in the Taft Houses on 114th Street, enjoying the moment, a black S-500

Mercedes Benz pulled up and the smoked tinted window rolled down.

"Yo, Wayne, what's up, my nigga? I heard you hit fifty-four points on them bitch-ass niggas last week," said Howie Tee, the neighborhood drug supplier. He was wearing more diamonds and platinum jewelry than Puff Daddy.

Jessie still hated him for slapping him up years ago because his father snitched.

"Oh, what's up, Howie? Yeah, I hit fifty-four points, but we still lost."

"Man, but forget about losing. You still did your thing, kid. By the way, Wayne, being that we on the subject of losing, I want to holla at you about something. Can I talk to you in private. No disrespect to you, Jessie, but can you give us a minute?" said Howie Tee.

"Whatever, man," said a peeved Jessie as he walked off.

Howie Tee said to Wayne, "Yo, son, check this out. Last summer my team, the Jordaniers, lost the Entertainers Basketball Classic by one point. I feel if we would have had you on the team, we would have blew the Cavaliers out, and I would not have lost that $100,000 bet. Later on today, I want you to come by my condo on Sixty-ninth Street and Central Park West and talk about maybe putting you on the team."

"Thanks, Howie. I'm wit' dat all the way. I'll definitely slide on through and check uh brother out," said Wayne. He was ecstatic.

Howie Tee smiled with a sly grin and said, "All right, son. I'll see you later then."

As Howie Tee pulled off, Wayne smiled from ear to ear, acting like he had just been asked by Lakers Coach Phil Jackson to join the team.

Jessie walked back and said, "Yo, man. What was that stupid prick spittin' in your ear?"

Wayne was so amped up he forgot about his friend's hatred for Howie Tee. "Yo, son. Howie Tee asked me did I want to get down with the Jordaniers and you know he only lets the nicest niggas in the city play on his team. Could you imagine me and Tomahawk playing on the same team? We'd be unstoppable. Howie Tee told me to come by his condo later to kick it."

Jessie was suspicious. Ever since Howie Tee murdered Junebug and took over his 136th Street drug spot, he had a reputation of being conniving and sheisty. Even his own drug crew was starving while he flossed in diamonds, fly whips, and kept a gang of beautiful women at his beck and call. But when Jessie saw Howie Tee trying to kick it to Crystal, the thought of him putting his slimy hands on his sister made his blood boil.

The stress of coming into contact with his arch enemy, Howie Tee, gave Jessie a pounding headache, and made him desperately need some weed smoke to relieve it.

23

Crossed Over

As Wayne, wearing an old blue and white Puma sweatsuit, walked past the doorman of Executive Towers, he was impressed by the building's beautiful interior.

"Man, this nigga Howie Tee is doing his thing. Anytime a brother got chandeliers and a fireplace in the lobby of his building, shit's got to be proper," whispered Wayne to himself as he entered the elevator.

A million things went through his head as the elevator took him to the sixth floor. Wayne wondered if Howie Tee put him on his Jordaniers basketball team, would the money start rolling in. And if it did, then he could buy all the Air Jordans and bling that he wanted.

Wayne heard that the players in the Entertainers Basketball Classic League were paid handsomely by the celebrities and big drug dealers who had their teams playing in it. The good players got a cut of the betting, too.

The elevator's slight jerk as it stopped on the sixth floor jarred Wayne. He got off and knocked on 6C.

A gorgeous Asian woman, with flowing long black hair and a skimpy, lacy negligee answered the door. She smiled and seemed relaxed.

"Come in, sir. Mr. Howie is expecting you," said the woman. She took Wayne by the hand and led him into a beautiful, spacious living room furnished with top-of-the-line

Queen Anne furniture.

"Would you like a drink of Cristal, sir? Mr. Howie is in the bathroom and will be out here shortly," said the woman, with a sly smile.

Wayne nodded, then said, "Oh yeah, yo, sorry, I mean yes, miss, I'll have a drink." He tried his best not to betray his eagerness at wanting to taste the expensive drink for the first time. He knew the rappers and big ballers always drank Cristal. Now he was going to get the chance to taste their indulgences.

The Asian lady smiled at Wayne like she could somehow read his mind as she gracefully sashayed towards the kitchen.

Wayne did not realize that little miss tiny hiney was as sheisty as any ghetto chick he would ever run across. The sneaky hoe was in the kitchen lacing his drink with the GHB date-rape drug. When she finished stirring her witch's brew, she walked back into the living room holding two champagne glasses of Cristal and passed Wayne one as she sat on his lap.

Immediately Wayne felt blood rush to his penis as she passionately massaged his neck and shoulders. Wayne, horny and woozy, smiled as he sipped his drink. He felt like a big baller getting his proper due. "Man, this is some good shit, sorry, I mean good champagne. I'm getting high already." His vision blurred and everything became hazy as the colors of a psychedelic light on a night stand flashed, giving him the same bugged-eye out-of-body experience of a Rave Club kid.

Then he spotted Howie Tee, in a black satin robe, emblazoned with a big pink letter H, and black Timberland boots standing by the high-tech Bose system.

As rapper Jay Z's "Hard Knock Life" blasted from the speakers Howie Tee said, "Looks like you're enjoying yourself over there partner. Li-Wen Lee's soft hands always hit the spot."

Wayne tried to talk but no words came out of his mouth. Howie Tee walked towards him and Wayne could swear he detected some swish in his step.

"Here, kid. Take some hits of this purple haze to get you more in the mood," said Howie Tee, as he passed Wayne the blunt.

As Wayne wondered *In the mood for what?* his question was answered. Li-Wen Lee sucked in his ear and Howie Tee slowly disrobed him.

Wayne made a feeble attempt to try and stop what the two lusty individuals were doing to him, but his limbs would not function and he slipped in and out of consciousness. The last thing he remembered was being slapped on the ass by Howie Tee and Li-Wen Lee grabbing his hand and leading him inside a bedroom with a glow-in-the-dark picture of a huge pink tongue on the wall, and more psychedelic lights. In a weird way, not being able to remember all that happened to him worked in his behalf because they treated him worse than a whore or common street booty. Wayne was fucked, sucked and stuck in every orifice of his body. Howie Tee had had a sexual fixation with him since the first time he spotted him practicing basketball skills one morning in Mount Morris Park.

Howie Tee blamed the state prison system for laying the ground work in his being attracted to men. Before his five-year jail stint in Elmira, he only fucked females. But during those years spent in prison he felt forced into a predicament of having to take matters into his own hands, like jerking off, and when that got boring, fucking niggas in the ass.

Never in his wildest wet dreams did he envision enjoying such a thing. But he did. And when Howie Tee got out of prison he continued having sexual relations on the down-low with men. Howie Tee got a thrill of popping the cherries of so-called real men. And if it took putting GHB in unsuspecting victims' drinks, so be it.

Wayne's only mistake was getting caught up in the mix

of a dirty low-down homo thug. The next morning Wayne woke up in a stupor, lying on a bench at the D train 155th Street stop, leaking from the ass. He sat up, engulfed with deadly rage.

24

Curious

Jessie sensed something was not quite right. Wayne had not been the same since he had been to Howie Tee's condo. Jessie suspected that something transpired that day that changed his best friend's whole demeanor and personality. Lately, Wayne had been flying off the deep end, getting involved in petty arguments, and was short-tempered. The key was when he stopped playing basketball, which had been a part of his life since age seven.

Wayne lived to play basketball, and there was never a day that Jessie could remember that he didn't play. Rain, sleet or snow never stopped him from playing the game he loved. Now Wayne wanted nothing to do with it. He did not want to play, watch or talk about anything pertaining to basketball.

Watching this drastic change only intensified Jessie's need to find out what had happened at Howie Tee's condo. So from time to time he would question Wayne. This only made Wayne mad as he steadily refused to answer.

Then one day out of the blue, Wayne blurted out that he wanted them to kill Howie Tee. It caught Jessie off guard because Wayne had never in his presence ever mentioned taking somebody's life. After some pressure, Jessie got Wayne to tell him what went on that day at Howie's condo.

The story told to him had his head spinning as Wayne

wove a tale of being violated to the fullest. Tears rolled down Wayne's face as the words sliced his vocal cords like razor blades, making him relive the whole traumatic experience over again. It was as painful for him as a rape victim testifying in court.

Wayne said he did not remember being penetrated by Howie. Jessie understood, because the hardest thing for a man who is not homosexual to do is admit that someone stuck a penis in his ass. It would be tantamount to telling somebody that his manhood was taken. Some men raped in jail have even committed suicide because they could not live with being violated in such a way. Jessie felt what happened to his best friend had to be avenged and the only justifiable punishment that would fit such a violation was Wayne's solution—Howie Tee had to be killed.

He felt, because of Howie, a promising future had been destroyed. Then add the fact that Jessie's own family had been in dire straits due to the fact of his father's incarceration. The feds took everything except the town house that Lorenzo managed to keep because of his cooperation. Jessie's family struggles made him feel pressure to be the breadwinner. All this made killing Howie, and at the same time taking over all his drug spots, seem that much more justifiable.

What really pushed Jessie over the edge was when he saw Crystal talking to Howie Tee by his car. She did it to make Jessie mad for not paying attention to her lately. It had made Jessie so angry that that night he snuck into Crystal's room and had sex with her while their mother was asleep in the next room. This was the first time he ever did it with his mother in the house.

At the same time Wayne was going through his drama, jealousy consumed Jessie. No other female made Jessie feel like his sister did, and he could not stand to see anybody look at her, let alone talk to her. How could something that was so wrong feel so right?

As the days went by all Jessie could think about was

killing Howie Tee. This would not be an easy task, so the plan that he hatched out was gone over and ironed out a million times. Nobody was told about Jessie's plans, nobody. Jessie did not even tell Wayne.

The plan was to catch Howie Tee leaving this dime piece named Trina's apartment where he was known to go every Tuesday like clockwork.

Jessie would wait for Howie Tee all night if that was what it was going to take to catch him off guard. Rumor had it that Howie Tee never left his crib without his 9 mm automatic and .38 snub nose, that he called Old Kissy. Many men were six feet under with bullets from those guns.

The only thing that stopped Jessie from putting his plan in motion was the fact that Howie Tee had gone to Baltimore to buy some drug weight. But Jessie knew that nothing would keep Howie Tee from missing his Tuesday night ritual with Trina. Trina was drop-dead gorgeous with a beautiful brown complexion, hazel eyes and a body to die for. Everybody around the neighborhood knew she had Howie Tee pussywhipped like a little puppy dog. Howie Tee did anything Trina wanted him to do.

He brought Trina mink coats, expensive jewelry, a red Porsche, and rumor had it that he was buying her a house in Baltimore. All the other girls were sweating Howie Tee like crazy, but all he did was fuck them and pass 'em to his homeboys. His running trains on girls was legendary. That's why when Jessie saw him kicking game to his sister, he pictured five guys taking advantage of her. This is another reason why Howie Tee had to die.

25

Howie Tee

The weather was sunny and bright and the fiends were fiending.

"How many you want, how many you want? 'Cause it's mad hot out here, so hurry up," said Zip Jack to the skinny dope fiend with long braids.

"Give me six bags. I hope it's as good as the last time, Zip," said the dope fiend, passing Zip Jack some money.

"Come on now, don't even disrespect me, my shit is murder. We got this shit on lock," said Zip Jack. Jessie and Wayne stood by the corner phone observing the hand-to-hand action on crowded 136th Street. It was the first of the month—a drug dealer's best day to do business because people got their checks and all the fiends got money.

Then add the fact that the sun was shining on a beautiful Friday and it was summertime and everybody was outside. Nothing could compare to the electrifying energy of days like this in Harlem. That is, if you were not broke like Jessie and Wayne.

"Yo, Wayne, I hate being broke and not having any loot. These niggas is doing it out here and it's about time we get some of this paper," said Jessie scratching his name on the phone booth's glass, with a sharp stiletto knife.

"Man, Jess, I'm wit' you, wearing last year's gear just ain't getting it. I want to get those new Air Jordans but them bad boys cost $200. I can't even afford the box that they come in," said Wayne.

"Don't worry, homeboy. Before long, me and you gonna be running all this shit and chumps gonna be sweating us," said Jessie, putting the stiletto knife in the pocket of his baggy blue jeans.

"Look at all these chicken heads riding these niggas dicks. If you got paper, they on yours, but if you broke, they ain't trying to hear you. That's why I don't fuck wit' 'em," lied Jessie.

"Yo, Jess, what you got planned? Is there something you're not telling me?"

"Don't worry about it, son, you will find out soon enough. 'Cause actions speak louder than words, feel me," said Jessie, with a sinister look on his face, honed from a year spent on Rikers Island.

"All right, if you want to play it like that, it's all right with me. Man, Jess, look at Trina with those tight-ass white pom-pom shorts. Little shorty fat ass is just busting out, that's one bad bitch. And look at her homegirl, Pam. Them bitches is straight dimes," said Wayne grabbing his crotch.

"Yeah, dog, and right about now me and you ain't got two nickels to rub together. Quiet as it's kept, if I had some money I could pull Trina from Howie Tee. Just look at her. All while he's OT, homegirl's out here looking for something to get into," said Jessie, angrily.

"Well, Jess, whatever it is she's looking for is right here in my pants." Wayne's comment made them both laugh.

"Yo, son, let's go to the town house and get something to eat," said Jessie, rubbing his stomach and spitting.

"That sounds like a plan. I'm hungrier than ten people. Let's get outta here," said Wayne.

When they got to the town house, Kathy was watering plants in the kitchen.

Wayne said, "Hi, Mrs. Thompson. Do you need some help with that?"

"Thanks for asking, Wayne, but I'm almost finished. By the way, how is your mother, Sandy? Is her sugar diabetes still bothering her?" asked Kathy.

"Yeah, Mrs. Thompson. I think she's getting worse. Her eyesight is real bad and she barely recognizes me sometimes," said Wayne, depressed just thinking about it.

"Don't worry, Wayne, when you get that big NBA contract you will be able to provide your mother the best care," said Kathy, using a metal pick to lift the dirt of some yellow begonias in a small green flower pot. Wayne stared at the white kitchen walls thinking about how in one night Howie Tee had shattered his dreams.

When his mom mentioned the NBA, Jessie became even angrier at Howie Tee. He could not wait for homeboy to get back in town because his next trip was going to be six feet under.

After Jessie made them cheeseburgers and french fries, they went inside his room to eat. While sitting down to eat and watch music videos on BET, Jessie and Wayne visualized living the lifestyles of platinum rappers.

"Yo, son, look at that Phat Bentley Phantom that Q-Tip is riding in. Them niggas is living large," said Wayne.

"Man, all them rappers is studio gangsters, none of them can't bust a grape, let alone a gun," said Jessie.

"Nah, son, some of them niggas is real. My man Tupac was a straight soldier, he died thuggin'," said Wayne, putting his burger on a plate by a nightstand and faking like he was busting a gun.

"Yeah, Wayne, you kinda right, but some of them rappers is straight pussies, and wouldn't make it a day in jail," said Jessie, thinking of his own traumatic experience on Rikers Island. "That's why they always get robbed for their jewels in the hood."

"Anyway, Jess, where's Crystal? I haven't seen her in a while. Is she all right?"

"Oh, she's okay, she just went to Florida for the summer to see some of our family. Why you asking about her?" said Jessie, fidgeting as he channel-surfed with the remote.

"Boy, you seem kinda testy whenever it comes to your sister. It ain't really nothing, I was just wondering how she was doing. You don't have to spaz out or nothing," said Wayne, looking dead at Jessie.

"I'm sorry, son, I'm just stressed out 'cause I'm tired of being broke and watching all these other niggas do their thing," said Jessie, no longer touching his food.

"Don't worry, son, at least we eating," said Wayne, making them both laugh as he chomped down on his burger.

Then Wayne spotted a poster on the wall of a young Michael Jordan flying through the air and dunking.

He immediately became so depressed and sick to the stomach that he stopped eating.

When Jessie tuned into his best friend staring at his poster, he knew what he was thinking. That put the last nail in Howie Tee's coffin.

26

I Know You Been Cheating

Three weeks later, while standing on 150th and Eighth Avenue, Jessie spotted Howie Tee and Slick Willie, the point guard of his basketball team, sitting in Howie Tee's Mercedes.

Jessie's heart beat at a crazy pace, not from fear but from an adrenaline rush. As the object of Jessie's attention sat in his Mercedes, Jessie could not keep still. He was thinking murderous thoughts. The first thing he had to do to put his plan in motion was to steal the gun that was given to his mom by his pops for protection. That would be easy because she always hid it in the closet by the kitchen.

After that, he would catch Howie Tee off-guard at Trina's apartment on Tuesday, which was tomorrow. But for now, Jessie just stared at Howie Tee with the look of a madman.

As Jessie stood there, he spotted Crystal approaching Howie Tee's Mercedes on the driver's side. Jessie wanted to go over there to see what she was up to, but decided to wait. Crystal went to the passenger's side, and a devious, smiling Slick Willie got out and she got in.

Jessie was so angry that he headed towards the Mercedes, but Howie Tee pulled off before he got there.

Not only was Jessie's heart beating real fast from thinking about what Howie Tee had in store for Crystal, his forehead and the palms of his hands were covered in sweat. The murderous rage burning up Jessie's insides made him run to the town house and get the gun and search all Howie Tee's haunts looking for him.

Every time Jessie thought of Howie Tee having sex with Crystal, his brain felt like it was going to explode. Jessie searched from sunup to sundown but he could not find them. He decided to go home and wait for her.

Finally, at 1:00 A.M. Crystal showed up with a fresh pair of Air Jordan sneakers and a bag of new clothes.

Jessie screamed at her like he was an angry husband, pissed off at his wife for coming home late. "I know where you been. You been messing around with that stupid nigga Howie Tee and he brought you all that new shit you got. You out there acting like a two dollar hoe. You and I both know you had to do something for all that stuff."

Crystal yelled back, "Mind your business. You are not my father, so don't try and tell me what to do!"

The ruckus woke up their mother. Wearing a brown nightgown she yelled, "What the hell is going on out here? Y'all out here yelling like y'all done lost y'all minds. Are y'all fools trying to get us kicked out of Strivers Row? It's too damn late for all this nonsense, so take y'all asses to bed."

They listened but said nothing because they did not want their mother to ask what they were arguing about.

After tossing and turning in bed for over an hour, Jessie snuck into Crystal's room and tried to have sex with her, but she would not let him. This only made Jessie madder, thinking she was turning him down because she had already had sex with Howie Tee. A vision of his enemy reaching for a third condom overtook Jessie's brain. He also pictured Crystal on her knees giving Howie Tee a blow job.

When Jessie's sexual advances did not work, he went back to his room and stared at the ceiling with only one thing on his mind. Murder.

27

Slap Me and I'll Slap You Back

Two hours went by and Howie Tee still had not shown up at Trina's apartment.

Jessie sat on the steps leading to the roof smelling piss, cum and crack, waiting and wondering what was taking Howie so long to come to his Tuesday sexual rendezvous. Earlier he had spotted Howie Tee in his S-500 Mercedes parked on 136th Street and Eighth Avenue. Some other light-skinned girl was sitting in his car, but Jessie already knew that no other chick could keep Howie Tee from meeting with the girl who had him pussywhipped.

After another forty-five minutes Jessie heard somebody coming up the steps, so he slowly got up and tiptoed down the stairs. It was Howie, wearing a Pele-Pele black sweatsuit, headed towards Trina's door. Jessie inched up behind him and shot him twice in the head with a .38 snubnosed gun. Howie Tee fell to the floor with half of his brain spilling out. Jessie quickly went through his pockets, stuffing two stacks of money and car keys in his pockets and ran downstairs. He suddenly realized that he forgot something. So, he doubled back, ran upstairs, lifted a dead Howie Tee's head up off the ground and slapped the shit out of him as he said, "Slap me and I'll slap you back." Then he went back downstairs, walked up the block humming a rap song like any other teenager. "Grabbed my gat, tat, tat, tat."

Jessie looked to see if anybody was around then, after spotting Howie's car in the project parking lot, he opened the trunk. He quickly grabbed a black briefcase and small bag and slowly walked toward his town house. When he reached 138th Street between Seventh and Eighth, he was relieved that nobody was outside. He walked up the stairs of the beautiful brown and brick town house and let himself in. Nobody was home. He closed the bedroom door.

On Howie Tee's key ring Jessie found the key to the briefcase. When he turned the key, the lock mechanism made a clicking sound causing Jessie to jump back as the briefcase popped open like a pirate's treasure chest. No gold or silver, but the contents held twenty kilos of cocaine, four stacks of $100 bills and pictures of a bunch of naked girls doing all types of crazy stuff of a sexual nature to Howie. When he did not see a picture of Crystal, Jessie smiled like a circus clown. Then he focused his attention on a leather pouch hidden behind a stack of glassine packets. When he opened the pouch, a 9 mm automatic dropped out and bullets ricocheted off the floor. One narrowly missed Jessie's face before becoming embedded in the ceiling. His life flashed before him as he thought he could have almost been killed by a dead man's gun.

As Jessie gathered his frayed senses, he quickly put everything but the money back inside the briefcase and placed it under the bed. The money, including what he took out of Howie Tee's pockets, totaled $68,000. Jessie's green eyes lit up like his mother's cat, Jimmy's, did at night.

Jessie had never touched one thousand dollars, let alone this much money. He thought about how he could help his family and best friend. The days of starving and watching other people floss as they stood watching like dumb asses was over. No more laying in the cut while the pretty honeys shook their butts for all the big ballers while he and Wayne stayed in fantasy land riding rappers dicks in videos.

Jessie felt a strange urge to yell "I'm going to

Disneyland!" like he had won a championship or something. But he chilled out, knowing that it was too early to be celebrating. Even though he felt it was his time to shine, he had to lay low not to bring suspicion his way.

* * *

A month went by. Howie Tee was put to rest with an elaborate ghetto funeral. In his gold coffin he wore a white Pele-Pele sweatsuit made by his favorite clothes designer, and some spanking-new black Timberlands. All the big time ballers, hustlers, drug dealers and pretty females attended.

Even many females abused, and mistreated by Howie Tee through the years were crying at the funeral. Jessie even spotted Crystal crying in one of the pews. This made him green with envy. Howie Tee was dead but still had the ability to make Jessie's blood boil.

Two months later, Jessie told all of Howie Tee's now-starving drug crew, that he had found one of his father's old black phone books and made a big drug connection. After believing Jessie's tall tale, more out of desperation than common sense, Howie Tee's former crew agreed to sell drugs for him when Jessie said he would double whatever they were getting paid before.

Meanwhile, word on the street was that somebody from Baltimore had followed Howie Tee up to New York and killed him because of a drug deal gone bad. The part about the drug dealer following him up to New York was true.

While Howie Tee had been in Baltimore he beat a big drug dealer named Cisco on a shady deal. Cisco had followed Howie Tee up to New York to seek revenge, but Jessie had killed Howie Tee before he could do it.

This worked in Cisco's favor and also in Jessie's, too, because nobody suspected him when he slowly took over the dead man's drug territory.

The only person Jessie told that he killed Howie Tee was Wayne. Wayne was shocked, but that did not stop him from sharing in the profits.

Jessie gave him $34,000 and made him lieutenant in his drug crew that he called the Crossover Crew, after Wayne's crazy crossover on the basketball courts. The first thing they did with some of the money was celebrate their birthdays. Jessie was eighteen and Wayne was seventeen, one week apart. They both went to 125th Street on a crazy shopping spree, buying Air Jordans, Timberland boots, fly jeans, sweatsuits and name-brand shirts, like Sean John, Enyce and Phat Farm. Then they bought matching blue-red Ninja motorcycles. Wayne decided to purchase a nice Cuban gold chain with a diamond basketball pendant. Jessie did not like to wear jewelry so he bought himself a video camera.

Later that night they showed up looking real fly in Nike sweatsuits, and their new Air Jordans at Jessie's godfather's bar, Big Red's, on 128th Street and Lenox Avenue, where all the big ballers, drug dealers and fly chicks hung out.

It was Friday night and the place was loaded. The DJ was bumping all the latest hip-hop jams, plus Tupac and Biggie. When Biggie Small's song "Warning" came on, Jessie just nodded his head up and down as he and Wayne smoked a fat blunt, and drank champagne to celebrate their birthdays. Jessie spotted Trina giving him the eye but he played her out the same way she used to do him. In his mind, none of these chicks had nothing on his pretty sister at home. Crystal had light brown eyes and he felt her chest and ass were better and bigger than any chick in there. A girl, who walked by his table smelling like the same Ysatis by Givenchy perfume his sister used, only intensified his feelings. While they enjoyed the atmosphere and their birthdays, Wayne danced with a beautiful, dark-skinned girl named Juicy who lived in the Polo Grounds projects.

As Wayne danced the night away, Trina came up to Jessie and made small talk. "Hey, Jessie, how you doing? Long time no see. Somebody told me it's your birthday. Happy birthday." Then she sang the Stevie Wonder version of "Happy Birthday." Jessie smiled because Trina had such a beautiful voice— a cross between Mary J. Blige and Anita Baker. Hearing her sing made Jessie forget about his pay-back-is-a-bitch game and say, "Girl, somebody should put you in the studio. You can sing your ass off."

"Well, Jessie, right before Howie died, he had made arrangements with this music producer to produce some songs. But then he got killed," said Trina, looking downward as her voice dropped.

Jessie said, "Oh, I am so sorry to hear that. Everybody's been talking about it. They said somebody from Baltimore came up to New York and killed him."

"Yeah, that's what everybody is saying, but who really knows. Did you hear that I sang at his funeral?" said Trina.

"Yeah. Somebody told me you tore the place down when you sang 'Missing You.'"

When Jessie said that, she cried and he grabbed a napkin and wiped her tears away, just like a conniving murderer would do at the funeral of the person he killed.

When Wayne came back from the dance floor he said, "What is going on over here? Don't tell me my homeboy making the girls cry already."

Smirking, Jessie said, "Nah, it's not like that. Trina's just going through a stressful situation, but she gonna be all right."

Trina smiled. At 4:30 A.M., when the place closed, Jessie gave her a ride home on his new motorcycle.

After that night Jessie and Wayne went about handling their business on the avenue. One thing about Harlem, if you were doing your thing on the streets, everybody knew, which could lead to all sorts of problems due to the fact that somebody always wants what you have. If you were known to be weak, you could not make it on the mean streets of Harlem. There are stickup kids, gangsters, thugs, and people looking to extort anybody. It was survival of the fittest, and only the strong survive. Jessie and Wayne, although they were young bucks, were well aware of this fact. They both made a conscious decision that the first sign of trouble they would go for the guns. This was something that Jessie was not afraid to do.

Their drug spot on 136th Street and Lenox was doing so well that Jessie was reupping his stash every other week. When the drugs that Jessie took from Howie Tee ran out, he convinced Red, to hit him off with kilos. This was not a small feat; Red was totally against him getting involved in such a dangerous game in the first place. But Jessie told Red that if he did not sell the drugs to him, somebody else would. This made Red go against his own wishes because he knew Jessie meant what he said, and Red also figured he could keep a closer eye on Jessie.

Since day one Red always treated Jessie like a son. Even after his father snitched, Red gave Jessie money and asked about his mother. Everybody in Harlem knew that Red had held a secret crush on her since they were kids. People suspected that Red never acted on his feelings due to the fact that she wound up with his best friend, Lorenzo. The fling that Red and Kathy had when they were young was so brief nobody knew about it.

Jessie did not care too much about any of this. He was just happy that Red was hitting him off with major weight and that he was on the road to the riches.

But not too long after making a drug pickup at Big Red's , the drama started.

When Jessie got on his motorcycle he spotted this stickup kid named Celo watching him from across the street. The way Celo was eyeballing him Jessie sensed there was going to be trouble. But after his first kill, Jessie had been looking forward to busting his guns again.

While Jessie put on his helmet, Celo came across the street.

"Yo, shorty, let me holla at you," said a cock-diesel Celo, wearing a played out tight-ass, black muscle shirt.

"Yeah, man, what you want cause I'm in a rush," said Jessie.

"Listen here, shorty, the first thing you betta do is take all that base out your voice. And second of all starting tomorrow, I want half of whatever you and your little man, Wayne, make every week, you got that?"

Without expression, Jessie looked at Celo up and down and pulled off popping a wheelie like a rough rider.

Jessie knew exactly what he had to do. He headed to the town house, got the 9 mm automatic out of the dead man's briefcase, then got back on the motorcycle and headed back to 128th Street and Lenox Avenue to look for Celo.

He spotted Celo heading inside one of the six-story buildings. Jessie slowly followed behind. These were the same buildings that Jessie and his friends used to jump across while people watched from the streets below. *Crazy Harlem kids,* Jessie thought. Celo walked up the stairs and headed for the roof with Jessie dead on his tracks.

Jessie figured that this meant Celo was going to get high so he patiently waited a few minutes, then busted through the door with the 9 mm automatic in his hand.

Celo screamed like the first time he got fucked in jail. The crack pipe fell out of his hand, shattering in bits and pieces.

"Now keep your dirty motherfuckin' hands where I can see them, you fuckin' crackhead," said Jessie. His face had transformed from the pretty boy, baby-faced type of nigga that Celo always robbed easily to that of the devil.

The sight of looking at a slightly red-faced Jessie, whose light-skinned complexion only got that way when he was real angry, made Celo become unglued. He was scared shitless.

"Yo, Jessie, I was just playing wit' you, homey. You know I wasn't serious," said Celo, shaking in his old, faded Levi jeans.

"Yo, son, I ain't gon' sweat that and being that I believe you, and I'm such a nice guy, I'm gonna give you two choices. Either you want me to shoot you, or you can jump from this roof and hope you survive. You got five seconds to make up your mind," said Jessie, as he started to count. "One, two . . . "

"Please, Jessie, I was just—"

Jessie continued, "Three, four . . ."

Celo yelled, "Fuck you and your rat father!" then flew off the roof like he was auditioning for a new role of a tight, black, muscle dress-shirt-wearing, black Superman.

All Jessie heard was a loud boom and a cracking sound as he walked downstairs and out of the building past a bloody Celo splattered on the top of a red Honda Accord. *Just another creepy coordinated ghetto visual*, he thought. He rapped, "Grabbed my gat, but no tat-tat-tat."

28

The Crossover Crew

"So and so got a tight crew," "Nah, so and so got a tighter crew," was all Jessie heard while growing up on the streets of Harlem.

Even his father bragged about how tight the SSJ Crew was and how they held shit down to the fullest.

But what Jessie quickly found out was that most, if not all of the drug crews, were just wick, wick, wack.

Jessie did not have to search too hard to find this out either, or did he have to look somewhere in the ether. Just watching how so called real niggas like his pops covered their own asses when the shit hit the fan told him all he needed to know.

Jessie learned never judge a person by the stuff they do when things are going good. Judge them by the actions taken under extreme pressure—where most people fail.

While Jessie was outside playing games like Run, Catch, Kiss, where the worst thing that could happen was catching a girl with bad breath, his father was playing a real game of Run, Catch, Snitch with deadly consequences. But that did not stop Jessie from feeling that he was from a different breed.

Yeah, Jessie heard the old-timers say the game was over, but to him they must have been talking about the kissing game, not the drug game. If they were not, Sorry, Charlie, gotta make moves.

Now that Jessie was a little older and had taken in all the lessons learned from watching his father and other drug dealers on the streets of Harlem, he felt ready to take things to another level, to step the game up.

By accident, Jessie learned from an early age that it was all about the Benjamins.

"Stay down, you stupid motherfucker. Stay down," eight-year-old Jessie remembered the crowd yelling when the Cadillac hit him. At the time, he did not have the slightest idea why everybody wanted him to stay on the cold, black-tarred street. All he wanted to do was get up and get out of there because he wasn't hurt. But what Jessie later found out was the reason they wanted him to stay down had more to do with suing the guy who hit him and less to do with really being hurt. The idea was to get the money. This was an enlightening lesson for a kid, because when people grow up poor in the hood, they learn that no one else is going to give them anything but a hard time.

So, when Jessie decided to get into the drug game, he had every intention of being a better drug dealer and a whole lot smarter than his father and the so-called tight crews that made costly mistakes. He thought about the type of people he wanted in his own drug crew. One thing he knew for sure was that he did not want snitches, bitch-ass niggas and two-faced wannabe gangsters.

Knowing all they were capable of doing was getting a brother locked up or killed. Jessie's father always tried to school him about hanging around people he felt fit this criteria. This was a good thing. The sad thing was that Pops turned out to be just like them. Although now Jessie was on some poppa-don't-preach shit, he fully agreed with his Pops' saying about, "Don't start nothing, won't be nothing."

The only thing Jessie thought he should have added was "Think and grow rich." When Jessie first got involved in the drug business, he made a promise to himself that he would capitalize from others' mistakes.

When he was younger, he watched his father and all the other guys that ran drug crews run around like chickens with their heads cut off when their supply did not meet the demand. The crackheads and dope fiends would be fiending and the dope dealers would be going crazy due to the fact of a drug drought.

To eliminate that problem, Jessie always made sure he bought extra quantity. By doing so, he could charge a cheaper price because the more he bought, the better the rate. Also, his product had to be a better quality than the rest of the competition if he was to succeed in having drug users cop from his crew. What you know and who you know can sometimes be the deciding factor in who makes it in this land of opportunity. And, Red had the connection and the top select that gave Jessie the keys to the city. Jessie's motto: "Ten thousand a key, come see me." Jessie's first choice of members for the Crossover Crew was a no-brainer because they were loyal. And no one was more loyal to Jessie than his best friend, Wayne.

Although Wayne was not the toughest guy in the world, he sure was not the weakest. Since day one, Wayne and Jessie always held each other down to the fullest. Forget being tight. They were brothers from a different mother.

The day an older guy kicked Jessie in the ass for sitting on his car and Wayne jumped in to help him, showed Jessie what Wayne was really made of. As Jessie kicked the guy's ass, Wayne almost killed the guy when he got the strength of Hercules and started banging his head on the hard concrete.

Wayne's actions were a true test of loyalty and character and he passed with flying colors. Wayne was a quiet dude, but not the least bit soft.

Jessie's next choices were two wild Jamaican brothers named Marvin and Mike. Jessie made friends with them in junior high school where they were treated like outcasts because other students could not understand their Jamaican dialect and because they wore funny-colored clothes. Although they were buck wild and always getting into fights, they liked Jessie because he never made fun of them. At the time, Jessie had no way of knowing that the school drama they endured was nothing compared to what they had to go through in Jamaica. Before coming to New York, things were very hard in their hometown. In order just to have something to eat, like porridge or stewed peas for their family, they had to resort to drastic measures like robbery, extortion and murder. *So here in the States, what do you think they would do for ox tails?* Jessie wondered.

After witnessing them holding their own, Jessie had to have them in his crew. The next crew member was a guy named Skeeter, who sold guns in the hood and could tell you anything you needed to know about artillery and self-defense. He learned all this from a crazy uncle who had been a career military man.

Jessie and Skeeter met in Gleason's Boxing Gym where Jessie's father had enrolled him when he was little. Lorenzo felt that Jessie needed to learn to defend himself and learn discipline so he had him in boxing and karate classes. This Jessie learned, but he also was taught all the dynamics of handling and using all types of weaponry like .38s, 9 mms, and Tech Nines, from his pal, Skeeter, in a project recreation room.

Skeeter would say things like, "Never forget about the bullet in the chamber. If you pull it out, use it, cock back and squeeze." Under his supervision, in no time at all, the student was up to par with the teacher when it came to handling weapons. Having been taught well gave Jessie an advantage over enemies. While in boxing class, Jessie had also lifted weights and managed to bulk up. He was no longer some puny little kid. Skeeter could swear he heard *Rocky* theme music "Getting Strong Now" anytime he saw his boxing mate kick some bully's ass that messed with him. *Stick and move. Stick and move.* Afterwards they would laugh about what technique Jessie used to finish the guy off.

After Lorenzo snitched, Skeeter watched many times from his third-floor window as a grown Howie Tee slapped, kicked and spit on little Jessie.

Skeeter felt real good for Jessie knowing all he had gone through from getting slapped around and beat up for something his pops did.

The physical and verbal abuse got even worse when other people around the neighborhood joined in. One time, when Skeeter felt he had seen enough, he sat by the same window with one of his uncle's high-powered rifles and seriously considered killing Howie Tee while he sold drugs directly across the street. But Skeeter's fear of the known, coldhearted killer Howie Tee made him chicken out. That's why when Skeeter watched Jessie get on some I'm-as-mad-as-hell-and-I'm-not-gonna-take-it-anymore-type shit, the tables turned. Jessie's knuckle game was crazy and it only added to his reputation when word got out that he told these three guys who were messing with him to give him a one-on-one and wound up kicking all their asses. After that, people knew shorty was not having it.

When Jessie decided to get in the drug game, Skeeter came to mind, because he knew Skeeter was intrigued by the drug game from his questions about his father's back-in-the-days exploits. Now instead of telling Skeeter about all that, he would give him the opportunity to experience the whole drug lifestyle first hand.

Howie Tee's drug crew had previously already crossed over.

29

Close Encounters

Down a few blocks from 139th Street and up on a corner, Terry-O said, "I don't care what nobody else thinks, but there's not a doubt in my mind that little pussy Jessie killed my cousin. Forget all that nonsense about some drug dealers from Baltimore doing it. I ain't the least bit stupid, cause it ain't no mere coincidence that Howie Tee is dead and Jessie is running his shit."

"Yo, Terry-O, I don't think it's a good idea to go messing with shorty. Big Red got his back and we all know that homeboy don't play when it comes to laying the murder game down," said Jay.

"Man, fuck Red. That nigga can get it, too. My heart don't pump no Kool-Aid. What I'm supposed to be, shook like he Suge Knight or some fucking body? Jessie and that bitch-ass Wayne was bums out here until my cousin died. I seen Trina riding on Jessie's motorcycle. Them niggas is as good as dead. Even though I did not get along with Howie Tee, still if anybody should be running 136th Street it's me. That shit got to stay in the family," said Terry-O.

A natural-born follower, Jay said, "So how you wanna do this? Wayne is always on the block running the workers, and niggas say that he's messing around with Crystal, so he's easy to get. But Jessie is another story because he's Mr. Seldom Seen, so we got to catch him right."

"Yo, partner, I got it all figured out. The same way he caught Howie Tee, is the same way I'm gonna catch him out there. What goes around comes around," said Terry-O, making a zero out of the smoke from his Newport cigarette.

* * *

"I fuck your girl and make you like me, but letting you jump on my dick ain't likely, you claim to be a thug but ain't never bust slugs." *Pow, pow, pow.* Before the rapper could finish busting a rhyme in this rap cipher on 136th Street and Seventh Avenue, some thugs in a black Ford Expedition were busting their guns for real.

The unexpected gunfire had everybody that was a part of the rap cipher, including innocent bystanders, running for cover, except for Crossover Crew members, Marvin and his brother, Mike, who returned rapid fire from their newly bought Glocks. One of them screamed, "Blast the bloody bumbleclods." But, the culprits were already speeding down the avenue like they were racing in the Daytona 500.

"Damn, dem niggas ain't playing," said the skinny rapper running into traffic trying to save his own ass.

The bullets never made any flesh contact with anybody on the street but ricocheted off buildings, and some became imbedded in a blue mailbox and some parked cars.

As the Ford Expedition sped off at 90 mph down Seventh Avenue, Wayne managed to get a glimpse of the truck and knew automatically that it was Terry-O's.

"Man, did you see how those bitch-ass niggas dove for cover," said Jay.

"True dat now them niggas know what time it is, and we ain't taking no shorts. Know what I'm saying, bruh man? In no time at all, son, we gon' be running shit, and them two pussies gon' be dead ass," said Terry-O, frantically trying to light a cigarette while driving.

A few minutes after the shoot-out, Jessie arrived and was briefed about what had transpired.

"Yo, Jess, we need to do them niggas, we can't have

chumps coming on our block shooting shit up. If we don't retaliate, niggas gon' think we pussies," said Wayne, shattering a Coca-Cola bottle on a brick building.

Jessie said, "That's what niggas expect for us to do—go off shooting up shit like the OK Corral. Then the spot gon' get hot and we really gon' have problems. Let niggas say or think what they want, but we don't have to stoop to their levels. Maybe them niggas was shooting at a dope fiend."

Marvin and Mike shot Jessie funny looks, while secretly hoping their homeboy wasn't getting soft.

Wayne also could not believe what he was hearing, but he figured his boy knew best so he left it alone. Wayne also wanted to tell Jessie that he had fallen in love with Crystal, but he decided to tell him some other time.

Jessie found it hard to keep a straight face while telling Wayne all that bull crap. But he felt it was best that blabbermouth Wayne not know his real plans for fear he would tell the Crossover Crew. In Jessie's mind the fewer people who knew about his plans of killing Jay and Terry-O the better. Plus, he thought, *Actions speak louder than words. Boo ya ka, boo ya ka.* But for now Jessie would have to play pussy and try not to get fucked.

* * *

When Jessie came home Wayne and Crystal were watching videos.

"Yo, man, you on vacation or something? Shouldn't you be outside watching the workers? I ain't paying you to sit here and watch videos," said Jessie, angrily, as he turned off the television.

"Chill, son, chill. We ran out of work and I came here to reup. That Blue Top and Duji is moving faster and faster. We got the best stuff out there and the fiends are loving it. I was supposed to tell you to hit me off earlier but all that shoot'em-up bang bang threw me off," said Wayne, tickling Crystal.

"Okay, I hear what you saying, but go back to the block and I'll hit you off after I bag up this new batch," said Jessie.

"All right, man, but let me tell you something before I leave. I been meaning to tell you that me and Crystal are dating and I'm feeling her in a major way," said Wayne.

Crystal hugged Wayne and they tongue-kissed right in front of Jessie. Jessie was angry that Wayne was violating one of the codes of the streets that dictates you don't mess around with your homeboy's sister.

Jessie said sarcastically, "Oh, so you trying to tell me that instead of handling your business outside, you been handling your business inside."

Before Wayne could answer, Crystal said, "You don't have to put it like that Jessie, because my man is on point and all he talks about is you and that damn Crossover Crew."

"Crystal, you need to shut up when two men are talking," said Jessie, talking grown.

"Dog, Jess, you ain't got to come out your face like that. You acting like you jealous or something. I'm your best friend, not your enemy. If anything, you should be happy for us," said Wayne.

Jessie looked at both of them with disgust then walked in his room and slammed the door.

That night Crystal went in his room and told Jessie to stop acting like a jealous boyfriend before Wayne started to suspect something.

"Crystal, I don't know what's come over me but I get mad if anybody even looks at you, let alone touches you. I love you like a husband does a wife and no matter how hard I try to change, my feelings get stronger and stronger."

Crystal knew how he felt, but she had also fallen in love with Wayne, but when their eyes met while talking, something came over the brother and sister. Soon they were kissing and hugging and had wild sex. Through it all, Crystal had tears in her eyes.

30

Truly Yours

Crystal, visibly upset, said, "Hey, Jessie, that girl Trina been calling here all day looking for you." She pranced around the town house in some blue, tight-fitting shorts.

Jessie, watching her every move, said, "How did she get my number? I didn't give it to her." He sounded like he was pleading his case to a girlfriend.

"Well, she got it from somewhere and she left a number for you to call her. Here it is," said Crystal, snidely. Crystal passed the number to Jessie and went to her room to watch television. Even though Jessie had not thought about Trina since his birthday, he decided to call her.

Jessie's mind had been occupied with handling a thriving drug business. His name was the talk of the town and everybody was talking about the young guy from Harlem, who was moving major weight and making things happen. Every so often just to let the streets know that his knuckle game was still intact, Jessie would start a fight with a local tough guy and knock him out cold. Nothing thrilled Jessie more because he possessed the skills to do that. If the streets had not pulled him in, Jessie could have been a pro-boxing contender—he was that good with his hands. Between that, and the fact he had a black 2004 Cadillac Escalade with the spinning chrome twenty-four-inch rims, this kid was shining. All of this only made his ego bigger, picturing him and the Crossover Crew running Harlem's thriving drug trade.

So many things ran through his mind as he called Trina, the neighborhood dime piece.

"Hello, Trina, this is Jessie."

Trina said, "Jessie, I've been looking all over for you since your birthday. One of your workers gave me your number. I can't lie to you, I told him I had it, but I lost it."

"Which one of them gave it to you?" said Jessie.

"Oh that guy, Jimmy, with the cock eye," said Trina, displaying her gift at dropping dime.

"I guess I was wrong. I thought Wayne gave it to you. Anyway, check this out, would you like to go to BBQs on 72nd Street and get some ribs?" he asked.

"Yes, Jessie, that would be real nice right about now because I'm mad hungry."

"Okay, Trina, I'll be over by your building in fifteen minutes, so wait for me outside."

When Jessie pulled up on his motorcycle, Trina was standing there wearing a pink and grey velour Roca-Wear sweatsuit that fitted her real nice. Trina's fat ass and ample breasts were damn near busting out of the fabric. She also had on some new white Nike Air Force Ones.

Homegirl was looking ghetto fabulous. As she got on the motorcycle and Jessie pulled off heading to BBQ's, all he could think of was, *This is what a drug dealer hustles for.*

* * *

At BBQ's Restaurant they ate ribs, collard greens, and potato salad, then went to the bar and ordered Long Island Iced Teas. As they drank they listened to Mariah Carey's "Butterfly" playing on the jukebox. This put them in an amorous mood.

"Trina, I forgot to ask you on my birthday about why are you taking an interest in me now, when before you used to look right through me?" asked Jessie, as Trina admired his fresh haircut and spanking new light-green Sean John shirt that matched his eyes.

"Jessie, Howie Tee used to be real jealous and he did not want me looking at anybody, let alone you. I always thought you were real cute but I only date one guy at a time," said Trina, lying.

"But, Trina, you sure it wasn't because I was just some broke chump without a dollar to my name? On the real, I always thought you looked at me like I was nothing," said Jessie, speaking his mind and not caring if he got some pussy tonight.

"Nah, never that, boo, but what I did see was ambition whenever we did make eye contact. Now look at you, doing your thing and all the females around the hood want to sex you," said Trina, softly touching his hand.

"Girl, I ain't sweating none of them chicks 'cause none of them was feeling me when I was broke. But let's get off that subject before I ruin the night. Anyway girl, you know I can't let you leave this place without me hearing that lovely voice of yours. Matter fact, on our way inside here I saw a sign that said it's karaoke night," said Jessie, with a big smile.

Trina grabbed Jessie's hand and smiled from ear to ear as they made their way to the back room, and she sang "Silly," the classic song by Deneice Williams. Her beautiful voice and song selection blew the packed BBQ's Restaurant crowd away and they gave Trina a standing ovation. Trina bowed like she was on stage at the Apollo Theatre.

After Jessie and Trina left the restaurant, she was feeling so good that she asked him to go to her apartment. When he agreed, she said, "I've got a surprise for you."

After they made it to her beautiful apartment in the Lenox Terrace Building on Lenox Avenue she went inside her bathroom and a few minutes later came out wearing a pink, two-piece laced bikini set. By Trina's crotch area it read TRULY YOURS in white letters.

As Trina started singing "Silly" again, Jessie felt like he was in ghetto heaven as she slowly swayed over to him.

Before she could even finish the last verse they were rubbing, kissing and touching each other all over.

But the weird thing was that Jessie could not manage to get an erection. Trina tried massaging and sucking him off but nothing was happening. Nada. They tried all night, but Jessie just could not rise for the occasion.

In the morning Trina tried to massage his fragile ego by telling him that it happens to the best of them. But that was the last thing he wanted to hear.

A disturbing feeling of wanting to kill the bitch to prevent her from spreading the words that every man fears, *Yo, homeboy couldn't get it up*, went through his head. So Jessie got up and left feeling like a chump for not being able to handle his business.

Jessie thought his body and mind were playing cruel tricks on him, until he realized that he had never had real sex with anybody but Crystal. This made him think that maybe that had something to do with it. *Could this be God's way of telling me to stop having incestuous sex with my own flesh and blood?* he wondered.

31

Secrets

Jessie was all ears as he listened intently to a rarely talkative Red in the John Lennon Strawberry Field section of Central Park.

"Jessie, I have tried my best to persuade you from getting involved in the drug business and you basically said in so many words that nothing was going to stop you from doing what you wanted to do. But I do feel that because I am your godfather and have been in your life since the day you were born, it is my duty to school you on some of the rules of the game," said Red, feeding the pigeons.

In the hood the same type of deranged person who murdered John Lennon for props came a dime a dozen on the drug games killing fields.

The thugs, extortionists, and people without consciences, who thought nothing of killing mothers, babies, children, anybody, when they want what another drug dealer has, made the drug game no picnic in the park.

"Jess, one thing that you have to understand is the streets are always watching, so trust no one, and have eyes in the back of your head."

Jessie nodded in agreement. As Jessie paid close attention, Red threw a peanut to one of the smaller pigeons. A bigger one with spotted gray dots on his head, different from the other pigeons, snatched it and gobbled it up. Red just laughed and continued to talk.

"You see, Jess, the jails and cemeteries are full of people who thought they knew everything, even your father. So what you have to do, kid, is learn from the mistakes of others. Some people on the streets are wondering why I let the son of a snitch come into my cipher, being that all I been through concerning your pops. On the real I'm telling you that you being my godson has nothing to do with it and more to do with judging you on your own merits, and not by the mistakes of your father, who I know you despise."

Secretly maybe that too had played a part in Red's decision to do business with Jessie. Everybody has secrets, including Red.

Jessie whispered to himself, "Damn, my hating my father is that obvious?"

But Red did not hear Jessie because he was preoccupied with feeding the pigeons.

Red, being a wise man, decided to teach Jessie a quick lesson on what he said about the "streets is watching."

"You see, Jessie, the reason you managed to kill Howie Tee is because you caught him slipping."

Jessie was flabbergasted. He could not believe how the fuck Red knew, because he thought he committed the perfect murder.

Red smiled as he looked at the shocked expression on his little comrade's face. Then he continued, "You see, kid, now there's somebody out there looking to catch you slipping and put you under. I know it shocks the hell outta you that I know you killed Howie Tee, but it just goes to show that if I know, there's other people that know also. So always watch what you tell other people and especially don't let no female out here twist up your brain and have you telling all your business and secrets like you caught up in believing some Alicia Keys I-won't-tell-your-secrets-bullshit." They laughed like crazy, making an old white lady sitting on one of the park benches look up from the book she was reading and stare at them.

Paying her no mind, Red continued. "Oh ya thought I wasn't up on all these new records, huh, kid? Jess, I just said that to lighten up a little bit on all the serious stuff I been kicking, being that nobody likes to be preached to. But don't get it twisted, this is still a very serious matter."

Jessie could not stop laughing as Red continued to kick the ballistics and enlighten Jessie with his knowledge, and wisdom on a beautiful sunny day in the park.

Although Red was a very wise man and kept his ears to the streets, there was no way humanly possible for him to hear Crystal twenty blocks away at the town house passionately singing Alicia Keys' lyrics, "I won't tell your secrets . . . break it down . . . "

32

In Too Deep

As Jessie and Wayne sat in his Escalade on a side block near 145th Street and Bradhurst Avenue, they both were real high and completely out of it from the Potent Purple Haze they were smoking. Wayne was nodding like a dope fiend with sleep apnea. Meanwhile, Jessie could not stop talking. "Yo, Wayne, Wayne. I wanna let you in on a little secret. I admit to having something in common with my father. No, it's not what you think, being a snitch. I'm talking about the philosophical side of him that came out when he felt like getting real deep.

"Here's an example. The whole family would be sitting at the dinner table on some Brady Bunch shit and out of nowhere he'd say, 'A lot of black people gonna always stay broke because they ain't got the slightest idea what the hell it takes to make money.'

"My mother would then ask, 'What do you mean?'

"Then he would continue, 'Well, in order to make some real money that you can survive on, first you gotta figure out a way to make somebody else some money. Look at Bill Gates when he first started out he had to convince some-body who had money that if they invested in his company there was money to be made. Now look at Bill Gates—he's a billionaire. Now let me flip something like that on a smaller scale. My workers make me a lot of money, and in return they make a lot of money. You see, in this world you can't expect to eat steak while everybody around you eats toast. So spread the wealth.'"

Wayne, drifting off and digging in his ear, said, "Make money wh . . .what? Wh . . where? H . . . h . . . how?"

Jessie said, "Nigga, shut your high ass up and let me finish. Like what I'm saying is that all of this kind of stuff that my father would say while getting deep had us all on some nod-your-head to this type shit.

"This brings me back to what I said earlier about having a philosophical side like my pops.

"Every once in a while I feel like getting deep and talking about stuff that's bothering me, but I don't for fear of being judged and looked at as crazy. So I keep those mental doors in my head closed real tight. But I can't lie, sometimes when I'm smoking a blunt somewhere by myself I tend to zone out and think about stuff like, why can't I be like a kid from the Harlem Boys Choir singing songs of joy going through life as if everything is gonna be smooth sailing, college degrees, good jobs and easy living? No siree, not in this life, but maybe when I'm reincarnated, because inside my ears, brain and in the front of my face I hear and see a vivid picture of my life playing itself out like a gangster movie script and sound track. No, nigga, I'm not saying I'm like Tupac and can predict my own demise. I'm just saying I got a crazy feeling that its gonna be eerie and dark as the sounds of my footsteps make you picture a scene of rapid-gunfire-dead-bodies everywhere, a ferocious barking rottweiler and a priest standing by to give the last rites, all the makings of a disastrous ending. But by the look on my face you can't tell it's about to go down because I got more tricks up my bloody sleeve than a magician and more subplots to my story than movie director Steven Spielberg.

"Wayne, I know the weed's got us real high but did I just hear somebody say DreamWorks?"

"Nah, Jess," said Wayne, blinking and rubbing his eyes

as he tried to stay awake.

Jessie continued, paying Wayne no mind as he babbled. "Yes, I got dreams but they don't seem to be working and this is the main reason I'm stuck selling drugs.

"I know exactly what you're thinking, my brother, excuses, excuses, and I agree. But why am I out here still selling poison to my own people when I know deep down it ain't right? But wait a minute, if selling drugs is wrong why do all my customers cop with big Kool-Aid smiles? Or why are my lines longer than the free cheese lines? Even when a dope fiend dies from using my product, it still doesn't stop the other fiends from copping. They just think the reason the fiend croaked was because their system couldn't handle the high potency and theirs can.

"So word spreads real fast about my bags of 'Do or Die' on 136th Street. Get it while it's hot. Once my shit flows through their veins they ain't got a care in the world. Then they drink their sugar-loaded fifty-cent sodas to mellow them out and it's all good. That's the power of my bags of do right, and I'm the dream provider."

Jessie inhaled two strong tokes of the potent weed, then, *swoo swoo*: "My dope makes a poor man think he's rich and a ugly bitch feel pretty. Just think, all that power in a little bag of white powder."

Jessie looked at Wayne, whose head was leaning on the passenger's side window. Jessie, not seeming to care, kept blabbing. "Chill, chill. Wayne, ya know I'm only bugging and I really must be higher than uh mu-fucker because why did I mention the name of movie director, Steven Spielberg's company called DreamWorks.

"But still with all things considered, who am I to deprive dope fiends out of an escape from their messed up circumstances?

"I got my own problems. I ain't no priest trying to save souls, I'm just trying not to die of hunger. And if somebody can't understand that then, F 'em. I'm a drug dealer and what do drug dealers do? We sell drugs.

"I sell drugs not because I want to but because I have to. What's a chump with an eighth-grade education, who can't rap or play basketball and has no marketable skills for the white man's world, gonna do? I sure ain't gon' teach geometry at City University. But, I sure can tell you a little something about ounces, pounds and kilos, plus I can throw in a quick chemistry course in how to cook some cocaine or heroin. Put a one or two on it and keep 'em coming for days. Sell for less, have 'em fiending, then up the price.

"Fuck it! Even a little semester in how to make some good Ecstacy. I may not know much about biology or a lot of other things, but I do know money can buy some shit and without it, you get treated like shit.

"So the streets say, stay down motherfucker, stay down. I'm gonna stay down for my crown, and any chump who gets in my way, I gotta make an example out of him, and if that means stabbing, shooting or even killing some fool, I just don't give a fuck. Like my Jamaican homeboy, Marvin, always says, 'Who gon' test the don-da-da.' Any sucker that got something that I want, it's as good as mine. Drug spots, money, whatever, I end niggas' miseries and problems, because after I lay my gun game down, they'll be lounging with sleep's best friend, death. Ain't no shame in my game. On the streets where I come from you gotta be hard 'cause skinny niggas die young. And, if I ever gotta go, I'm definitely taking somebody along for the ride.

"Somewhere under the rainbow there is a dead man walking, but I'm always gonna be the last man standing, so let me vent, Wayne, Wayne."

33

Smoked

The opportunity Jessie had patiently waited three weeks for was finally being set in motion as he watched Jay and Terry-O standing by his former junior high school, Wadleigh I.S. 88, trying to talk to all the young girls walking by. As they stood on the corner it did not matter to them that two damn near thirty-year-old grown-ass men should be messing with females their own ages. The excuse given for their perverted actions and lapses in judgment was that they felt cheated because the younger girls these days were built like grown women and had bigger asses and chest than the females they grew up with. Excuses, excuses. They felt no harm could come out of two positive brothers looking to give back by providing their own much needed after school program that consisted of buying bags of weed, beer, new Nike sneakers and possibly some useful advice for them on not falling victim to some horny young buck. If that's what it would take to fulfill their devilish lusts, they were more than willing to provide their services with a smile.

As Jessie watched them from his Cadillac Escalade he whispered angrily, "Look at them slimy bastards kicking it to the little girls. Don't they know Jessie is for the children? Ha, ha, ha!"

Terry-O and Jay never suspected that Jessie had stalked them for three weeks, watching their every move. Jessie followed them when they left their apartments in the morning. He followed them to their drug spot on 105th Street and Second Avenue, and even to their girlfriends' cribs. Now it was prime time and they would have to pay for choosing to play in a game that plays for keeps.

Their dreams of being shot-callers, big ballers and part-time child molesters would be short-lived because they chose to mess around in the wrong part of town. So Jessie waited.

"Brother Jay, what ya say? Brother Jay, what ya say? Man look at shorty's nice ass over there sucking on that lollipop. Ain't that the one who thinks she's a rapper and be acting like she's Lil Kim and shit?" said Terry-O with a toothpick in his mouth.

"Yeah, yo, and last week I told her I was a video producer and I gave her an audition on my casting couch. She's got skills, but it ain't in rapping, if you know what I'm saying, yo" said Jay, making them both laugh.

The smell of cherry Now & Later candy, sunflower seeds and Old Navy cheap perfume flowed through the air as a police van pulled up and made the two sheisty individuals, and everybody standing on the corner, move.

Terry-O and Jay then walked around the corner and got in their rented black Ford Expedition with the dark-tinted windows and Terry-O pulled off.

"Yo, Jay, before po-po popped up, I was just about to bag that light-skinned shorty that went in the store," said Terry-O.

"Yeah, homes, and her body was banging," said a voice coming from the back.

Terry-O, shocked and confused, looked at Jay because the words they just heard did not come from them. They were both greeted by a smiling Jessie crouching in the back pointing a shiny chrome 9 mm at them. He said, "Look at here. Look at here, y'all two chumps done made my little girlfriend here jealous. Don't y'all know we been uh watching y'all? And to top it off, she's still mad that y'all did not invite her to y'all little shoot around a few weeks ago up on my block."

"Please, Jessie, don't kill me. I didn't have anything to do with your block getting shot up. It was Jay," said Terry-O, giving himself away.

Jay viciously slapped him and said, "He's lying, Jessie. He's the one that did it. He said you killed his cousin, Howie Tee."

Jessie laughed like a crazy man, then hit Jay with the butt of the gun as he motioned for Terry-O to pullover by a popular weed spot on 145th Street.

The last thing they both heard before bullets penetrated their brains was, "Who wanna get smoked?"

Then to send a message to all the thugs who had any aspirations of taking over shit, Jessie did something he learned from a book he read about the ruthless Westies Gang in Hell's Kitchen. He cut their penises off.

As Terry-O and Jay lay slumped over in the tinted vehicle Jessie got out then went inside the weed spot and ordered two bags of purple haze, like a student fresh out of school.

34

Funny Style

As they sat at the table of a five-star restaurant on 145th Street and Broadway, Wayne tore up a blue napkin and said, "Yo, Jessie, for the past hour that bald-headed old guy with the suit and bow tie over there in the next table been eyeballing us. The next time I catch him, I'm gonna slap the shit out of him."

Jessie thought Wayne was over reacting and secretly wondered if his being raped by Howie Tee had anything to do with his discomfort concerning the old man.

"Son, don't sweat that. Every time I come here, he be staring a brother down. A few times he even passed me some weird notes on his way out the restaurant. For all I know, the nigga might be crazy. Sometimes I think he be following me 'cause I even seen him at Slyvia's restaurant. But Wayne, that big-headed wankster be having some bad bitches," said Jessie, tilting back in his chair.

Wayne said, "What do you mean he be passing uh nigga notes? That seems kinda funny style."

"Some of the notes be saying stuff like 'Trust no one, not even yourself,' 'Hit it and quit it.' I remember another one was, 'Change your game, change your destiny.'

"I guess when ya eat in a Chinese restaurant ya gotta expect some fool to be telling you some fortune cookie crap," said Jessie, making them both laugh so hard that the old man was not the only one staring now. "I don't know about that other nonsense, but I know a lot of brothers who won't see nothing wrong with the hit it and quit it part, because brothers do that all day and every day, if you know what I'm saying," said Wayne, hunching his shoulders, with a smirk on his face.

The camaraderie that Wayne and Jessie were sharing was a pleasant change for the two best friends, who lately had been at each other's throats.

Sometimes the more money people make, the edgier they get. When Jessie started selling kilos for $10,000, his business skyrocketed. But most of their problems had to do with a certain someone.

"Maybe you're right, Wayne, but something tells me the old man's sayings are a little bit more complex than that," said Jessie.

"True dat. Yo Jess, by the way, there's something I been wanting to kick to you," said Wayne. "Man, don't tell me you want to tell me some more shit concerning Crystal, cause I don't feel like going there," said Jessie, staring hard at Wayne.

"Nah, it ain't got nothing to do with her. I been meaning to tell you that I been thinking of investing some of my money in this rap group outta the Polo Grounds. They got mad skills and they already got two albums full of material done. All they need is some capital for promotion. They said if I started up an independent record label, they'd sign up," said Wayne, looking for some encouragement.

"That's all well and good, Wayne, but why not open up a laundry mat, or a liquor store, 'cause that rap business is real shady and kinda risky. Man you could even open up a Chinese restaurant," said Jessie, trying to be funny.

This time Wayne didn't laugh because he felt that Jessie was in some way mocking his intelligence, and being condescending so he got off the subject. Not only that, something else was on his mind. Wayne wondered why Crystal always seemed to be on Jessie's mind.

After finishing up their meals, they got up from the table and Wayne decided to lighten things back up. So as he passed the old guy's table, he said to him in a serious tone, but really playing, "Don't eat the food, it's spoiled."

When Jessie realized Wayne was making reference to a line in an old episode of the Little Rascals that they saw on Nickelodeon a few years ago he laughed right along with Wayne.

The old man stared at them the way Bill Cosby might stare at some cooning Amos and Andy type comedians.

35

Common Bond

Roxanne's eyes zoomed in on her prey the same way a tiger stalks a deer that doesn't know its going to be eaten. Every week, religiously, she made it a priority to be up in the place that she used to strip at, hoping to meet the guy that her bull's-eye was aimed at.

Finally, after almost a year, the object of her attention was up in Sue's Rendezvous, the hottest strip club in Mount Vernon.

Tuesday happened to be the best days to be up in the place because all the hottest rappers, drug dealers and celebrities liked to party when they felt the working stiffs of the world were sleeping.

Roxanne's persistence paid off. Her womanly instinct told her that Jessie was going to make his way over before the night was out. All females know that a pretty face and a banging body draws guys to them like bees to honey. Roxanne's prediction was right on the money, but it happened faster than she thought. Jessie, in full Hennessy mode and with more lust in his eyes than a rapper in a video, was headed straight towards her.

"Hey, sweet thing, I don't mean to bother you, but would you mind if I asked your opinion on something that's been on my mind ever since I stepped in the club?" said Jessie, wearing a blue Sean John outfit and new tan tims.

Nonchalantly, Roxanne said, "Be my guest."

Jessie smiled and said, "I don't know you from Adam but I already got jealous feelings of not wanting you talking to another dude. I feel I could kick someone's ass or even take an ass-whipping for somebody just looking at you. Why is that?"

"Because I'm fine as hell conceited, and niggas will say anything to hit it," said Roxanne, smiling and full of confidence.

"Girl, you so cra-zay," said Jessie, jokingly. "I like a woman who doesn't pull any punches. Plus, you're a diamond in the rough. So what's a nice girl like you doing in a place like this?"

"Well, Mr. Private Dick, since you're investigating and trying to solve this crime, I'm getting my drink on and I love being around an anything can happen atmosphere," said Roxanne, sliding her manicured pink and gold nails down the rim of the glass of her almost finished Long Island Iced Tea.

"Ain't nothing wrong with that. By the way, would you mind if I refill your drink?" said Jessie.

"I gather you like buying drinks for older females who you don't even know their names," said Roxanne, making reference to her twenty-nine years of age. She liked the fact that her youthful look could attract even the young bucks like Jessie.

"Oh my bad, you just got a brother so messed up that I forgot to ask. What's yo name, girl?"

"My name is Roxanne, but people call me Roxy for short."

"Wasn't there a classic song named that?" Jessie asked.

"Yeah, and don't go there," said Roxanne, remembering having to put up with people asking her if she was the real Roxanne when the rap song "Roxanne" came out in the '80s.

"So what's yours?" said Roxanne, faking like she did

not know his name.

"My name's Jessie, and you can call me Jessie," said Jessie, jokingly.

While the pretty Dominican bartender filled Roxanne and Jessie's drinks, Roxanne said, with a big Kool-Aid smile, "Oh you got jokes."

"I got more than jokes and something tells me I done found me a down-ass chick," said Jessie, massaging her soft hands with two rings encrusted with yellow and pink diamonds. His street smarts told him he was dealing with a diva.

"And who is that may I ask?" said Roxanne, already knowing the answer and looking good in a tight white Christian Dior outfit.

"The Ebony Queen with the beautiful hazel eyes that sits beside me and whose name is Roxanne," said Jessie, smirking.

Hearing those words made Roxanne moist and wet. "Jessie, it ain't hard to tell that I am not a sista who bites her tongue, so I'm going to get straight to the point. I'm feeling you in a major way and I like a guy who is confident and sure of himself. I know a lot of females be sweating you and a handsome guy like you are used to getting what you want and I am the same way. I would love to spend time with you and I don't care about your other chicks. The only thing I ask is that you treat me with the utmost respect," said Roxanne in a serious tone.

Roxanne thought it would be real smart to use some of the same tactics on Jessie that had manipulated his father. Jessie nodded and said, "Your every wish is my command," as he took a long sip of his Hennessy.

The spotlight was on them as they sat at the bar vibing and listening to R&B singer Usher's song "Confessions."

Before Jessie walked up to Roxanne he had his eyes set on a stripper who looked like Left Eye from the group TLC, who died a few years earlier in a car crash. And she had more ass than R&B singer Beyonce from the group Destiny's Child. But now Jessie had a change of plan. Roxanne's lusty look made a brother go left and follow his third eye, which told him the beautiful female that sat in front of him would be down for anything.

His intuition happened to be right on the money. Homegirl had tricks for the kid. Some tight gripping poo-nanny, better head than Linda Lovelace in the porn classic *Deep Throat* and *Setup* ability.

In one night Roxanne had earned a prime slot on Jessie's booty call list, not counting Crystal.

But Roxanne had her own list. A hit list. And Jessie's name had been on it since Roxanne vowed to destroy any-body linked to the SSJ Crew for contributing to her brother's death.

However, Jessie attributed Roxanne's being at his beck and call to his money, good looks and charisma.

On their midnight rendezvous, Jessie rambled on about how he hated his father.

Early on it occurred to her that a lot of thugs hated their fathers for not being in their lives. But Roxanne noticed that Jessie's feeling went beyond hate. Whenever he mentioned his father it seemed like the whites of his eyes turned blood-shot red, the veins on the side of his head would pulsate as sweat trickled down.

Roxanne and Jessie had a mutual hate for the same man.

One day while they both were at a hotel in New Jersey, Roxanne went in her Coach bag and pulled out a hundred dollar bill filled with cocaine and began sniffing. It kind of threw Jessie off because he assumed she did not mess around with cocaine. Every time they got together, all they did was smoke weed, drink alcohol and have sex. But as they chilled in the hotel room the more cocaine she sniffed the freakier she got. The head was so good she damn near was sucking the skin off his dick.

In the heat of passion and lust, Jessie went against his

better judgment and made the mistake of not saying no to something that could turn his whole world upside down. He made the decision to just take a one-on-one of some of the cocaine, figuring indulging just once could not do him any harm, and also thinking the drug could make him just as freaky as Roxanne. Jessie felt so good after taking a hit of the white powder that he almost wanted to sing "The Star Spangled Banner," but he just did not know the words. In a moment of clarity, Jessie's street survivalist instinct told him to slap Roxanne for introducing him to something that would only wreak havoc in his life. He paused and stared at her briefly, then decided against doing that.

But instead he slapped the little bag of cocaine in his hand two times then poured some more out and sniffed his way into the promised land.

After the both of them would get high together, the cocaine's euphoric effect made them get deep and tell stuff they normally only told people they trusted. This made her reveal how she held the SSJ Crew responsible for her little brother's death and when the feds took them down she secretly celebrated their downfall. The one thing she left out from Jessie was the part she played in it. She even got up enough nerve to tell Jessie that when they first hooked up her intentions were to set up Lorenzo's son.

But now that she had gotten to know him better, her feelings had changed. Roxanne even almost blurted out that she was falling for him big time, which was not surprising because a lot of fly girls are attracted to thug types and sometimes even fall in love with them.

Jessie had already picked up on this fact as it pertained to Roxanne, but by this point he was down for anything.

36

Crystal Clear

"Evonne, look at that chicken head sitting in Jessie's Escalade. That bitch Roxanne fronting like she all that," said Crystal, looking fly in her burgundy, leather pant suit and Prada boots, as they stood in front of the fish joint on 129th Street and Lenox Avenue.

"Let's go mess wit' that bum bitch," said Evonne, whose model looks were the cause of her getting into fights with chicken heads.

So off they went strutting across the street, headed to Jessie's truck. Rapper LL Cool J's hit song "Head Sprung" blasted from the speakers as Jessie and Roxanne bobbed their heads.

They were so caught up in the music that they did not notice Crystal and Evonne standing by the vehicle. Crystal talked over the music and said, "Jessie, I need you to give me a ride to 125th Street. I got to get my watch out the shop before it closes."

"Not now, Crys, I'm kinda busy right now. I'll take you later," said Jessie, as Roxanne sat beside him on the leather seats with a sly grin on her face.

"What you smiling about you dumb bitch? Do you think something's funny? Matter a fact get out of my brother's car," said Crystal.

"Who you calling a bitch? You messing wit' the wrong

girl, so you best get ta stepping," said Roxanne, sounding like rapper Foxy Brown.

As soon as she said it, Crystal snatched the passenger side door open and grabbed Roxanne by her long braids and dragged her to the dirty street. She stomped Roxanne's head into the ground, punching and scratching at the same time. Evonne never got a chance to jump in because Crystal was fighting like a mad woman caught in a fit of jealous rage.

Jessie finally made it around to the other side of the Escalade and pulled his sister kicking and screaming off Roxanne.

"Girl, you dun lost your mind. This shit is so uncalled for. Roxanne ain't do jack to you," said Jessie, who was close to slapping her out of a trancelike state.

Crystal stood there panting like a tiger with her hair all messed up and totally at a loss for words. Jessie helped Roxanne inside the Escalade then he got in and pulled off as the chromed-out rims spun in the shiny Pirelli twenty-four-inch tires.

Evonne took out Kleenex tissues from her brown Coach bag, and wiped sweat off of Crystal's forehead.

"Girl, I thought you was going to kill that bitch the way you went at her. I never saw you lose it like that," said Evonne, attempting a quick touch-up on her friend's hair that looked like Broome Hilda's.

After gaining composure, Crystal said, "I just can't stand these bitches that try to use my brother for his money and when I saw that stupid grin on her face, I lost my mind for a minute."

"Mrs. Laila Ali, I can tell you one thing, girl: to that bitch, Roxanne, I bet that beating you put on her seemed longer than a minute. You had her scared to death to get her ass back in that Escalade," said Evonne, making them both laugh their heads off.

Deep down Crystal sensed there had to be ulterior motives behind her actions that went above and beyond what the situation called for. Crystal was not the type of female that let her emotions get the best of her.

The way she acted out told her something was not right. Anybody witnessing what just took place would have thought Crystal had caught her man cheating. Not her brother.

And the way Evonne was staring at her as they walked down Lenox Avenue on this cool Friday night made her think she suspected something was a little shady.

Could it be that Crystal's seeing Jessie with another female led to her jealousy surfacing?

Crystal tried to lie to herself, thinking, *No way. Jessie's my brother, not my lover. Wait a minute, if a sister has sex with her brother who she already has brotherly love for, could that be considered making love? Wait a minute, for me to even be rationalizing this crazy mixed up stuff is bugged out.*

They headed toward Strivers Row, tears rolled down Crystal's face, leading Evonne to think something real shady was going on.

Meanwhile, a battered and bruised Roxanne was taken to Harlem hospital by Jessie where she learned that having a hard head saved her from serious injury.

37

Who Can See What I Can See?

Bishme had a date later on with a female whom he met at an after-hours spot so he took his son, Christopher, to his mother's house in the Taft Housing Project so she could babysit. When Bishme arrived, he decided to chitchat while waiting for his date to pick him up.

"Look at my boy. Look at my boy, Ma. This little handsome nigga right here gon' make me rich 'cause he's gonna be in movies. First me and Carla gonna get him in commercials," said Bishme, playfully shaking his smiling son's square and peasy head that Bishme mistook for curls.

Tessy, sitting in her favorite rocking chair, chewing snuff and spitting the contents in an old coffee can, busted out laughing at her son.

"Nigga, you must be losing yo damn mind. How the hell a child that looks like a grown-ass Sammy Davis Jr. gon' be a star when people won't be able to tell if the little nigga seven or forty-seven?"

Christopher ran crying into a bedroom. Hating his mother's cruel words, Bishme said, "Ma, why you gotta go say something like that in front of your grandson?"

"'Cause if I don't tell him the truth, your mixed-up ass sure as hell won't. Nigga, did you forget that ugly runs in our family?" said Tessy, straightening out her sand-colored wig. She was so black she looked blue and her discolored lips were cracking. Hearing little Christopher laughing at her from the bedroom made them join in.

Bishme smoked some good chronic with his mother, and after shooting the breeze a little longer, he went downstairs to the front of the building to wait for his date to arrive in her car. While standing there, he observed two guys shooting dice.

The two petty gamblers and wannabe ballers were all up in another person's business as they killed time on the block.

"I don't care what anybody says, that chump Jessie is fucking his sister Crystal," said Leroy to his homeboy Booger as the green dice hit the building's wall.

"That fool Jessie goes ballistic if a nigga just looks at her. That chump knows that Crystal is one fine bitch and it's only normal for niggas to try and kick it to her. But I been busting Jessie's whole ceelo and anybody with eyes in their head can see that the way he be acting is a little bit more than brotherly love."

Bishme felt like beating them down right then and there for talking mad reckless about his homeboy Jessie, but he decided to keep listening.

"Yeah, Leroy, I been peeping that shit out too for a while, but I just didn't want to speak on it for fear of niggas thinking I was hating because Jessie's father snitched on my pops, Country. Man, I can even remember when we was in elementary school and Jessie hit Eric over the head with a lunch tray in the cafeteria just for sitting by Crystal," said Booger. "Then his parents transferred Jessie and his sister out of school and put them in Catholic School."

Bishme remembered Jessie saying sarcastically that the Catholic school was supposed to be a more positive environment. But his friend got into trouble there, too.

As Leroy tossed the two green dice against the wall of the front of the building's entrance that smelled like old urine, he crapped out and yelled, "Damn!" Then he said,

"Let me tell you something son, **Crystal's friend** Evonne told me homegirl spazzed out the **other day on** some chick that Jessie had in his truck. She said **Crystal acted** like she was his woman and beat the crap **out the girl.** That shit confirmed my suspicions. They **fucking."**

Bishme was steaming.

All this jibber jabber was not **coming from** two gossiping females but from two knuckleheads **who were** just hating because they wanted to be doing **what Jessie** was doing—fucking his sister.

Secretly they did not care what **went on behind** closed doors due to the fact that they knew **all types** of sick and disgusting things went down in the hood. **While they** rambled on and on and shot dice, Jessie's **ears were ring**ing as he chased cheddar somewhere else in **the hood. If he** only had the privilege of listening to them **gossip, he** would have found out that ain't no such thing **in the hood** as I won't tell, you won't tell.

If two slow knuckleheads could **figure out the** methods of Jessie's incestuous madness, any**body could.**

Now Bishme was getting a sa**mple of what** had been floating around the rumor mill. He **did not believe** one bit of it. He thought they were just play**er haters. Bish**me could not stand to hear another word, so **he bumrushed** them and clunked their heads together. The **two shook ones,** scared out of their wits, ran for their lives.

Bishme laughed his head off as **a pretty chick** in a red CLK 430 coupe Mercedes pulled up. **He got in.**

38

Who's Ya Daddy?

As Crystal and Evonne stood on 114th Street and Seventh Avenue talking, they watched little kids getting all soaked up as they played by an open water hydrant.

"Sista girl, I have been feeling real sick lately. Every morning I can't stop throwing up or shitting, plus I haven't had my period in two months," said Crystal to Evonne.

"Girl, you betta get ready, 'cause you pregnant. And that baby gon' be fly and handsome just like his father, Wayne. That brother's a cutie," said Evonne.

A lot of females found Wayne to be handsome and said he resembled NBA basketball player, Chris Webber.

"Evonne don't even go there. You talking like I'm definitely pregnant. Anyway I don't think I am ready to have no baby. I'm only seventeen. Plus I plan to go to college."

"I say if you old enough to be boning, you old enough to have a baby. And Lord knows how you like to have sex, that's all you talk about. I know tall-ass Wayne must have a strong back to satisfy you, because you're too much for one guy to handle," said Evonne.

When Evonne said that, Crystal just cringed at the irony in her words, being that she was in love with two men at the same time. All she could think was how did she manage to get caught up in such a crazy situation. Crystal wondered how a bunch of fun and games like playing house could spiral into something she did not have the slightest idea how to handle.

Then there is the big problem of who impregnated her. Jessie or Wayne? Crystal had already heard in school that incest caused a lot of problems if a baby was conceived in this manner.

If her brother Jessie was the father, how would the baby turn out? Would it be deformed, retarded or crazy? Would the baby look like Jessie? Then Wayne and everybody would know right away that it was her brother's.

These were just some of the unanswered questions that bogged Crystal's mind as they watched the little kids play water games by the hydrant on a beautiful summer day.

"First of all, what we got to do, Crystal, is go to the clinic and find out for sure if you really are pregnant. Then afterwards you can decide what it is you really want to do," said Evonne, throwing a big orange and yellow plastic ball back to the kids by the hydrant.

"Yes, Evonne, you are so right, that's exactly what I need to do. But let me get my head together first, then I'll tell you when I want to go."

39

Pop Swayze

While driving by the Pathmark on 125th Street and Lexington Avenue, Jessie spotted Pop Swayze waiting in line by a can depository machine with a cart full of cans. He had not seen him in a long time.

Before Pop Swayze's downward spiral he was a frequent visitor at Lorenzo's town house and would do magic tricks and give twenty dollar bills to little Jessie and Crystal, who reminded him of his own kids before his wife ran away with them.

Jessie yelled, "Hey, Pop Swayze, leave the shopping cart. I want you to take a ride with me."

"Jessie, I can't leave my cart. I got six bucks in cans. I gotta collect my money," said Pop Swayze.

"Don't worry, Pop, I got you. Just come on," said Jessie as he double-parked.

Before Pop Swayze stepped off with Jessie, he told a Puerto Rican lady standing in back of him, "Listen, mamacita, I'm gonna make you an offer you can't refuse. Take my spot and my cans and when I see you out here later, just give me half the money and my cart back and everything will be square."

The lady with the old worn-out wig on her head smiled and agreed.

As Jessie pulled off with Pop Swayze he said, "Pop, I

see you haven't lost a bit of your game or your sway. I like how you macked that broad. I see a nigga still game tight."

"Jess, you know the game don't change, Just the circumstances. By the way, where we going?"

"Oh, I just want to spend some time with you, 'cause I ain't seen you in a minute. And I also need to pick up a few things at the 116th Street Mart."

"Okay, Jess that's cool, plus there's something I been meaning to kick to you. I know you been hearing a lot of nasty things about ya pops, but to me he was a bit more complex than people make him out to be. Even though Renzo sold drugs, do you know that he used to give the drug clinics around the hood money so that they could give the fiends free needles to prevent them from sharing their works and getting AIDS? I even remember the time he had a beef with this other dealer and people thought he killed the guy over some drug shit, but the real reason was the guy had the monster and was giving that shit to a lot of females in the hood. Ya see, Jess, Renzo wasn't just some jive turkey drug dealer giving out turkeys on Thanksgiving to soothe his conscience. I ain't tryna sit here an' say ya pops was an angel, but he sure wasn't the worst."

Pop Swayze's opinions held a lot of weight because Jessie knew Pop Swayze had spent years in prison after a guy named Sticky Hines snitched on him and the Harlem drug syndicate. Jessie nodded slightly as he spotted a guy from the hood slapping up his elderly mother by a church.

After arriving at the 116th Mart, Jessie started looking at some of the clothes that the vendors were selling. Then he asked Pop Swayze what size clothes he wore.

Pop Swayze smiled and told him. Jessie picked out a bunch of clothes that he figured an older buck would like and also brought Pop Swayze some black Timberland boots. After that, Jessie took him to get a haircut at the Muslim barbershop on 116th Street and Lennox Avenue and gave him two hundred dollars.

Pop Swayze had the biggest smile in Harlem and could not thank Jessie enough.

Before Jessie left, Pop Swayze told him numerous stories about his father and how they both used to run things back in the days. He even called Lorenzo a down-ass brother and said that sometimes a person gotta do what they gotta do. Even though Pop Swayze brought up things about his father that showed another side—opposite of other negative opinions of him—the old man still could not change Jessie's feelings concerning his father.

The big smile that graced Pop Swayze's face was gone in less than three hours because he had sold all the clothes and spent all the money shooting up heroin.

40

Baby Girl

"Girl, that ass of yours is getting bigger and bigger every day since you been messing around with that boy, Wayne. I hope you been using protection if you're having sex. I ain't about to take care of nobody else's kids, and I'm sure not ready to be no grandmother. You hear me, Crystal?"

"Ma, you been talking about me putting on weight ever since I started getting breasts at ten years old. You and I know that I'm getting a big ass 'cause you got a big ass. You and Pops always laughed about that when my body began to take shape at an early age."

"Yes, I know, girl, but yo ass and tits is spreading out a little bit too fast. Crystal, do you remember when that kid came to our house to ask you for a date? Your father took one look at him and said, 'Get your little horny ass on away from my door before I lose my religion.'"

Crystal almost laughed along with her mother, but she said, "Yeah, Ma, I remember, but can we please talk about something else?"

The pregnancy talk and her mother bringing up her incarcerated father, who had refused to see them since he went to prison, was too much for her to handle.

"Okay, girl, but you watch yourself on them damn streets. I don't want to have to put a bullet in one of them stupid niggas out there for disrespecting my girl," said Kathy.

"Whatever you say, Ma. Whatever you say," sassed Crystal, as she opened the refrigerator to get cold cuts for a sandwich. Lately she had been eating everything she could get her used-to-be-sleek, now-chubby hands on. Every day, her body was changing.

All the signs pointed to one thing but she refused to believe that a baby might be growing inside her. And if she was pregnant, who was the father? The father could be either of the two people she was sexing—Wayne or her brother, Jessie.

Crystal knew that putting off finding out would not solve her problems but she still could not figure out the answers. That is until she watched and listened to Oprah Winfrey's talk show about being responsible for your actions. Oprah Winfrey stated that if a person considers herself to be strong, that means when she encounter problems and decisions need to be made, that person has to face adversity head on. This made a whole lot of sense to this sista in trouble.

Even Oprah, Halle Berry, and other strong black women made it out of all types of drama in their lives. *Now look at them, shining through all the rain,* thought Crystal. After watching that show, she decided that she had to find out the truth and decide what to do.

She felt there was only one decision to make. That would be if she was pregnant, to tell Jessie and everybody else that Wayne was the father.

Crystal had a hard time coming to grips with the fact that positive females are not supposed to go out like that, but she felt she didn't have a choice.

Her family and the hood could never understand incest. Never, never.

41

Choices

Crystal's stomach rumbled as her eyes glanced at the article about incest in *Essence* magazine. When she reached a paragraph stating that women who become pregnant through incest risk having babies with multiple complications, she became nauseous and almost passed out while lying on the red leather couch in the living room.

"Crystal, are you all right?" yelled her mother from the kitchen while washing dishes. "You look kinda sick. Is everything okay?"

"I'm all right, Ma, I think my period is about to come down any day now." She felt bad lying to her mother because her "little friend" had not showed up in two months. The thought of being pregnant was just tearing her up inside. And what if she was pregnant by Jessie? How could she explain that to everybody? Would the world turn on her and treat her like the bubonic plague or like she had The Monster, AIDS?

What would her parents think about their daughter who had been having sex with her own flesh and blood? Who do you talk to about subjects that hardly ever get talked about. Every time she and Jessie had sex, she felt dirty afterwards. But while the act was being played out, everything felt so good, so good. *How could something so wrong make a person feel that way?* she wondered.

Whenever she thought about the pregnancy, she tried unsuccessfully to block it out. She thought, *What if I am pregnant by Wayne? Would he want me to keep the baby, abort it, or worse, would he think the kid was not his?* One of her girlfriends had a kid and she doesn't even know who the baby's daddy was due to sleeping around. Now she was destined to suffer the same possible fate. As Crystal curled up in misery she wondered why all this drama was happening to a person who never did any dirt to anyone. Why? Every time Crystal thought she had all the answers to her problems confusion would soon set in.

"Hey, baby, do you think you are coming down with the flu? It's been going around lately. Some people at my job are out sick now. That's why I've been getting all this overtime at the post office," said Kathy. If Kathy only knew what was going on under her roof, it would be enough to make her go postal.

"Nah, Ma, I don't think it's the flu, I just got to take me some Midols and I'll be okay. Ma, where's Jessie? I ain't seen him in a few days."

"Girl, that boy's out on them damn streets doing something he ain't supposed to be doing. He's just like his daddy, couldn't stay his ass off those streets."

"Yeah, Ma, you sure is right. Didn't you almost give birth to him while sitting on some park benches outside?"

"Let me tell you girl, when my water broke, I jumped up real fast, told my homegirl, Sara, to get me to Harlem Hospital quick, I ain't having no baby on no damn streets," said Kathy. They both laughed hysterically.

Then the thought of being pregnant penetrated Crystal's brain again. And for some strange reason Tupac's "Brenda Got a Baby" video that she saw while watching a BET video throwback series came to mind. This made her have crazy visuals of throwing a baby in a garbage can.

As tears fell, she got up off the couch and headed to her room.

* * *

As Crystal sat in the Planned Parenthood Center called Choices on 95th Street and Madison Avenue, the last day's events played out in her head.

She could not escape feelings of desperation and despair as she tried to fool herself into thinking that maybe the pregnancy test was wrong because sometimes it gives incorrect readings.

So she realized it was time to accept the consequences. She thought, *What's done is done, and like Daddy always said, 'Keep your head up and keep it moving.' So I'm just going to have to have an abortion and go on with my life. Besides, I'm too young to think about having anybody's baby. I gotta get my education, find a job and make something of myself. I don't plan to be stuck in the hood with a bunch of crumb snatchers waiting on some knucklehead like a project chicken head. Mama and Papa ain't raise no fool, I'm a strong black sista. But wait a minute. Do strong black sistas have sex with their own flesh and blood? No, so that makes me a dirty stinking hoe.*

The slim Filipino nurse in a white uniform called her to the back. "So, young lady, did you read our pamphlet concerning choosing to have an abortion?"

Crystal came up out of her slumber and responded, "Oh yeah, uh yeah." But she really wasn't hearing what had been said.

"I see here that you checked the 'yes' box on our form we gave you to fill out. So that means you have decided to abort your four-month fetus."

"What do you mean four months? I'm only two months," said Crystal, totally disgusted.

"Yes, ma'am, you are four months pregnant, and if you look to your right at our fetus chart on the wall, pay very close attention to the picture with four months next to it. That's a fully developed fetus." When Crystal first walked off with the nurse from the reception area she felt the nurse talked too much, and looked at her in a demeaning type of way. Now the sly little bitch telling her about some chart was a little too much for her confused mind to handle. So she stood up and backed away from the desk and uncomfortable wooden chair and left without saying a word to the blabbermouth nurse who stared in bewilderment. Crystal had heard and seen too much. At that moment she made her choice at the place called Choices. She was going to keep the baby.

42

My Favorite Things

Things were going real well for the Crossover Crew. They were at the young ages where you think you know everything but really know nothing. Nada, jack, zero. And the Crossover Crew had a hero-like worship of guys named Jackson, Franklin and Grant, all dead presidents, with their love of money, violence, and pretty females, combined with a little help from their friend, Red, they managed to take over several drug spots. The streets knew that the Crossover Crew was not to be messed with.

They were known to squash problems quickly and keep it moving. Not only was Jessie the leader of the Crossover Crew, he also became the man to see when product got low on the streets of the city that never sleeps. If you needed keys, Jessie was the man to see. Jessie had so much money rolling in that sometimes even his money-counting machines would malfunction. His first big purchase was a beautiful brick house in the suburbs of Fort Lee, New Jersey. It was put in an elderly relative's name so as to not arouse suspicion. Jessie did not spend much time there because the streets of Harlem kept him busy.

Other drug dealers heard through the grapevine that Jessie was the one who killed Jay and Terry-O. The gory details of them being found with their penises in their mouths had the other dealers shook, thinking anybody who was capable of doing that had to be crazy.

Wayne also suspected that Jessie killed them and wondered why his best friend felt the need to be so secretive. He felt offended. Wayne detected a wedge coming between them. Ever since they got in the drug game, he noticed their relationship was different and he could not figure out why. Then the last argument Wayne had with Jessie about Crystal told him something was not quite right and deserved further looking into. But for now Wayne had to keep handling his business on the streets, knowing all too well that other thugs would love to take his place as lieutenant of the Crossover Crew.

While he stood on 136th Street in deep thought, Jessie drove up in his new Black Cadillac Escalade.

"Yo, Wayne, I feel like partying. Why don't all of us meet up at Red's spot later on and get our drink on. The champagne and Hennessy is on me tonight," said Jessie, smiling.

Bishme, one of the drug dealers from the Crossover Crew, said, "What are we celebrating?"

"Man, we celebrating street life, money, bitches, and so called thugs," said Jessie, making everybody laugh as he pulled off.

Jessie parked at Red's town house on Strivers Row, situated on the same block as his family. Everybody who lived in this part of Harlem had major dough and Red fit right in with the lawyers, stockbrokers, doctors and celebrities. Jessie admired the way Red had managed to do his thing on the streets for so many years and never did any major time in prison. Sometimes Jessie wished that Red had been his father and not Lorenzo.

As soon as Jessie rang the bell, Red's beautiful wife, Nina, answered the door. Nina was about forty-five years old but looked ten years younger. She was a straight dime piece with long reddish brown hair and light-skinned complexion. Nina resembled the beautiful actress Debbie Allen.

"Hi, Jessie, how's your family doing?" said Nina, wearing tight blue jeans that fit her like a glove.

"Oh, everybody's doing fine. Matter fact, I'll tell them you asked. By the way, you sure look good, and Red must be one very happy man," said Jessie.

"Thanks, young man. You are such a charmer, you remind me of my husband, Red. Ya know my Red still has a crazy crush on your mother, Kathy. "He talks about her all the time," said Nina showing the confidence of a lady with class.

Jessie just laughed as Red yelled for him to come upstairs. Jessie climbed the long steps with beautiful African-inspired artwork on the walls. One in particular, "The Poet," by artist John Holyfield caught his attention. It showed a tall lanky guy sitting by a tree reading to his tall lanky girlfriend. When Jessie got upstairs he saw Red messing with an expensive back-in-the-days phonograph that looked like it came from the 1930s.

"What's going on, Red? It seems like your kind of busy," said Jessie, sitting on a burgundy leather sofa with brass studs.

"Oh, Jess, I was just listening to some of my old jazz records—Miles Davis, Thelonius Monk and Charlie Parker. Ain't nothing like listening to John Coltrane's "Love Supreme." All these cats' music put me in a relaxing state of mind. And by the looks of you, it seems that you're not feeling too bad yourself," said Red, placing Coltrane's "My Favorite Things" on the turntable.

"Red, life's been treating us damn good and I got a lot to be thankful for. The money's coming in so fast I can't even count it. I'm just gonna make my money real fast like I been doing, then get out of the drug game," said Jessie, tapping his fingers in sync with the music on the sofa.

"Well, my brother, if we just hold our heads, there's a whole lot more paper to make," said Red, smoking a fat Cuban cigar.

"Yo, Red, the reason I came by is that we running kind of low on product at some of the spots. I need you to call Lester and tell him to have something ready for me."

"No problem. I'll make the call as soon as you leave," said Red, slowly blowing the cigar's smoke toward a gold ceiling fan.

"Thanks, Red. You the man, and I'm just the man standing next to the man," said Jessie, making them both laugh as he got up from the sofa. Then Jessie left to make the pick up.

43

I Been Thinking

Ever since Crystal told Wayne that he was going to be a father, he had experienced weird food cravings, body aches and a fluctuating emotional mental state. Wayne heard these were the same symptoms that pregnant women go through, and that it was fairly normal for men to feel this way when their other half was expecting. Yet, since he sensed that Jessie and Crystal's relationship was not normal, he wanted to have his questions answered.

While standing outside a movie theater on 47th Street and Seventh Avenue, Wayne got the nerve to ask Crystal if something was going on between her and Jessie.

"Crystal, sometimes you and Jessie act more like lovers than brother and sister. What's up wit' that?"

Crystal immediately cried. Wayne thought it was because he offended her, but the real reason had more to do with the truth in his assumption.

Crystal quickly regained her composure and lied like a person trying to pass a lie detector test for fear of her secret being found out.

"Wayne, how could you disrespect me by even coming out your mouth with some crazy shit. You been watching too much of that Jerry Springer. Because me and my brother got mad love for each other you gon' turn it around and turn that into something sick and twisted? Would you like it better if we hated each other and fought all the time? If so I can't mess with you."

Wayne felt bad for asking such a thing, so he flipped his script. "Yeah, Crystal, you're right, and I'm dead wrong. I just been stressing and wilding out these past few weeks. My mind's been in a daze wit' all the street drama and being on the grind. Can you forgive a brother?"

Before she could answer, he grabbed her by the waist and started to tongue her down, totally oblivious and not caring about the people staring at them on the crowded midtown street.

As Crystal became moist, hot and tingly all over, she smiled and said after their slob down, "I know why your mind's been in a daze, it's all that damn purple haze you been smoking."

Wayne just laughed along with her and said, "Don't go there, my little chocolate Thai." While they made up, little did Wayne know that he was not the only person whose mind had been in a daze.

Lately all Crystal's thoughts gravitated to the things that were unfolding in her life, like the twisted love triangle and her pregnancy.

44

What's a Girl To Do?

Crystal paced back and forth in her room for several hours and then finally got up the nerve to tell Jessie what was on her mind.

"Jessie, I am pregnant and I don't know who the father of the baby is," said Crystal, sitting on the tip of the bed in his old bedroom. The previous night Jessie had decided to sleep there after being too tired to drive to his new home in New Jersey.

"What do you mean you don't know who the father is?" said Jessie, groggy from just waking up out of a deep sleep.

"Jessie, don't try to lay there and play stupid. You know exactly what I am talking about, it's either yours or Wayne's."

Jessie was now wide awake after hearing the penetrating words his sister just spoke. Rage crept up inside him at the thought of Wayne having sex with her. But Jessie knew that losing it was not going to solve this problem.

"Okay, I feel you, so what do you plan to do?" said Jessie, sitting up in his bed, staring at Crystal. His head felt like it would split with pain. The excruciating headaches he had been having since he was incarcerated had been getting worse.

"What do you mean, what do I plan to do? You mean what do *we* plan to do?" said Crystal, getting pissed off.

Jessie put two fingers by the side of his head as if he was the president trying to figure out the answer to a complex question.

"Okay, first of all, if you plan to keep the baby you gonna have to fake like the baby is Wayne's. And second, you and me got to keep this amongst ourselves. Nobody can't know about this, not even your friend, Evonne, okay?"

As Crystal made her way out of the room, she nodded in agreement. She had already told Wayne he was going to be a father, and remembered how the news made him jump for joy, like an NBA basketball player winning his first championship.

45

Punk City

Lorenzo's mind was made up and nobody not even the suit-and-tie-wearing white individual in front of him could change it.

"Lorenzo, I think you are making a serious mistake. If you sign yourself out of protective custody, you will be signing your own death warrant," said Federal Agent Smith as they sat in a room at the Otisville Federal Penitentiary.

Lorenzo, with slightly graying black wavy hair, shook his head in disagreement, as he rubbed his callused fingers across the black numbers on his green prison uniform. A gray dusty fan on the off-white wall made an annoying clicking sound, disturbing his already-frayed emotions.

"Mr. Thompson, you can shake your head if you want to but there has been a $30,000 hit out on you since you first came to Otisville Federal Penitentiary seven years ago. And on top of that, the minute you step into population there will be other inmates just waiting to try to kill you so that they can get a notch in their reputations."

"To tell you the truth, sir, and taking into consideration everything you've expressed, nothing is gonna change my mind. The only reason I agreed to be put in Punk City in the first place is because I wanted to hide like a rat. I felt I could not deal with people staring at me like I had leprosy or judging me for the actions I chose to take, that of a no

176

good, dirty snitch. So I chose to hide in Punk City. But I had a long time to think and I found out that in prison there is nowhere to hide. Let me school you on something, Agent Smith. Even the child molesters and rapists in protective custody think that they're better than me."

Before Agent Smith could answer Lorenzo kept talking. "I ain't saying that I been rejected by God, but do you know that the Muslims and reverends don't want nothing to do with me?"

"But, Mr. Thompson, think about your family that love and care about you," said Agent Smith, trying hard to change his mind.

"You must be kidding me. I have no friends. My kids hate me, and I told my wife when I got incarcerated to go on with her life because mine's been over since the day I decided to cooperate with you assholes—I mean guys."

A skinny, frizzy auburn-haired white female CO tapped on the room's glass window, signaling the federal agent to end the meeting. Agent Smith nodded in her direction then said to Lorenzo, "Mr. Thompson, it seems that you have really thought this thing through and you are adamant concerning your decision to go into population. But I strongly advise you not to do it because we cannot protect you against the forces that threaten to rise up against you."

"Thanks for caring, but a man's got to do what a man's got to do, so don't cry for me Argentina," said Lorenzo.

Agent Smith knew then and there that he was sitting in a room with a man who had lost his mind.

46

A Stranger Calls

After waiting several minutes, the prison operator finally clicked over and Lorenzo received the dial tone to place his call. He dialed all the digits then started talking when he heard the familiar voice.

"Listen, Red, you got every right to be pissed off at me for going out like a sucker, but I'm living on borrowed time and I need you to do something for me for old time's sake," said Lorenzo.

"What do you want me to do, chump," said Red, a little upset from hearing Lorenzo's voice for the first time since the trial. Lorenzo continued talking and acted like he did not hear the "chump" comment.

"I know you heard about how my boy, Jessie, been catching hell all these years because of my actions."

"Yeah, but he'll be all right. Your little man's a trouper and he reminds me of someone I thought I used to know," said Red, trying to shake off a nervous tick that he had suddenly developed in his trigger finger.

"Red, I need you to look out for my boy and hold him down to the fullest. You know like how the white man says, 'Be a mentor.' I need you to be there for Jessie when he's going through the bullshit."

"Nigga, you talking like you headed to your eternal rest and your burial plot's already picked out," said Red.

"Nah, brother, it's a little bit different than that. You and I know that in prison they just bury you in the back with the rest of the other sorry bastards, then put a white cross on the dirt and keep it moving," said Lorenzo, feeling queasy at the thought.

"I can't say you're wrong, Lorenzo, and that other stuff concerning little shorty I already been talking to him. But with the kids today you can't come at them too fast, so I been slowly chipping away at Jess and don't worry, I'm gonna hold him down."

Red had his own secretive reasons for wanting to "be a mentor," and it had nothing to do with helping Lorenzo. After Red finished talking, Lorenzo said, "Thanks, man."

Then the phone went dead.

47

Fist of Fury

Since the moment Jessie showed up on 136th Street and stepped out of his Escalade, he felt like all eyes were on him. As everybody stared and watched his every move, he made it over to Crossover Crew members Marvin and Mike. His head was pounding.

"What the fuck up wit' everybody eyeballing a nigga? Niggas need to get off my dick." As he laughed it made his homeboys laugh, too.

"What up, Jess? Long time no see. I was gonna put up some wanted posters for the kid, where you been?" said Mike.

"Nigga, I'm the Matrix, even when you don't see me I'm right there watching y'all niggas." Then he smiled and playfully punched Mike in his chubby stomach. "Homes, I'm playing, I just went on a little ghetto sabbatical. Brother just needed a break," said Jessie, smiling.

"Ain't nothing wrong wit' dat, Jess. I need a little rest and relaxation myself. That's why when I finish moving these last few bags of thing-thing, I'm gonna call up that big-butt hottie, Maria, and hit the skins," said Marvin.

"Is you gonna put uh nigga down or what 'cause ain't no fun unless the homeboys get some," said Mike, making everybody in listening distance laugh.

Before Marvin could answer, a guy named Frankie, who used to run with Howie Tee, pulled up in a green Range

Rover, got out and started talking to one of Jessie's workers by the grocery store. He knew Jessie was in earshot.

"Whut up, whut's craka lacking?" said a dreadlocked Frankie.

Bishme said, "Nothing much, playboy, just grinding, but if I had your hand I'd turn mines in. That Rover you driving is looking real proper and the color reminds me of that nigga Riff Raff's fly whip, who use to get money a while back. Man, he was one of the first cats to roll up on the block in a drop top aqua-blue bugged-eyed Benz."

Frankie nodded in agreement and said, "Yeah, son used to get mad dough."

Jessie, standing in close proximity bit down harder on a chew stick in his mouth as he snarled at Bishme and at Frankie.

"Yo, Bishme. You need to get off all those used-to-be major players in the drug game dicks. I am tired of hearing everybody always talking that so-and-so-was-the-first-to-do-it bullshit. They can all kiss my ass. Most of them niggas y'all talk about went from tattle-telling to dry snitching to outright ratting on their whole crews. And you know where most of it all started from. Mommy. Mommy, Johnny drank all the Kool-Aid! Those lame niggas been snitching from day one."

Jessie did not mean what he said to be funny, but everybody on the block, but Frankie and Jessie, busted out laughing. Some of what Jessie said was brought on because of his hatred for his father. This was no laughing matter.

Frankie shot Jessie a nasty look, then said, "Bishme, I don't know what's up with your man talking all out of his head, but that shit sounds kind of personal. And if I remember correctly, his pops did some snitching himself."

Bishme, seconds from punching him in the face, said, "Yo, Frankie. I ain't really tryna hear all that."

"Yo, pussy, you really got some balls coming out yo mouth like that," said Jessie, slowly approaching.

"Who the fuck you calling a pussy, chump? Your pops is a snit—" said Frankie.

Before he finished saying the word, Jessie and the Crossover Crew members pounced on Frankie. They punched, stomped and kicked him in an unrelenting attack.

All the people out on the street enjoying the hot and sticky August night bore witness to this horrendous act. In the hood you learn rather quickly that sometimes examples have to be made out of chumps who jump up to get beat down. And Roxanne, who happened to be swishing down the block, looking fly in a tight blue and white Phat Farm short set, and holding a white polka-dotted puppy bull dog, was well aware of this fact. She yelled, "Bust 'em down, Jessie." She loved Jessie's thugged-out ways.

While Frankie lay on the ground, a bundle of damaged goods, Jessie ran to his Escalade and got a Louisville Slugger aluminum bat and proceeded to bang up Frankie's Range Rover like he was a demolition technician.

Crystal, who happened to be riding by in Wayne's Lincoln Navigator, spotted Jessie breaking windows, and lights and denting up every piece of metal on the vehicle. Crystal and Wayne flew out the truck and tried to grab Jessie, who turned around quickly with bat in hand like he was going through steroid rage and almost took a Barry Bonds' swing. But before he could do it, he got a moment of clarity and noticed it was fam. Crystal did not know how close her head came to being mistaken for a baseball.

He dropped the bat and they all got in Wayne's bone-colored Navigator and pulled off.

As they drove away, Wayne, Crystal, Mike, Marvin, and Bishme, looked at Jessie, but they were scared to say anything for fear he might spaz out.

To break the awkward silence Jessie jokingly said, "Hey y'all, let's go to City Island and eat some scrimp," making everybody in the car laugh. They all knew only ghetto chicken heads called shrimp "scrimp."

"Yeah, I'm hungry," said Crystal, who lately had been eating enough for two.

"That sounds like a good idea," said Bishme. "A brother's gotta get full if me and Marvin gonna satisfy Maria, Maria. Y'all know the key to a brother's dick is through his stomach," said Bishme, rubbing his stomach.

"You stupid ass, the saying goes the key to a brother's heart is through his stomach," said Jessie, as everybody laughed again.

"Yeah, Jess—I just like flipping my own shit. I'm like that west coast rapper E-40. We on another level with our word play. We innovative," said Bishme.

"Ina-who, whatever. Oh, so that means ya bumbleclod sweatin da next mon. Get off his dick," said Marvin, who resorted back to his Jamaican dialect making what he said even more funny. Since coming from Jamaica and being in the states for years and hanging around Harlemites, Marvin and his brother talked like native New Yorkers.

Bishme never took it the wrong way when his homeboys gigged on him so he slapped him a pound.

All the pleasant camaraderie and chilling with his people slowly released all the built-up tension inside Jessie that was caused by the beat down they inflicted on Frankie. Jessie liked the fact that nobody even mentioned anything about it. The sad part was, deep down inside, he knew things were only going to get worse for the Fist of Fury.

The murderous rage he displayed up on the avenue scared the mess out of him, knowing he easily could have killed Frankie if Crystal and Wayne had not popped up on the scene. As they made their way to City Island, Jessie's mind drifted off as he thought about potential witnesses that would have seen the murder. Jessie knew his actions were reckless. This made him wonder what would he do the next time somebody tried to draw him into some type of "What's up with your pops?" snitch drama.

48

Putting in Work

While standing by the observation deck of his assigned dorm in the Otisville Federal Penitentiary, CO Astwood yelled, "Yo, Azar, let me holla at you for a minute. Peep this. I know you heard that Lorenzo is out of PC." CO Astwood carefully observed the surroundings of the dorm to make sure no one else was listening.

"Yeah, I heard he signed his snitch-ass outta Punk City," said Azar.

"So, I ain't gotta tell you what time it is, y'all niggas handle y'all business and make his punk-ass regret what he did. And don't worry 'cause I'm gonna hit y'all niggas off lovely, feel me. It's time to show that snitching nigga Lorenzo a perfect ending to seven years of bad luck," said CO Astwood.

Azar nodded his bald head then headed to his work detail in the prison mess hall.

Then CO Astwood went to call the person who had paid $30,000 for him to set up the hit.

CO Astwood justified his slimy actions because he was fed up with seeing big drug dealers and criminals who had dough beat cases due to loopholes in the law found by their high-priced lawyers. His reasoning did not make a bit of sense, being that he should have been glad Lorenzo snitched and helped get some criminals off the streets. But CO

Astwood was just a crook in a prison uniform trying to rationalize his own larceny and greed. The real reason had more to do with pleasing the pretty young thing that he met while doing visitor room detail.

He first spotted the red bone, big booty chick when she was visiting this drug dealer from his dorm. And now that he was hitting the skins in order to keep her happy, more money than a correction officer's salary was needed. This meant setting up Lorenzo to be murdered.

Azar had his own reasons for wanting to kill Lorenzo that had nothing to do with snitching. Quiet as it was kept, he had snitched out his homeboys, so he was definitely in it for the money and not trying to fool himself. By killing Lorenzo, Azar could accomplish two things. One, make some money, and two, by helping CO Astwood, Azar knew in time he would be obligated to help him get drugs in the prison.

* * *

"Hello, Jody, what's up, boo. How's it shaking?" said CO Astwood.

"Listen, you jake bastard, let's stop the bullshit. Just tell me if you handled the business that we talked about," said Bolo's woman, Jody.

"Jody, everything's been taken care of, Lorenzo is gonna get what's—"

"Shut up you stupid bastard. Where are you calling me from?" said Jody, angrily.

"Oh my bad, I forgot I'm at work," said CO Astwood, his lapse of judgment making him feel real stupid. Before CO Astwood could finish talking he heard a click.

"Damn, what the heck that bum bitch hung up on me," said CO Astwood, but at the same time understanding that Jody was 100 percent right.

He thought, *If anybody should know the phones are tapped, he should, being a correction officer and all. But forget that, who does that bum bitch think she is, talking to me like a knucklehead. Next time she disrespects me, I'm gonna whip her ass, then put my big dick in her mouth. Who the fuck she gon' go get, her stupid-ass man Bolo is in jail doing twenty-five years behind Lorenzo's snitching. And I'll bet my last dime that she's out on the streets sexing one of his homeboys. Stanking hoe. Bitches ain't shit but hoes and tricks.*

That's why to hell with all these sons of bitches, I'm just gon' sit back and make some cheddar off all these bitches.

49

Dear Mama

Sitting in his cell at the Otisville Federal Prison, Lorenzo wrote a letter to his mother.

Mama, people always like to mention rats, cheese and snitches in the same sentence whenever they find out somebody dropped a dime on someone to the police. These are three things I have found out that don't quite agree with my system.

Since my youth I have always had a fear of rats. First of all, they're beady-eyed, slimy and creepy little creatures that even eat their own. And if you try to back them into a corner they will do anything to get away.

I guess that's why people connect snitches with rats. Snitches have been known to rat out their own mothers, kids and loved ones when they get trapped into a corner, because to them nothing is sacred. Snitches do not give a rat's ass that they are the main cause of their sorry predicaments. Mama, these are just some of the things that make me want to puke, but before I do let me finish. When I was a little kid I always hated the free cheese that you got at the neighborhood church. Every time I ate it, my stomach would start boiling. This in turn always gave me bad stomach pains and a bad case of gas. Any time I farted, anybody that was around me would say I smelled rotten inside. Nobody wanted to be around me whenever I cut loose, so I got

*into the habit of cracking jokes and blaming my gas epi-
sodes on "Mama's good ole cheese-baked biscuits." Sorry,
Mama. This would always make them laugh.*

*But that still did not stop my system from not agreeing
with cheese, because I hated having to eat it so much due to
our family's dire situation.*

*Now years later, and as the feds put it, being of sound
mind and body, I have to come to grips with becoming the
federal government's star witness against my own drug crew.*

*This is something that deep down at the bottom of my
core and conscience, goes against everything I have ever
stood for. I'm forced to live with the fact that I chose to eat
cheese, like a rat. Nothing more than a beady-eyed, slimy
and creepy creature. A low-down, dirty rotten snitch. Every
time, Mama, that you used to catch me doing something I
was not supposed to be doing, you would always say, "Son,
one day you are gonna have to pay for all the wrong things
that you do in life."*

*Well, Mama, I'm caught in a bit of a bind and I know
you said there was gonna be days like this, but what about
the years? The years of maybe being stuck in a eight-by-
nine-foot dreary cell with nothing but heartache, pain, tears
and an asshole full of time. And to make matters worse,
Mama, is that I'm a snitch, the worst thing you can be in
prison. Mama, even the feds that I made the deal with don't
like snitches.*

*Mama, I feel like a rat caught in a glue trap destined to
die a cruel death because in prison they say "snitches get
stitches" and the cock-diesel inmate in the cell next to mine
is just waiting for the chance to use his long rusty shank,
that I hear him sharpening up, on yours truly. Mama, it's so
dark on the tier that although I can't see anything, my sense
of sound is magnified tenfold. This transferring of the senses
makes hearing the slivers of metal dropping off my enemies'
crudely made weapons that more frightening. Mama, right
now I got a bad feeling in the pit of my stomach and it's not*

from hunger. It's a queasy rumbling that's banging up against the walls of my insides. Excuse my French, Mama, but I know I ain't gonna take a shit because I just went in the dirty little thing called a toilet. Maybe it's my subconscious mind trying to tell me something, but it's too much for my brain to handle, so my body's playing tricks on me.

Mama, as I stare at the prison walls in my suffocating cell that smells like sweat, blood and tears, I find myself trying to figure out what the hell is going on.

I can't quite grasp this feeling I'm feeling so therefore I'm trying my damndest to forget about it, but it keeps coming back.

Mama, is it my intuition, God, or an angel sent down by him to warn me to keep my guard up and get ready to roll with the punches? Maybe deep down I know that the answers to my questions have already been answered by a higher authority. And all I really have to do is sit back and wait for what's already written in God's log book of debts to be paid—that is, you reap what you sow, Bye, bye, Mama.

"CO, crack the cell, I got work detail!" yelled Lorenzo, getting up from his bunk and hiding his writing pad under the hard and stiff thing the prison called a mattress. From the observation deck a red-necked CO yelled, "Opening cell number twelve!" The bars on Lorenzo's cell started to move.

As Lorenzo stepped on the tier, several inmates lingered.

"Yo, Renzo, how's it shaking this morning," said a black guy with scars across his face.

"Listen, homes, you don't know me from a can of paint and I don't know what types of games you tryna play, but I suggest that you keep it movin'," said Lorenzo.

The frightening and deadly serious way that Lorenzo looked at the inmate was the same look that most of his murder victims would see right before they flatlined. The guy shot Lorenzo his own nasty look and headed down the tier with a skinny Puerto Rican guy Lorenzo suspected he was fucking.

"You see, baby, that piece of scum right there is an informant and he's living on borrowed time. I don't know who the fuck he thinks he is, but, honey, all the money they say he got can't save his snitching-ass now," said the musclebound inmate.

His little plaything just smiled like he was in homo heaven and, in an effeminate voice, said, "Rock, don't let that stupido get ju all stressed out. Ju know I don't like to see ju like dat. But I know, papi, how to make my mang feel betta. So step inside mi little casa wit' a view and I'm goin' to take care all ju problemos."

As soon as they got in the cell, the Puerto Rican guy pulled down Rock's green prison-issued pants and proceeded to suck him off in a frenzy.

Meanwhile, on the other side of the tier in the well-lit dayroom, another scenario was playing itself out. Lorenzo would be playing a major part.

"Yo, cracker, you betta turn that TV channel back to Jerry Springer before I catch another damn case up in this piece," said Alonso, head of the prison house gang.

"I'm sorry, Alonso, I thought y'all wanted to watch Rickie Lake," said the red-necked, white boy, who secretly hated niggas with a passion.

"Man, forget that fat bitch. Now that she gained all that weight, niggas can't even get they dick hard. Now my man Jerry Springer got bitches showing ass and tits," said Alonso as all the other inmates in the crowded dayroom laughed, some out of fear.

All while this was going on, Lorenzo watched the pouring rain hit the tar-covered basketball court in the yard through the dirty window protected by reinforced wire.

A vision of God crying crossed Lorenzo's mind as he thought about what his family, especially Jessie, was going through because of him.

Then somebody jarred him out of his depressing thoughts and said, "Lorenzo, I can tell by your dreary look and puffy eyes that it's been kind of hard all these years getting adjusted to prison life after having all that money, bitches and fly-ass cars," said CO Astwood, who was known in the prison to be responsible for a lot of the drama. He liked to play both sides against one another. Then he stepped back in the mix and acted like he didn't know anything when somebody wound up dead.

"CO, it's no skin off my back. What's done is done. We all gotta make decisions in life and I made mine. I can't sweat shit that's outta my control, so all that nonsense you talking is just a bunch of bullshit," said Lorenzo.

CO Astwood almost laughed when Lorenzo talked about making decisions in life, thinking, *Yeah and you chose to become a snitch.* But he didn't laugh, he just said, "Yeah, man, but I know you gotta miss being with that beautiful wife of yours that I seen you with in the visiting room."

Lorenzo saw right through his mind games. He knew he was the same slimy bastard who always tried to kick it with the other inmates' women after they left the visiting room. One time he heard him tell a pretty Dominican chick that her boyfriend was getting fucked by a big black guy who had AIDS. Lorenzo also knew that CO Astwood helped another inmate smuggle a gun into the prison.

Lorenzo pointed right in CO Astwood's face, which got everybody's attention, and said, "Listen, you conniving bastard and listen good. Keep my woman's name out of your mouth, you asshole!"

Then Lorenzo walked toward the entrance of the dayroom. All of a sudden CO Astwood nodded to Alonso, who jumped up out of his seat and lunged towards Lorenzo with a sharp shank in his hand.

Lorenzo's sixth sense told him to move to the side, but a little voice in his head said, *Let it happen,* as the sharp blade pierced his jugular making blood spurt everywhere.

At the same time Lorenzo was on his way to meet his maker, Rock was busting his load on his lover's face.

50

Tell It Like It Is

"Sit down, Jessie, I want to talk to you," said Red, as Jessie stood by the counter of his bar.

"No problem, Red, how's everything going? I heard you been making a killing hitting them numbers. Didn't your number 751 come out the other day?" said Jessie.

"Yeah, and I had five thousand dollars on that sucker. Paid a brother off lovely."

"Man, you must of got a nice piece of change off that hit. Red, youse a big timer and one lucky brother," said Jessie in a jolly mood.

"Thanks, Jess, but what I have to tell you is a lot more serious than hitting a number. It's no easy way to say this, but I have to let you know. Your father got killed in prison. He's dead," said Red, staring straight at Jessie, fumbling with a coaster.

Jessie said nothing because for an instant he felt nothing. Then he said, "I guess that snitch bastard finally got what was coming to him. I hated him with a passion and I hope he rots in hell." The words came out like he was spitting out arsenic.

"Yo, Jess, deep down you don't really believe that. Your father loved his family more than anything in this world. Forget what the streets say—he was more than a snitch. The real person was a good brother that did a lot of things for some of those same people that talk bad about him. Sometimes things get out of control, nobody's perfect. Not even you or me."

Red briefly thought about his own deep secret.

"Red, I can't put my stamp on that, 'cause no matter what, he didn't have to go out like a sucker. A real nigga wouldna went out like that. He woulda just took his case to trial and fought the feds to the end. Real niggas do real things," said Jessie. He slid the coaster down the counter, as a story about black sports legends like Muhammad Ali, Jack Johnson and Hank Aaron played on a small color television by the bar.

"All that sounds good, Jess, but in life things happen. Now don't get me wrong. I don't agree one bit with the decision he made. But it was his decision to make, not mine."

"Red, you and my father were best friends, and it's only right that you defend him to the end. But, no disrespect to you, nothing's gonna change the hate and disdain I have for that rat bastard," said Jessie. Then he got up and walked out of Red's bar.

Red thought he saw fire in his eyes. Jessie was angry because he knew that as soon as word hit the streets that his father had finally been killed for his snitching, it would revive old issues and give the other thugs and haters reason to mess with him and Jessie was not going to put up with that. In Jessie's mind there would be no smack-down part two.

Jessie got in his black Cadillac Escalade, and headed to 158th Street and Amsterdam to get guns from the Dominicans. Going shopping always relieved Jessie's stress.

There, he got out of the truck and with the stride of a man on a mission he proceeded to go handle his business.

Domincans selling Pedico in front of a dirty charcoal-colored building, gave approving head nods as he walked past them and knocked on apartment 1C in the back. A curly-haired guy, who looked like a young Julio Iglesias, answered the door with a silver Glock in his hand. He waved him in.

"What's up, Jessie? How's it shakin' poppa," said the muscular Dominican wearing a wife beater T-shirt.

"I'm chillin', papito. Everything's copacetic. I'm just tryna spend a little paper—ya know, spread the wealth," said Jessie, already feeling at home. The soothing music coming from a radio in the apartment made him feel like he was buying groceries at a supermarket.

"That's all right wit' me, poppa. Whatever you need I got it. Ya know, I always look out for the cool moreno," said the guy, slapping Jessie a pound.

"Well, papito, I need to reup on some artillery. What you got for your hombre?"

Papito did a funny little two-step in his Timberland boots and said, "You've come to the right place. Step into my little office 'cause I just got a nice shipment the utta day."

As they entered the brightly lit room, Jessie's eyes focused on a red wall covered with Tech Nines, Uzis and all types of automatic weapons and silencers.

Papito smiled and said, "You see sun-din you like, poppa?"

"Yeah, give me everything on the first row, third row, and that Tech Nine you got on that little table."

Papito got serious. "Jessie, man, you on your way to Iraq or sun-din?"

"Nah, but a brother likes to be prepared. Know what I'm saying?"

"You so right, poppa, but if you need any help wit' that war you 'bout to fight, me and my homies are down for whatever."

They both laughed as they made their transaction, and Jessie kept it moving.

All while Jessie was handling his business, word traveled fast around the hood about Lorenzo.

Jessie decided to get his mind off the current happenings by calling up a hottie.

"Yo, Tanya, how's it going girl," said Jessie, faking like he really cared.

"What do you mean, how's it going? I ain't seen yo ass since a month ago when I let you talk me into running a ménage à trois on me and my homegirl," said Tanya, wearing nothing but a light green thong and bra set as she stretched out on her bed.

"Yeah, girl, but a nigga's been busy handling his BI trying to stack that paper. But forget all that, a nigga wanna see you," said Jessie.

Tanya smiled on the other end and said, "What time you gonna pick me up?"

"Right now, Tanya, I'm downstairs," said Jessie.

"Oh, you just knew I was going to be wit' it, huh?" said Tanya.

"Stop yapping your gums and come downstairs," said Jessie as he closed his silver cell phone.

After a few minutes of waiting in front of her building on 112th Street and Park Avenue, he spotted Tanya headed towards the Escalade in a tight grey and pink velour sweatsuit with Phat Farm written across her bodacious ass. Tanya looked a little like the rapper Eve combined with some chinky eyes.

Just looking at her pretty face and banging body was already getting the stress off Jessie's back. When he finished banging her back out, she would be asking him to let her get his name tattooed on her ass.

As they headed to the Poconos in Pennsylvania they listened to a tape with Mary J. Blige classics. When her song "You All I Need" with Method Man started to play, he switched to another track. It made him think about the Coca-Cola commercial with the father listening to Marvin Gaye's version in the living room while his son listened to the Mary J. Blige and Method Man version upstairs. And right now he was on some fuck-all fathers type shit.

When they arrived at Caesar's Palace, they went into a

big reception area with purple velvet couches, chandeliers and mirrors all over the place and ordered the Champagne Towers Suite. After drinking a few bottles of Cristal and smoking chocolate Thai that had them higher than ten people, they both were ready for a little skin on skin. Tanya's pussy was moist, tight and sweet. They fucked and sucked for hours. The more she sucked the more he squirmed. In the heat of passion he lost control and at last began to bust off.

He yelled, "Crystal, I'm coming!"

Tanya looked up at him while bending on her knees and said, "Oh, no you didn't! Who the hell is Crystal?"

51

Listen Closely

Jessie tried to explain his way out of calling Tanya another female's name during sex, but to no avail. What made matters worse, was that he called her Crystal again during the ride home. This made Tanya angry. She told Jessie that because he couldn't remember her name not to call her anymore. Jessie's foolish pride made him promptly curse, and kick her out of the Cadillac Escalade.

Then he sparked up a blunt to relieve the stress of knowing that he had blown some real good poo-nanny. A cop in a police cruiser spotted the blunt in his mouth as Jessie sped by and pulled him over.

The white rookie cop with bad acne, and who looked like he was not much older than Jessie, arrested him for speeding and possession of marijuana.

On the way to the 25th Precinct, the rookie cop tried to preach to Jessie about how marijuana was a gateway drug that leads to using other highly addictive drugs like cocaine and heroin.

Jessie looked out the window and ignored him as he thought about the previous night's events. When they arrived at the 25th Precinct, the rookie put Jessie in a room that smelled like stink-whore cunt, Budweiser beer and stale pretzels. As the cop processed his desk appearance ticket, Jessie concentrated on what he heard in the other room.

"So, you say you're going to let me go and drop all the charges if I agree to bring back some substantiated evidence that could be used to help convict Dollar Bill and the rest of the Black Top Crew, that you claim I'm down wit'," he heard someone say.

Another voice, perhaps a cop, said, "Yo, Einstein, you better stop your shucking, jiving, and talking this, claiming to be down wit' crap or else the deal is off. Our whole drug task force already has the handle on what the fuck you and your boys have been up to. Either with you or without you, we're going to get convictions. So if you want to sit here and play games, I ain't got time to listen to your nonsense."

"My bad, Sarge. I understand exactly what you're saying. I just don't want to get a promised deal then, and after I do what y'all say, y'all turn around and renege. Then my homeboys find out I'm the one who's been dropping dimes on them. If that happens, I'm a dead man," said the snitch.

As Jessie sat in the dirty and smelly room, waiting for his DAT for getting caught speeding and smoking weed, he smiled thinking he was going to make the snitch's fears become a reality. While he waited, he wondered who could the guy with the loose lips be? Jessie had no clue, but on the streets that he roamed, loose lips sink ships and this one is going down like the Titanic.

After a few minutes, the cop who busted him came into the room and said, "You don't know this, Jessie, but I'm cutting you a break big time. I could put you through the system and take you down to central booking, but I'm gonna look out for you. Also, let's not forget that nice Escalade you got could have been confiscated. I just hope one day you remember what I did for you when I need a favor," said the red-faced blue coat.

Jessie could not believe his ears as he listened to the stink-breath rookie cop trying to set him up for down-the-road-becoming-a-snitch bullshit. The tactics the cop tried to use on him were taught to the rookie in the academy. Course

101, How to Turn a Snitch. But what they taught the sneaky cop only worked on suckers like the guy in the other room, who most likely would even sell out his mama if he thought it would get him a get-out-of-jail-free card.

As he listened to what was going on in the other room, Jessie thought about what tactics were used to get his father to rat out the SSJ Crew.

He knew the cops had to come better than what this asshole was trying. Jessie just smiled at the cop, said nothing and snatched the DAT out of his hand, then went outside to wait for the guy who was a willing participant in a cop's cruel game of tattletale.

Because the snitch liked to play games, Jessie had a brand-new one fresh out the wrapper called, "I see Death Around the Corner." First and last question of the game: If a guy snitches out his partners in crime, what is the proper punishment: (1) death by natural causes; (2) death by heart attack while having sex; (3) death by gunshots and torture at the hands of an unknown assailant.

The snitch better choose wisely because the wrong answer could lead to being dead wrong.

* * *

As Jessie patiently waited for the snitch within eyesight of the precinct, he smoked a bag of chocolate Thai that the rookie cop did not find. It helped ease the pain in his head.

He laughed to himself as he thought about the rookie's weak attempt to turn him into an informant.

After waiting an hour, Jessie watched a brown-skinned guy with braided hair, a green army fatigue outfit and broccoli-colored Timberland boots walk down the precinct steps *straight solider*. He looked around nervously.

Jessie suspected the guy was making sure nobody spotted him leaving the place of ill repute, the precinct. The snitch walked off fast heading towards Seventh Avenue. Jessie followed half a block behind. As he ran across to the other side, he totally forgot the first rule you learn as a kid.

And that is, you have to look both ways before you cross the streets. When the guy made it to the 135th Street train station on Lenox Avenue, he went downstairs and got on the number two train, never suspecting he was being followed every step of the way.

As the fidgety guy squirmed in his seat, Jessie watched his every move from a distance. The chronic had Jessie so high that he almost busted out laughing after noticing that the guy bore a striking resemblance to the comedic actor Chris Rock, who played a snitch in the old movie *New Jack City*.

As Jessie looked away, he spotted a pretty redbone checking him out so he walked over to her while keeping an eye out for his target. Jessie had to be ready to get off the train when he did.

"Hey, gorgeous, I spotted you over here checking a brother out. Would you mind if I ask, do you know me from somewhere?"

Shorty dime piece smiled, showing her pearly whites and said, "Yeah, ain't your name Jessie, and don't you live on Strivers Row and you drive a black Cadillac Escalade?"

Her questions told Jessie that he could fuck this chicken head with quickness. Jessie smiled and said, "Yeah, shorty, I'm that guy but forget about all that. All I wanna know is can I come one day and pick your pretty ass up, so that I can wine and dine you?"

Shorty dime piece was so hard on Jessie's dick that she did not even answer him. She just started writing down her house number, cell, and pager number. Talk about getting the seven digits. As soon as she passed Jessie the numbers, the two train pulled into the 116th Street station and he spotted the snitch standing by the doors.

When the train stopped Jessie followed him out of the station. After a quick pit stop at the corner store where the snitch bought a vanilla blunt and a Heineken beer, he crossed the street and went inside a newly renovated building. Jessie went in right after him and they both waited for the elevator. The snitch was so lost in his thoughts he did not even notice Jessie getting on the elevator with him. But he did notice the silver 9 mm Glock in Jessie's hand when the doors closed. The same automatic that the stupid rookie cop failed to find because he never checked Jessie.

"Yo, Jess, what's up with the gun bruh, I ain't got no beef with you," said the snitch as the stench from his sweat and fear permeated the enclosed area.

"Oh, yes, I do got a problem with a snitch-ass nigga knowing my name," screamed Jessie as he unloaded every bullet from the automatic weapon.

The first bullet tore off the top of his head, while the rest of the bullets shattered teeth, bones and splattered blood and insides all over the elevator. The snitch was dead before he hit the pissy floor. Jessie got off the elevator smiling as he whispered, "How do all these people know my name?"

.

52

Snitch Detector

From time to time, Jessie had heard one person or another say that whenever you buy clothes, jewelry or material items, you suddenly start to notice that a lot of other people have bought the same things, and your stuff is not unique.

Take for instance the time he copped his first jeep, a red Pathfinder. When he bought it, he envisioned driving up on the block, windows down and music blasting, just flossing on niggas. But, on his way to the avenue he spotted the same jeep ten times. It seemed like everybody and their mother had one. In his mind he tried to trick himself into thinking that the other chumps had seen him with his and jumped on the bandwagon. But, deep down Jessie could not lie to himself when the real reason was he never paid attention to it.

But the situation with the jeep taught Jessie a valuable lesson. That is sometimes finding your path means keeping in tune with everything and anything going on and around you.

This is why lately, because of all the drama concerning his father, all his senses tuned into anything that had to do with snitches.

Jessie's ability to weed out a snitch anywhere in his vicinity took on supernatural proportions. If a conversation to do with snitching was taking place, his ears took on a cat-like ability to hear it from far away. Like a smoke detector could detect smoke, he was like a Human Snitch Detector.

If Jessie spotted somebody whom he thought looked, acted or did something that made him suspect they might be a snitch, his body temperature would rise hotter than fire and somebody would get smoked. Not only that, he wanted to piss on their wounds, smell their blood, and make any potential snitch witnessing the act feel the pain.

In Jessie's warped sense of thinking, he was providing a much-needed public service. He thought the fewer snitches walking around the better. And to top it off, he did not even want to be praised or given the key to the city for ridding society of people whom he felt fit this category.

His father always said, "Boy, find what you're good at, and do it." *Well, well, well. Pops, it took a minute for me to find my calling in life, but better late than never. And the answer to your often-asked question of, "Son, what do you want to be when you grow up?" has finally been answered.*

The revelation came to Jessie like a thief in the night: "Daddy dearest, I'm gonna be a snitch killer."

53

Loco-Loco, Jessie's Gonna Kill Somebody

While sitting in Bishme's blue 600 Coupe Mercedes on 155th Street and Eighth Avenue waiting for the Entertainer Basketball Classic game between Jay-Z and Fat Joe's teams to start, Jessie, decided to ask Bishme about something that was bothering him.

"Yo, Bishme, I heard you are dissatisfied with the money you been making, and that you feel you deserve a bigger cut," said Jessie.

"You see, that's that bullshit. Who the fuck been telling you some shit like that," said Bishme, pissed off.

"Bish, the streets talk and word done leaked back to yours truly that you got your head bad one night drinking that thug Passion along with that Ecstacy crap and you started popping off at the mouth. I always tell everybody in the crew, if niggas got a problem, let a nigga know and I'll try my best to solve it. I ain't never tried to come across as a know-it-all type uh nigga or some selfish bastard that wanna eat steak while his homeboys eat toast. But what gets me vexed is when I hear my own niggas is bad-mouthing the crew."

As they sat in the car, Bishme suspected that Jessie was a bit paranoid and delusional from all the coke he heard Jessie had been sniffing lately.

"Yo, Jess, I can't believe you gon' let some crab-ass playa-hating motherfuckers even come at you on some divide-and-conquer bullcrap. You should know by now that I don't even get down like that. I don't care how high they say I got, I ain't never put our business on the street," said Bishme, raising his voice. Bishme was lying through his teeth and Jessie was not fooled. Scratching behind his ear and talking real fast—things Bishme only did when lying—confirmed everything.

Then the fact that Jessie heard about Bishme's bitching from a reliable source, convinced him that if Bishme would lie about this petty stuff, what else would he lie about? The more Bishme lied, the madder Jessie got. Some of it had to do with Jessie being weary of Bishme and all of Howie Tee's crew members that he put down in his crew.

"Jessie, we go too far back for me to disrespect our crew. Plus, me and you done too much dirt together."

All Jessie heard is, "We done too much dirt together." Then Jessie heard some voices in his head, *Loco-Loco, Jessie's gonna kill somebody. Loco-Loco, Jessie's gonna kill somebody. Loco-Loco, Jessie's gonna kill somebody.*

"Bish, cut off the radio, it's too loud, I can't hear myself think," said Jessie, his eyes buggy.

"Yo, kid, you bugging. Ain't no radio on," said Bishme, confused, as he continued to plead his case, figuring Jessie was just hallucinating from the potent weed they were smoking.

And as Bishme blabbed away, everything he said took on an underlying meaning to Jessie. Jessie envisioned Bishme spilling his guts at a precinct, ratting out the Crossover Crew, just like the snitch he killed.

Bishme's voice became the voice of that snitch. *My homeboys find out I'm the one who's been dropping dime on them* . . . Jessie wondered if a good-cop-bad-cop routine, played out in a hot room of a precinct under glaring bright lights combined with a cigarette and a free cup of coffee, would be enough to make Bishme become a snitch.

Jessie wondered if a guy who had been telling lies since a kid all of a sudden let his conscience get the best of him and decide to start telling the truth at the wrong time. *Yes, the Crossover Crew are drug dealers and killers. Yes, Jessie is the mastermind. And yes, I'm willing to cut a deal to save my ass,* Jessie thought when he heard Bishme tell lie after lie.

Jessie thought, if his own father, Lorenzo, could drop dime, why not Bishme? Even so-called real niggas have snitched. Just the promise of a get-out-of-jail-free pass by some conniving cops was enough for them to sell their souls. Never even taking the time to think that nothing is ever really free and such a proposition only leads to getting their ghetto passes revoked. Cops can't keep a secret. They snitch on snitches.

While Jessie and Bishme were in deep conversation, a gray Crown Victoria with tinted windows pulled in back of the 600 Coupe Mercedes. Right off the bat they spotted Drug Task Force Detectives Kennedy and his partner O'Grady getting out. The detectives tapped on the windows of the Mercedes and told them to get out.

When they opened the doors and stepped out of the vehicle Detective Kennedy said, "Sorry to bother you two assholes, but we received a call about some guns in the area, so we got to perform our duties by checking out you decent, law-abiding citizens."

"That's right, you dickheads, get on the floor spread-eagle so we can get this over with," said O'Grady, smirking at Jessie.

Then, with a slight grin he said, "Jessie, sorry to hear about your pops being murdered in prison."

Jessie acted like he did not hear him and said nothing. He knew O'Grady helped put Pops away.

Bishme, pissed off, said, "That's that bullshit. Anyway, why we got to get on that dirty-ass floor, we ain't got nothing and we ain't done nothing, so why y'all harassing us?"

Jessie kept quiet, observing everything along with the big crowd that had gathered to watch the ghetto drama unfold. The crowds at the 155th Street Entertainers Basketball Classic that used to be called the Pro Ruckers, had gotten bigger since the NBA players and hip-hop stars joined up. Now the crowd was getting a special added treat.

"Listen, knucklehead, if you keep your fuckin big mouth shut we can get this shit over fast," said O'Grady as he motioned them to the ground. As they both complied, Jessie still kept quiet.

Lying on the floor, Jessie could hear a guy on a microphone from the Entertainer Basketball Classic League Court screaming, "Man, did you see that? Nobody dunks it better than 'the incredible half-man half-amazing.'"

Hearing this made Jessie think of himself as being half a man, and of Wayne wasting his truly amazing basketball skills in the drug game. Jessie sighed. While Detective Kennedy checked them on the ground, Detective O'Grady ransacked the Mercedes, secretly finding pleasure in the task. He thought, *Why do I have to ride around in a 1998 Galant while these pricks floss in luxury cars? When the Drug Task Force eventually takes down the Crossover Crew it will make my day, and busting Lorenzo's son is going to be icing on the cake.*

Trying to help a friend out, Pop Swayze wearing a dirty white sweatshirt yelled from the back of the crowd, "Leave 'em alone y'all red-necked bastards," making everybody, including the detectives, laugh. While frisking Bishme, Detective Kennedy found a 9 mm tucked by the waist of his Carhartt blue jeans.

"Look what we got here," said Detective Kennedy as he pulled out the shiny chrome automatic and placed Bishme under arrest. "Didn't your mother tell you not to play around with guns when you were little, you stupid bastard?" said Detective O'Grady, wishing they found the gun on Jessie.

"Yo, that ain't mine, I don't care what you say, it ain't mine. You planted that on me," said Bishme. Detective O'Grady slammed the 600 Coupe Mercedes car doors then ran over and helped his partner lift Bishme and Jessie off the ground.

"Jess, I guess this time you're the lucky one. We're gonna let you go being that we didn't find nothing on you, but next time you won't be so lucky. Now get yo mute ass outta here," said Detective Kennedy.

Detective O'Grady acted like he wanted to kick Jessie up the ass but having people watching made him rethink that.

"Why y'all always messing wit' us, why don't y'all go mess wit' those crackers in the suburbs? They the ones doing all the dirt," said Pop Swayze, trying to get the crowd riled up. That's when a few other cop cars pulled up and made the crowd disperse.

Jessie walked off, heading to his Escalade that was parked around the corner. When he got there Tracy and her big-butt friend, Tina, were standing by the truck.

"Jessie, them punk police is dead wrong, they just jealous. If you need a witness, I'm there for you, that's police harassment," said Tracy.

Shorty fat ass, with the short braids and chinky eyes, nodded in agreement and said, "If y'all need us Jess, we got y'all back."

Jessie, dazed and pissed off that he was still reaping backlash from the cops who busted his father, came up out of his stupor and said, "That's real. That's real. Us brothers need the sistas to hold us down. By the way, what y'all doing, y'all want to hang out?"

Tracy, who had a crush on Jessie for years, said, "Yeah, Jess, me and my homegirl are not doing nothing, plus those po-po on the corner right there are watching us." Tracy was just fooling herself into thinking she was important.

They all got in the truck and jetted.

When the girls spotted the plasma screen TV inside the vehicle, with its plush leather and brown wood-grain interior, they asked him if it was all right if they sparked a blunt and watched one of the DVDs on the bone-colored leather seats.

Jessie, playing the nice guy, said, "Whatever y'all honeys want to do, be my guest." As they rode around smoking blunts, the girls watched a DVD called *Pablo Escobar: The King of Coke* while Jessie drifted off into deep thought.

The day's previous events had Jessie craving a hit of that thang-thang, so he reached in his pocket and retrieved the bag of white powder and a straw. And being that the girls thought he was such a nice guy, he offered them some before he took a hit. He passed the bag of coke to Tracy, who took a few hits then passed it to shorty fat ass. The females were in ghetto heaven as everybody got blitzed off of the coke.

Then it started in his head. *Loco-Loco, Jessie's gonna kill somebody. Loco-Loco, Jessie's gonna kill somebody.* Jessie yelled, "Shut the fuck up! Shut the fuck up!"

The girls were startled, thinking that he was talking to them. Jessie put his hands on his head and closed his eyes.

Then he got a moment of clarity and the voices quieted, but Jessie still had some of the angst that the words in his head made him feel. This made him come out of his Mr. Good Guy bag, and say, "Y'all bitches gonna fuck or what?"

54

Side Show

After passing an antsy crackhead two jumbos and three bags of dope, Mike said to Marvin. "Hey, I ain't seen Bishme since he got out of jail the other day after catching that case by the Polo Grounds while hanging with Jessie. That's not like him, that greedy nigga be grinding from sun up to sun down," said Mike as they were standing by the corner store.

"Come to think of it, son, Jessie was here on the avenue a little while ago and he said he ain't seen Bishme since he got busted. Maybe Bishme met some jumpoff and she got that brother's head messed up. Not to blow up his spot but tricking and Bishme go hand in hand," said Marvin, making them both laugh.

"Mike, do you want to go see the Kings of Comedy show at the Apollo? My homeboy, Wendell, that be scalping can get us some tickets if you want to go," said Marvin.

"Yeah, Marvin, let's do the damn thing, that sounds real good right about now—we done put in enough work since this morning slingin' dem thangs. Let's get outta here," said Mike, lighting up a stogie.

As they headed down Eighth Avenue on a warm and pleasant Friday night, they acted like they did not have a care in the world. It was a nice day for everybody but Bishme who, at that very moment, was somewhere buried in a patch of ground on Randalls Island being eaten by maggots.

* * *

As they reached the Kentucky Fried Chicken joint on a crowded 125th Street and waited for The Kings of Comedy Jam show at the Apollo to start, Marvin said, "Yo, Mike, there go crackhead Larry. Man, ever since his cousin hit him over the head with that bat he ain't never been the same. They say it messed him up so bad he acts like one of those guests that be on some talk show bugging out. I think they call it Tourette's syndrome. One minute they be talking normal and the next minute being saying stuff unintentionally like nigga, asshole, cracker and other curses," said Marvin.

"Watch this, Mike. Yo, Larry, come over here, I got something for yo ass," yelled Marvin, as they stood there killing time.

Larry, who was on the other side, flew across the crowded street and almost got hit by a female driving a light blue Honda Civic.

Just the thought of somebody giving him something made a bummy and dirty Larry's mouth water as he made it over to them.

"Man, Larry, I haven't seen you in a minute. Where you been hiding? Don't tell me you been going somewhere else to cop. You know the Crossover Crew got the best product in Harlem," said Marvin as Larry approached, wearing ugly, multicolored women's shoes.

"Nah, Marvin, uh brother just been going through a little hard times, but I'll be all right once I get on my feet," said Larry, through a mouthful of yellow, rotten teeth.

"Larry, since you've always been one of our good customers, here's two jumbos," said Marvin, as he nudged Mike on the side and winked.

Larry caught Mike off guard when he grabbed the two cracks out of Marvin's hand and said, "Thanks bitch, bitch, bitch, suck my dick hoe, bitch, bitch, bitch." Then he said, "Yo, Marvin, how's Jessie and Wayne doing?" flipping back into normal conversation.

Mike stared at Larry and then at Marvin in shock by what had just transpired and said, "Nah, no way."

Then Larry pulled out a dirty stem, and with no regard for all the people walking by, placed a piece of the crack that looked like soap inside it and lit it with a butane lighter. The hit made his eyeballs flicker uncontrollably and his cheeks swell up bigger than Dizzy Gillespie's as he strained not to let the crack crease his crusty lips.

"Y'all some all right dudes, bitch, bitch, bitch, suck my dick. Bitch, bitch, bitch, I'm coming girl—give me my money back. Man I don't know how I'll ever repay y'all two cats, good looking out. Bitch, bitch, bitch, holy shit, goddamm, bitch, bitch, suck me off, bitch," said Larry, carrying on two conversations at the same time.

This was too much for Mike to handle. He said to his brother, Marvin, "Yo, man, let's step off. This nigga's a total nut case."

As they walked down 125th Street towards the Apollo Theater on their way to the comedy show, they both laughed, knowing that nobody on stage tonight was going to top crackhead Larry's mental side show.

55

Somebody Save Me

The time was 1:00 A.M. Mount Morris Park was dark. The only thing casting a slight glow was a rusty lamppost with a little fluorescent light bulb. Mosquitos flew around it.

A dope fiend sitting on a green, paint-chipped bench, placed a black scuffed-up belt around his dirty scabbed-up arm and searched frantically for a vein. When he found it, he pushed out the air of the syringe and shot up the heroin.

Pop Swayze smiled and made mucous-filled snorting sounds. His eyes rolled up in his head and he nodded off. Coming up from his drug-induced stupor, he almost leaped off the bench when he saw Jessie's piercing green eyes staring at him.

Jessie's downtrodden and depressed look made Pop Swayze damn near lose his high as Jessie stood there saying nothing. Pop Swayze gathered his composure and said, "Sit down, my brother, and tell me what's going on."

Jessie did as he was told without uttering a word. For a minute, he just sat there and said nothing looking like a mentally disturbed person in a psych ward. Then Jessie said, "Pop, have you ever been caught between a rock and a hard place?"

The irony in what Jessie said almost made Pop Swayze bust out laughing because he was sitting on a hard bench with a syringe in one hand, a crack pipe and a few vials of crack rock in his pocket. But, he did not because he felt his friend was going through some painful inner turmoil.

"Yeah, Jess, I'm Mr. Troubled Man himself and at my age it's not too many things in life that I haven't experienced. And, I ain't gon' waste my time worrying about dying because death is guaranteed. Anyway, talk to me, Jess."

"Pop, I don't want to get you caught up in my drama, but let's just say I have done some pretty bad things. And the funny part is, I can't ask for forgiveness from God when it comes to the things I've done because deep down I know I'm gonna turn around and do the same things again."

Pop Swayze pondered his words and said, "Jessie, who am I to judge the next man. I'm a dope fiend. . . . To tell you the truth, I don't even have to know the things you've done because I already know that there are good people that do bad things and there are also bad people who do good things. Nobody's perfect. And the answers to whatever it is you're going through can be found somewhere deep inside your soul."

To a sane person, what Pop Swayze just said concerning Jessie's dilemma, would be a valid answer. But, Jessie's sorry mental state, combined with looking at Pop Swayze's drug-ravaged body, had him wanting to repay all the kindness and love Pop Swayze had shown him through the years by way of a mercy killing.

So, he got up off the park bench, stared real hard at Pop Swayze again, then walked off into the stillness of the night whispering under his breath, "God, protect me from myself."

56

Pissed Off

"Hurry up and take off that skirt, don't make me hurt you. All you little bitches are all alike," said the ugly pockmarked-face man.

"Please, please just take my earrings. Uh, uh, take my book, uh, uh, bag. I won't tell nobody, just, uh, uh, leave me alone," said the young Catholic High school senior, who was scared out of her wits. She had been on her way home when she was approached from behind by a man. He told her he had a gun, and led her behind a building.

Slap, slap, slap! The man hit the young Puerto Rican girl with an open hand, busting her lip and making blood leak from the side of her mouth.

"Now do you think I'm playing? Take all your shit off, for I can give you what you need and want, you little cunt."

As he spoke, she touched a rosary hanging from a chain on her neck and said a silent prayer hoping God or an angel would rescue her from being raped.

After being slapped around and then seeing the deranged look in the ugly guy's eyes, she knew that if she did not do exactly what he said, he was going to kill her. So as she started to nervously pull down her plaid skirt, the rapist ripped off her white blouse, part of her school uniform, making the buttons drop to the garbage-littered ground.

The rapist heard some rumbling by the garbage cans

and, thinking it was just some rats looking for some food, continued to take advantage of the young defenseless girl. When she was naked, the rapist pulled down his brown trousers, letting off a whiff of raw smelly ass before he could sexually assault her.

Bam, bam, boom, crack! Jessie clobbered him with a big silver garbage can top, and when the attacker fell to the ground, Jessie gave him a swift kick to the temple, instantly knocking him unconscious.

As the rapist lay on the ground like the piece of garbage he was, Jessie said calmly, "Everything's all right, Brandy. It's me, your old classmate, Jessie. Nobody's gonna hurt you now, just put on your clothes and wait for me in the front of the building and I'll take you home. And don't worry, I'll take care of this scumbag."

While putting on her clothes and crying, Brandy could not thank Jessie enough.

In Catholic school Brandy was taught that God really does answer prayers. She didn't realize that the only reason Jessie happened to be in the alley was because he had been drinking a lot of Heinekens and had to piss. Jessie being there was like divine intervention.

As she looked down at the rapist laying crumpled on the floor, then back at Jessie, she suddenly remembered that terrible day in school. A vivid visual of an angry Jessie taking their classmate Felix's eye out with a pencil flashed before her watery eyes. Then, a slight devilish grin appeared on her face knowing all to well what Jessie was capable of, and secretly hoping that he showed the rapist no mercy. She thought castration could be the proper punishment for a rapist. Jessie was going to make sure that the rapist got exactly what he deserved.

57

Who Shot Ya?

While Jessie was in the bathroom of Club Speed, two guys came inside and started whispering, "Man, did you see that honey with the white spandex? Man, them red bikini panties was just slicing her big ass," said one.

"Yo, Russ, forget that bum bitch. Check this out. If everything goes as planned concerning what we been kicking, you'll finally get your gold at the end of the rainbow and I will have made a name for myself, which translates into more clientele and more money. We got such a sweet arrangement because you'll be handling business on the outside and I'll be taking care of business on the inside. Plus, I got a good relationship with young Assistant District Attorney Rebecca Smith that's looking to make a name for herself."

"She got that hanging Judge Richard Klein whipped and he'll do anything she says," said the other guy.

While they blabbed on and on, they never suspected that Jessie was sitting on a toilet sniffing coke and listening to everything. Jessie's light-skinned complexion turned bloodshot red and his temper boiled as he assumed that they were two conniving drug dealers out to make it big in the lucrative drug game, including snitch.

So, without making a sound, Jessie slowly removed his silver 9 mm automatic from his waist and connected the small black silencer.

"Feel me, partna? This means anybody on the streets that's up to no good, can be taken down. We just got to hold our heads," said the guy as he continued to talk.

Before they knew what hit them, Jessie was busting out the bathroom stall like he was Richard Roundtree in the movie *Shaft,* letting off shot after shot, striking one straight in the head and the other one hit his lower and upper body extremities. Blood splattered everywhere. When they fell to the ground, Jessie stepped over them, put a spearmint gum in his mouth, and calmly walked out the bathroom.

As LL Cool J's song "Hush" blasted from the club's speakers, Jessie grabbed the hand of a pretty female wearing white see-through spandex that revealed her red bikini underwear and he headed to the crowded dance floor.

Jessie had no idea that the guy he had seriously wounded was an ambitious lawyer, and the one he murdered was a cop, who had hoped to earn a detective's gold shield.

58

Please Don't Kill Me

"Crystal, Jessie has been missing in action for a week and he hasn't called me, and I can't reach him on his cell phone. I'm starting to get worried," said Wayne, lying down next to Crystal on her bed.

"I'm worried too, boo. The last time I seen him it seemed like he was real distant and had a lot on his mind, like mentally he was in a bad place."

At this very moment, the place that Jessie happened to be, to some people would be considered a bad place, a Bellevue psych ward. After feeling down in the dumps from the stress, chaos, turmoil, and killings, Jessie decided to check himself into a hospital.

Jessie told the doctors he had been experiencing painful and pounding headaches along with depression. They admitted him after doing some head x-rays and finding something that they felt needed more looking into.

While at Bellevue and waiting for more tests to be conducted, Jessie met with a team of psychiatrists who tried to figure out the reasons for his depression. This was real hard for the psychiatrists to diagnose because Jessie was vague with them about what was troubling him—incest, snitching and killing.

While sitting in a day room with a bunch of other mentally disturbed patients and staff, Larry, the crackhead with

Tourette's syndrome, walked over to Jessie.

"Man, if it ain't my motherfuckin' favorite drug dealer, the legendary but never a legend Jessie shoot-'em-up Thompson. How ya doing? How ya doing? 'Cause I'm doing fine," said Larry, talking real loud and looking buggy-eyed.

"Yo, Larry, chill, chill. Nigga, is you crazy? Stop putting me on blast in here."

Everybody in the day room had their eyes and ears tuned in after hearing Larry's loud voice.

"Nah, nah, nigga, I ain't crazy. Can't you see I'm cured since I had a dose of that shock therapy and I stopped using them damn drugs you been selling. I'm a new man," said Larry.

Jessie decided it was time to leave Bellevue Hospital, so he got up from his chair, stared at Larry, and walked away.

Larry screamed, "Jessie, please don't kill me! Jessie, please don't kill me! Crack a lacking, crack a lacking, suck, suck, baby, gimme my money back bitch . . . "

The Bellevue Hospital orderlies in white uniforms went to get a straitjacket.

59

Wayne's Murder

As Jessie entered the warm town house he said, "Crystal, where's Ma at?"

"First, you just pop up out of the blue, looking like you just left Devil's Island and now you want to act like you really care where Ma's at. Give me a break! I bet it never even once crossed your mind to pick up a phone and call your family or friends that's been worried sick about you during your disappearing act," said Crystal, pouting.

"I'm sorry, Crystal, I'll never do that again. I just had to take time to do me and get away from it all. Now can a thug get a hug from his beautiful sister?"

Crystal smiled, kissed him on the lips, and hugged Jessie tightly.

"I feel better already, girl. Now tell me where is Ma at," said Jessie, moving away from his sister.

"Oh, Ma and Sheila went upstate to a jazz festival." What Crystal just said was like music to Jessie's ears as he grinned like a kid in a candy store. He immediately started thinking with his bottom head as he looked her up and down and stared at her tight-fitting shorts.

"Crystal, I think I'm gonna go take a shower, plus my back is hurting and I don't' feel like driving to my crib in New Jersey. I must have slept on the wrong side of the bed last night."

It was just another lame excuse to justify his ulterior motives of wanting to be there so that he could have sexual relations with her.

As she nodded, Jessie headed to his old bedroom and placed a big black bag that held a cache of weapons, drugs and money inside a closet. Then he went to take a shower.

After finishing up in the bathroom he put on new boxer shorts, then went to his bedroom and unexpectedly dozed off.

Why did you kill me, Jessie, I ain't never done nothing to noo-bod-dee. Okay, let me stop lying. Yeah, I hit that, no not your sister, nigger. Yeah, I fucked the shit out of my brother's woman, but that ain't had nothing to do wit' yo ass. Yes, I admit I did a lot of bad things in my life due to my messed up circumstances, like stealing and selling drugs. But nigga, you did the same shit. Ain't nobody kill you chump. Jessie, it's cold, dark, and it's starting to stink down here. Plus, I'm scared to death. Ha ha ha, man, I almost crapped on myself again from laughing too hard when I said 'scared to death.' Nah, but I'm gonna let you do the laughing for now and I'll just be comforted in knowing that one day a murdering scumbag like you who goes around killing his friends will one day get his just due. And I'll be waiting, waiting, wait—

Jessie was shaking and sweating as he remembered Bishme's words.

Why you kill me, Jessie? Why you kill me, Jessie?

Bishme, if you don't know by now, you betta ask some-body! yelled Jessie, at the same time trying his best to gather his composure. Bishme, remember that time when you said "me and you did so much dirt together," how was I sup-posed to interpret that? Right off the bat I pictured you rolling inside a precinct and dropping dime. Then in the same conversation you lied straight to my face and said you wasn't talking behind my back. It was like you was saying to me in so many words, what you gonna do now, sucka?

Well, actions speak louder than words and all you got to do now is look around your final resting place and all your questions will be answered. Nigga, I do my dirt all by my lonely.

Then Jessie woke up from the horrible nightmare for real, for real.

After drifting back into reality, Jessie released the vice grip he had on a pillow and yelled, "Hey, Crystal, can you come here for a minute?"

When Crystal came inside the room, she said, "What do you want, and why are you sweating so much? You look like you just saw a ghost."

Jessie responded, "I'm all right, I just had a bad dream. Crystal, the reason I called you is because my back is still hurting. Can you give me a massage?"

She gave him a funny look and then walked towards the bed as he lay on his stomach. As Crystal rubbed his back all over, Jessie made exaggerated oohs and aahs.

"Ooh, Crystal, you have such smooth hands. Yeah, rub right there. I'm starting to feel better already. Ooh, that feels so good, ooh baby right there," said Jessie, feeling horny. As she rubbed his back, what an older guy once told Jessie about pregnant pussy being the best pussy came to mind. *Maybe it is true. But, when you add sexing a sister to the equation, it becomes sick and twisted*, thought Jessie. Crystal's massaging lasted fifteen minutes, then Jessie sat up and said, "Now let me give you a massage 'cause you have been real stressed out lately and you look a little tense."

"I guess I have been a wreck since I found out about the pregnancy. And at my last appointment they said I was definitely carrying twins—twin boys. Maybe I do need a massage," said Crystal. Jessie rubbed her back sensuously as she sat beside him on the bed.

"Boys. They better be good-looking like their mother," said Jessie, as he parted his long fingers and rubbed her lower back really slowly. Then he picked up the pace when

Crystal started moaning. This went on for a few minutes. Then he slowly turned her around towards him and kissed and touched her breast and stomach, which still did not look very big, even though she was seven months pregnant. As she sucked his nipples, he slowly took off their underwear and inserted his penis inside of her. Then they stroked each other like two dogs in heat.

Wayne rang the bell but they were so involved in what they were doing that they did not hear him. He tried the doorknob because he had just left Crystal not long ago, so she had to be home. The door opened and he went inside.

When he heard moaning and groaning, he figured somebody was having sex.

It couldn't be coming from Crystal's mother. She had gone to the jazz festival. So who could it be? His heart raced as he got close to where the noise and scent of raw sex was coming from.

When he got to Jessie's room, he spotted him stroking a female but he could not tell who it was, so he moved closer. The sight of Crystal moaning and groaning in pure ecstacy was enough to drive a young man wild.

Wayne yelled like a crazy man, "Get the hell off of her, you pervert!" Jessie and Crystal were so engrossed into their stroking and kissing that he caught them totally off guard. Jessie immediately stopped what he was doing as Crystal, ashamed and not knowing what to say, pulled up the sheets to cover her naked body and turned her head.

Wayne's "pervert" comment made Jessie angry and he yelled, "I'll be that, but you the one who got fucked in the ass by Howie Tee!"

Crystal did not have the slightest idea what her brother was talking about. But Wayne did, and Jessie mentioning it put an enraged Wayne in kill mode. He snatched a buck-naked Jessie off the bed and they fought like they were in an HBO death match.

As they punched, kicked, and bit each other, Crystal

yelled, "Stop, please, stop, it's all my fault!" Tears rolled down her face.

They ignored her as they tussled and fell on the floor, trying to kill each other. Jessie managed to get his hands on his pants that were on the carpet by the bed. In one quick move he snatched his 9 mm automatic out of a pocket. The last thing Wayne saw was Jessie with a gun in his hand, firing shot after shot. One bullet struck Wayne in the chest and another one hit him in the face.

Blood splattered all over. Crystal yelled and screamed like a mad woman as Jessie got up off the floor with tears in his eyes.

"You killed him! You killed Wayne! Why, why? You didn't have to shoot him! Why did you do it? Ahh, ahh!" Crystal fainted.

60

On the Run

Jessie, limping, grabbed his big black bag in the closet and, before leaving the town house, looked at Crystal rocking back and forth on the floor next to Wayne's body, and said, "I'm sorry Crystal. You know I didn't mean to kill him. It was, uh, uh, an accident, but the cops ain't gonna believe me. I gotta get outta here until I can figure something out. I'm, I'm, uh, so sorry," said Jessie.

Crystal did not seem to hear anything Jessie said as she stared at Wayne, mumbling to herself. As Jessie's eyes watered and their salty contents rolled in his mouth, mixing with blood-tinged saliva, he ran outside and got in his Escalade parked in front of the town house.

After putting the key in the ignition he hit the steering wheel in a frenzy. "Damn, damn, damn, I'm a sick bastard! What have I done? I killed Wayne, I done fucking killed Wayne!" said Jessie. He let out a scream that vibrated off the truck's windows. When he gained composure, he sped off towards Lenox Avenue not really giving thought to his destination. After coasting a few blocks down the avenue, he lost it again.

"I didn't mean to do it, Wayne, I didn't mean to do it!" He banged like a mad man on the steering wheel. Suddenly, he heard tapping on the passenger side window that took him back to reality.

He was relieved when he saw that it was Roxanne instead of police coming to arrest him for killing Wayne. When he let down the window, Roxanne said, "Man that music must be good the way you were banging on that damn steering wheel."

Jessie was so caught up in his crazy emotions he never even heard the radio playing the rapper 50 Cents' song "Magic Stick." But he played along.

"What up, Roxanne? How ya doing?" said Jessie, trying his best to stay composed. Before he could even say anything else, she took it upon herself to get into the truck.

"I'm sorry to hear about what happened," she said. Her question scared Jessie as he wondered how news of Wayne being murdered had gotten out so fast.

"Who told you?" said Jessie, nervously.

"Oh, I ran into Marvin, and he told me that your mother had gotten real sick with stomach ulcers a few weeks ago and had to be taken to the hospital."

Jessie gasped a sigh of relief.

"Thanks for asking, Roxanne, my mother is all right. Matter of fact, I just left her," said Jessie.

"That's good to hear. So where you headed, stranger," said Roxanne, smiling from ear to ear.

By this time Jessie had made up his mind to go to his crib in Fort Lee, New Jersey, figuring only a chosen few even knew it existed, and the police would never find him there.

"I'm on my way to New Jersey. I just feel like I wanna get out of the city for a little while. Do you wanna come?" said Jessie, thinking having a little company could not make things any worse than they already were. And it would relax his mind while planning the next move. Plus, they could get high together and get his mind off the realization that he was a wanted man living on borrowed time.

But Jessie thought asking her to come had more to do with him not getting a chance to ejaculate due to Wayne's unexpected interruption of his sex session with Crystal. Before she answered, he was already on the George Washington Bridge headed to New Jersey, knowing she was down for anything.

When they arrived at his plush two-story brick house, Roxanne commented on how nice it looked. She had been there before but it was late at night and she was higher than a dust head on crack. Jessie bought the house because it had all the trappings of all the beautiful cribs that rappers floss in music videos. It had a spiral staircase, big ceilings, a Jacuzzi, step-in living room and top-of-the-line furnishings. The only difference between the rappers and himself was that he really owned everything. Red, who also owned several properties, helped him get it for a steal when the owner, possibly a rapper, went bankrupt. But, having all that now meant nothing to a condemned man.

"Roxanne, before we both go in the house, I need you to stay in the truck while I go check something out," said Jessie. He left the car and went inside.

Roxanne found it kind of strange, but that is not the only thing that happened to make her feel something was amiss. Since the moment she got into Jessie's Escalade, she realized he was not acting normal. But her thoughts shifted to a party mood when her favorite song, "Seven Days" by Mary J. Blige, came on the radio. As she sang, Jessie scoped out every room in his immaculate house.

When he reached the spacious master bedroom, the phone rang several times, but before he could pick it up it stopped.

This made him wonder who the caller could have been. Red? Crystal? These were the only people who know the number. The police?

Then Jessie's eyes drifted to the half-ounce of Purple Haze beside the phone on the dresser drawer. Leftovers of a hot night and a hot honey. He reached in his pocket, pulled out a blunt and rolled a fat spliff, lighting it up as he went to the truck. Little did Jessie know that while he was in the house Roxanne had heard about a $50,000 reward being offered to the person who could give the police information that led to the arrest and conviction of murder and suspected cop-killer Jessie Thompson. The announcer said that Jessie had been tied to the murder through forensic evidence—they found a straw used by Jessie to sniff cocaine in a bathroom stall.

When she heard the broadcast, her palms got sweaty and her blood pressure went up like a contestant on the game show "The Price is Right" who had just guessed the answer to a $50,000 question.

At the same time that Jessie was knocking on the passenger side window telling her to get out of the truck, the attraction she thought she had for him went out the window.

She could not wait to call the police, but first she had to regain her composure so she wouldn't make Jessie suspicious.

"What's up, boo? Did I scare you?" said Jessie, as she got out of the truck.

"Nah, Jessie, I'm all right, it's just that looking at your beautiful place got me all excited and flustered," said Roxanne. "You know this is the first time you ever brought me here in the day time."

"Yeah, you're right," said Jessie, as she got out of the truck and he passed her the fat blunt.

The potent smoke helped ease his mind about killing Wayne.

Roxanne was relieved that he believed her quick lie. The blue bikini panties she wore sliced the thin fabric of her white and tight spandex capris on their way up the stairs leading to the house. When they got inside, Roxanne immediately went to the bathroom, hoping that a phone was still hooked up there. But it was gone, so she proceeded to take off all her clothes, except for blue pumps, blue bikini and matching bra set. Roxanne had a body to die for—34-28-36—and whenever she walked through a block, niggas lost their minds. And this is exactly what was happening to the guy in the next room.

As Roxanne entered the enormous living room, she spotted Jessie sitting on the plush black leather couch sniffing cocaine and staring at Al Pacino's *Scarface* on the fifty-one-inch plasma television screen. Jessie should have known that he was bugging out when he wondered if Al Pacino secretly wanted to screw his sister. For a moment Roxanne felt sorry for him, knowing that this might be his last day as a free man. But that did not deter her from keeping her greedy eyes on the prize. More money—his problems.

Jessie came up out of his deep stupor as Roxanne stepped right in front of him. Her plan was to rock him to sleep by sexing him to sleep, then dialing the lucky seven digits to the police hotline, putting in her bid—for the dough. Roxanne definitely had the skills to pull it off because behind her back guys called her "Blow Pop" for good reason.

"Jessie, stand up I want to tell you something," said Roxanne. Jessie smirked, breaking the tension.

"What do you wanna tell me, boo?" said Jessie as he stood up at attention.

Roxanne smiled and puckered up her succulent lips, then pulled down his baggy Sean John jeans and let them drop on his size 12 Timberland boots, revealing a long cock the same size as his big feet.

She then began to do what she was famous for—*slurp, slurp, caknop, caknop, slurp, slurp*—and at the same time taking the blunt out of his hand and then blowing weed smoke all over a throbbing cock. Her little twist to giving a "shot gun."

Jessie's legs shook and he dropped down on the couch and Roxanne stayed at the job at hand.

"Boo, baby, boo, baby," Jessie squirmed, busting off a mouthful and as sperm met tonsils, Roxanne drank every drip drop. Long ago, Roxanne found out that giving head was the cure for her tonsillitis.

She looked up at Jessie with a smile on her face and said, "That's what I wanted to tell you."

In a serious tone, Jessie said, "Roxanne, I got to tell you something, too."

The way he said it made her immediately sit down and put a comforting hand on his shoulder. "What's wrong, big man?" said Roxanne.

"I might be going away but before I do I want to make amends and apologize for your brother getting murdered in the drug game that I, myself, am a part of. I put that on me, my dead father and the streets."

Roxanne cried, then said, "Thank you, Jessie, but it's not your fault. People make choices."

"Nah, but still shorty didn't deserve that and I know you miss him a lot just by how you always talk about your brother. Me and my sister used to have a relationship like that but my sick ass messed it up."

Jessie's comment about his sister made Roxanne think about the rumblings on the streets that he was sexing his sister. Roxanne thought maybe that was why he said, "My sick ass." All of this, plus Jessie bringing up her brother, almost made Roxanne forget to ask, "Jessie, where are you going?"

"Roxanne, this is for your own good. I don't want you to get caught up in my drama, so it's best that I don't tell you," said Jessie.

"Jessie, you can trust me," said Roxanne.

"Sure I can, boo, but it's better this way."

Then they got high and Jessie pounded her like there was no tomorrow. After having sex, just like Roxanne anticipated, Jessie drifted off to sleep. So she thought.

Roxanne slowly got out of the king-size bed in the master bedroom, grabbed her blue bikini, all of her clothes and tiptoed like a cat burglar to the kitchen. As she dialed the cop shot hotline, she rationalized snitching on him—that any sick individual who is capable of fucking his own sister did not deserve to be on the streets. She was also agitated because Crystal had whipped her ass one time. Roxanne did not care about a cop being murdered. All she wanted was the reward.

"Hello, my name is Roxanne Mitchell and I heard the bulletin on the radio about the reward for the cop ki—" *Crack, bam, boom!* Jessie clobbered her with a bat after sneaking up from behind. Then he snatched the phone from beside unconscious Roxanne and placed it on the receiver.

He screamed, "You dirty cum-drinking, conniving bitch! Red always told me trust a bitch as far as you can see them."

Jessie kicked Roxanne in the stomach; she did not move. What looked like blood mixed with a load of cum oozed out of her mouth. Then he ran to the living room and turned on the television, trying to see if there was a news report about him killing Wayne.

As he sat there nervously watching the news and sniffing cocaine, after a few minutes a commercial came on promoting the benefits of getting plastic surgery. For some strange reason flashes of the old guy in the restaurant kept popping up in his head and he thought it was the cocaine bugging him out.

Then all of a sudden something came to him. He put the cocaine on the television set, ran to the bedroom and searched frantically in his walk-in closet for some old issues of *Fed* magazine, and found the copy he was looking for. Fumbling through the pages, he found the article. The writer's story talked about a legendary drug dealer that snitched on the Harlem drug syndicate back in the day. In the story, the writer also had a picture of the guy with a cigar in his mouth, posing in gangster mode.

"You rat bastard, you thought you could fool the kid. I can spot a snitch's little beady eyes anywhere," said Jessie out loud, laughing his head off like a crazy Charles Manson.

61

Off Limits

As Wayne lay dead on his back leaking from bullet holes and looking more like he was in a deep sleep than someone on their way to meet his maker, the police, conducted their investigation.

After all the questions had been asked, crime scene forensic evidence gathered, and the body taken to the morgue, the police left the town house to hunt down Jessie, never telling Kathy about the evidence that was found at Club Speed that linked him to the killing of one of their own.

Kathy decided to get to the bottom of the bloody murder scene that had managed to turn her family's world upside down. She called out to Crystal, who was in the bathroom staring blindly at her reflection in the mirror. She was trying to come to grips with the part she played in being the catalyst to someone winding up dead.

"Crystal come out here, I want to talk to you," said Kathy.

"Okay, Ma, I'll be right there!" yelled Crystal, trying to gather her composure by throwing cold water on her face.

Then she left the bathroom and took a seat at the kitchen table while Kathy stood by a window surrounded by a bunch of vases and colorful roses. The pleasant scent of rose petals did nothing to soothe their frayed emotions.

"Crystal, I listened to every word that you told that homicide detective, and I figured that you were trying to protect your brother, but right now I want you to tell me what really happened, and I mean everything, do you hear me?"

"Yeah, Ma, I hear you," said Crystal.

"So what are you waiting for? Tell me what happened," said Kathy as the tension and the ticking of the black and gray owl clock on the wall lent an eerie feel to the room.

"Me and Jessie were making love, uh, I mean having s-s-sex and Wayne ca-ca-caught us, and they started fighting, and Jessie shot him," said Crystal, nervously trying to get it all out. She never once made eye contact for fear of what her mother's eyes would reveal, so she slowly picked at the pink polish on her pristine, manicured nails.

Crystal did not see her mother's disgusted look that revealed that she was not shocked by Crystal's incest revelation.

Kathy had secretly suspected for a long time that something unsavory was going on in her household. Her motherly instinct told her that the sibling bond her children shared went way beyond the ordinary. Ever since Jessie and Crystal were kids, Kathy picked up on that they both acted more like lovers than individuals who shared the same blood line.

One time, when Jessie was eleven years old, she caught him rubbing his sister's neck in an erotic manner while they watched cartoons. She sternly told him a brother is not supposed to touch his sister that way. Then, a week later, she caught them playing hide-and-seek and humping on each other in a closet. Back then, as Kathy beat them senseless, she wondered if things would have been different if their father had been around instead of in prison.

She tried her best to beat the forbidden lust out of them, but she had not succeeded. Deep down, in the back of Kathy's brain where she held her deepest secrets—things that she did not even consciously want revealed to herself— hid a family's nasty secret. Incest. While trying not to let her mixed-up emotions get the best of her, Kathy said, "You mean Jessie shot Wayne by accident."

Crystal, picking up on the clear message that was being sent through her mother's eyes that indicated that the incest part of the story was off limits, said, "Oh yeah, it was an accident. Jessie and Wayne were fighting and things got out of hand, and they both fell on the fl-fl-floor and they both grabbed for the g-g-gun that was hanging out of Jessie's gym bag and it went o-o-off. Wayne got shot. I'm sorry, Ma, uh, uh, I'm sorry, it's all my fault," said Crystal, as tears flowed down her face.

Kathy walked over to her daughter and provided much-needed motherly comfort. Then, after gaining some mental clarity, she said, "Baby, here's what we are going to do. No matter how hard the police try to manipulate you to change your story about all this happening, because of two friends horseplaying and a gun going off by accident, you stick to your story. Although our family loved Wayne with all our hearts, Jessie going to jail is not going to bring him back. Another thing, when people on the street start getting nosey and asking questions, you say your lawyers advised you not to say anything. Plus girl, I don't have to tell you that what goes on in this house stays in this house. Do you hear me, Crystal?"

"Yes, Ma, I hear you," said Crystal, wiping away her tears.

62

Pastor Lee

As Kathy tidied up the town house, trying to ease her nerves, her friend, Sheila, yelled out frantically, "Kathy did you hear the radio report? There's an all points bulletin broadcasting every five minutes saying the police are now looking for Jessie for killing a cop."

Kathy listened intently knowing the words her friend just spoke meant a death sentence for her son. When Wayne was killed, Kathy thought Jessie had a chance of not being charged with murder because she thought it was a case of self-defense. But when he went on the run and people on the streets said Jessie lost his mind and was on a killing spree, she could figure out that the worst was yet to come. Now this. Anybody with a brain knew killing a cop meant the other police had license to shoot the culprit down in the streets. Cop justice.

As tears rolled down Kathy's face, she said, "They must be mistaken. My son would never do that. He's not a killer."

Her own words made her cringe. The stress and pressure of the last days events were too much for her to handle, making her lose it.

"Damn, damn, damn, Sheila, they gonna kill my boy, those bastards gonna kill my boy. God help me," screamed Kathy, shaking uncontrollably and sounding like the mother on the back-in-the days sitcom *Good Times*.

Crystal, who had been listening to the whole conversation in her bedroom, rushed to help Sheila comfort her mother. As Sheila rubbed Kathy's back and Crystal held her mother's hand, she said, "Ma, everything is gonna be all right. We just have to find out what's going on and get Jessie to turn himself in."

"Yeah, Kathy, and we can get Pastor Lee to help us, he has a lot of powerful connections in high places. He'll know exactly what to do," said Sheila, acting like she had just solved all their problems.

Crystal turned her face away from the both of them because she did not want them to see her look of pure disgust.

Unbeknownst to her mother and Sheila, when Crystal first thought she was pregnant while feeling down and depressed and not knowing what to do, she went to seek guidance from Pastor Lee at their church. Instead of offering help and assistance, he tried to take advantage of her fragile emotional state by asking for sex. So she did not agree with Sheila's suggestion of going to see the sleazy pastor one bit. But she stayed silent for fear of having to reveal anything about her traumatic experience.

"Everything is gonna work out just fine, Kathy, just let me call our pastor and set up a meeting," said Sheila as she headed to the kitchen of the town house to make the call.

* * *

"Sheila, baby gal, the way you sung that solo last Sunday in chuch had me dancing like I was living in sin at some club on a Friday night. You sho' is a gifted baby gal," said Pastor Lee, grinning and slyly looking at her ass.

Kathy noticed her daughter's look of pure disdain as they entered his plush office where he sat in a big burgundy and gold velvet chair that was fit for a king.

Pastor Lee stood up in his two thousand dollar blue pin-striped suit and spoke as if he was preaching to the church choir. "I'm ve-ry sor-ray for the chu-ch fam-lee to be meeting under such troubling cir-cum-stances, but I have made a few phone calls to the pro-par authorities and they have expressed their feelings about resolving this hare situation without it resort-ing to anymore vi-o-lance," said Pastor Lee with a Southern twang as everybody took a seat in his church office.

"Pastor Lee, I don't think that was a good idea for you to call anybody without first talking to my mother," said Crystal, in a tone that showed her anger.

"Oh, baby gal, you sure have grown up since the last time I seen you," said Pastor Lee.

Crystal immediately interrupted him before he could finish. "No disrespect but can we forget all that and handle the serious situation at hand."

"Calm down, young lady, I know what we are going through, but please don't talk that way to the pastor. He's just trying to help us," said her mother.

Sheila nodded in agreement as she shot Crystal a nasty look for disrespecting her secret sex partner. While looking at Crystal, a fake smile graced the pastor's face, then he continued. "Baby gal, I mean Crystal, you have ev-ray reason to be an-gray, being how the press has been par-traying your bruda, making ole boy out to be some deran-ged psychopath. We all know that Jes-say's a good boy and he will give eva-body some reasonable explanations for all the things he's been accused of doing, once we get ole boy to sa-ren-da."

Pastor Lee did not believe a bit of the words he just spoke. He thought Jessie was just another violent young thug wreaking havoc on the community, just like his father before him. Pastor Lee thought that once Jessie was apprehended the streets would be a little bit safer without one less street thug to worry about. As the pastor spoke, Kathy's thoughts drifted off wondering if her son was being shot down by cops on some dirty street as they sat there in a church. Deep down she knew more action and less talking was the only way they would stand a chance at saving her son's life. She nervously began to speak. "Pastor, I don't care what anybody thinks. My son Jessie's innocent of everything he's being accused of. I'm not gonna sit here and tell you my son is some choir boy, but my boy ain't kill no cop. They just want to put another black man in jail because they think that's where all black men are supposed to be. But not my son, you hear me, not my son."

Then the tears left her eyes like waterfalls. Crystal, who had read the sleazy pastor's thoughts concerning her brother, angrily looked at him.

"Pastor Lee, what do you think we should do? We don't want the cops to kill Jessie," said Sheila in a voice cracking with emotion.

"First of all, baby gal, I need y'all to tell me where Jessie is hiding. And then I can personally talk to my good friend, Mayor Robert Edwards, so he can arrange for Jessie to sa-ren-da peacefully."

Crystal lost her composure and screamed, "We don't know where my brother is, and besides we have not even made up our minds yet about exactly what it is we really want to do! And we all know that so-called mayor of ours don't care nothing about us black folks and I don't trust him or y—"

"Crystal, please, please stop it. Pastor Lee is not our enemy. He's only trying to help the situation," said Sheila, looking at Kathy for support.

Kathy slowly got up out of the chair she was sitting in and angrily looked at her daughter, and then at the pastor, who by this time was standing and staring hard at Crystal.

Then she said, "Pastor Lee, you have been a big help and I'm going to take everything you said under consideration, but at this time I feel I need to think things over carefully. When I figure out what I want to do, you will be the first person I call."

Pastor Lee, eager to find out Jessie's whereabouts so that he could claim the $50,000 reward given to anybody who dropped a dime on a cop killer, and also hoping for some good press to possibly help his secret political aspirations, tried to persuade Kathy to see things his way. "I seriously think that you are making a big mistake by putting all of this off. The longer you wait works to Jessie's disadvantage," said Pastor Lee, grasping at the last straw.

"Well, we'll just have to put it all in God's hands," said Crystal, sarcastically, as they walked out of the church office.

63

Fiddy Thousand

On the same day and time, members of the NYPD were pulling their cars up on all the known drug locations in the city, informing all the drug dealers that not a drop or morsel of drugs would be sold until Jessie was apprehended. Basically everything was being shut down.

"Yo, Marvin, come here," said Detective O'Grady. "I want you to listen and listen good because I'm only gonna say this shit once. Your pal, Jessie, has stepped over the line. Now going around killing other drug dealers is one thing, but when you kill a cop it's gonna be hell to pay. If it takes me and my partners coming out here and busting heads open, that's what we will do. You and I both know that we have a sweet arrangement and those of you who pay your gratuities get free rein out here. But all that shit will come tumbling down like the Twin Towers if we don't arrest that asshole Jessie," said Detective O'Grady.

Marvin looked up and down the avenue to see if anybody was watching, then he nonchalantly nodded his head without saying a word.

This pissed off Detective O'Grady and he slapped the crap out of Marvin, making him rub his face and wince from the stinging pain.

"Yo, O, man why you do that man?" said Marvin.

"Shut up, chump. Now you spread the word that the

heat is on," said Detective O'Grady, loudly. Suddenly, some-one from a third-floor window screamed, "Get outta hare muhfuckers, 'cause ain't nobody heard, seen, or know jackshit about nuttin'. Kill 'em all. Kill 'em all."

Before Detective O'Grady got in the black Crown Victoria, he looked up and yelled, "Get a job, you good-for-nothing lowlife."

Everything his partner, Kennedy, witnessed and heard while sitting on the driver's side of the vehicle made him laugh hysterically as he pulled off, mimicking Marvin winc-ing and holding his face.

Marvin immediately placed a call on his Samsung cell phone. "Yo, Skeeter, that cracker O'Grady just slapped the motherfuckin' taste buds out my mouth because crazy-ass Jessie done spazzed out and killed a cop. Nigga, I almost came close to John blazin' one of those pussies myself a minute ago. Don't no bumbleclod put his dirty hands on me. Especially not no corrupt-ass cop who we be hittin' off."

"Yeah, son, I feel you big time, but what else did that fool O'Grady say," said Skeeter, as some pretty chick mas-saged his neck.

"Man, he said that until Jessie gets caught the po-po was gonna shut everything down. So what do you think we should do? Plus, I heard from some people on the streets that there is a $50,000 reward out on Jessie. I don't even have to go into again about our discussions of running our own shit," said Marvin.

"Yo, son, all this shit plays right into our hands. Let me make a few phone calls and put a few things in motion and I'll get right back at you," said Skeeter. Then he hung up the phone.

"Popi chulo, when you get the fiddy dousand, please popi can you buy me a mink coat and Couch bag?" said the Puerto Rican chick in a voice that sounded like the actress Rosie Perez.

"You stupid bitch, it's called a Coach bag, not a couch bag, and keep your nosy ass outta my business. Now suck my dick bitch, 'fore I stomp a mud hole in that big ass of yours."

"Okay, popi, I'm so sorry, popi, I always treat you real good, popi chulo," said the Puerto Rican bonita as she sucked him off in a frenzy.

After blowing her back out, she fell asleep and Skeeter went to the bathroom in his condo and placed a call. "Man, I just got off the phone with that conniving-ass nigga, Marvin. Remember what we kicked around?" said Skeeter.

"Yeah, I remember. That's all that's been occupying my mind. I can't wait to eliminate Marvin, Jessie, and all them lame-ass niggas, so we can be running shit," said Skeeter's cousin, Smitty. Smitty was wearing a faded black T shirt with the words "Stop Snitching" in white letters on it.

"Whoa, whoa, slow down nigga, stop speeding. That's why you broke now. Just shut the fuck up and listen. I want you to talk to that blabbermouth Sheila you be boning. Ain't she Jessie's mother's best friend?

"Yeah, Skeeter, they cool like that," said Smitty.

"Okay, here's the deal. That pussy Marvin just told me the cops are looking for Jessie for murdering a cop and Wayne, and there's a $50,000 reward. All you got to do is talk to your blabbermouth jumpoff and get her to find out where Jessie is hiding, then get back to me," said Skeeter, secretly doubting his dumb cousin could pull it off.

"Brother man, your wish is my command," said Smitty, then he hung up.

Smitty went back inside the dirty, roach-infested SRO and stared at a mouse eating a cockroach.

Even though his brain was toasted from too much crack usage, he suddenly had a brainstorm. He ran back to the hallway phone and did what sheisty niggas are known to do by calling a cop who pays good for useful information.

"Hey, hey, hey, what's up, Officer Franco?" said Smitty.

"Oh, I'm all right, Smitty. Why do I have the honor of receiving a call from the number one guy in the know?" said Officer Franco, smiling as he sat at his desk drinking a hot cup of coffee. In Officer Franco's book of confidential informants, Smitty was listed as Charlie Yap-Yap.

"Thanks for the compliment," said Smitty. "Man, do you remember my big-baller cousin Skeeter, who's been letting a good nigga like me starve?"

"Yeah, what gives?" said Officer Franco.

"Well, he just hipped me to the fact that you guys are looking for Jessie for killing Wayne and one of the boys in blue, and there is a $50,000 reward. Is that correct?"

"Yeah, we looking for him and I would love to be the one to put a bullet in his ass. Do you know where he is?" said Officer Franco, as blood rushed to his head.

"Nah, but I can definitely find out, and when I do, will I be entitled to the reward money?"

The police officer, trying his best not to seem overly anxious for any information that could possibly land him a cop killer, and a promotion to detective slowly said, "Yes you will, but we got to move quick."

Smitty, with his mouth wide open, smiled like one of those Hee Haw rappers and said, "Thanks, Officer Franco. And to show my appreciation, when I get my reward money, this time I'm gonna be the one hitting you off with money. And my cousin ain't gonna get a dime," said Smitty, unknowingly sounding like a little kid.

64

Sticky Hines

A person who has nothing to lose can really wreak havoc when certain buttons get pushed. Under the wrong set of circumstances anything can happen. And ever since the day Lorenzo chose to snitch, his son had been forced to bear the full brunt of his dastardly deeds.

Although the real reason for all of Jessie's pain was dead and gone, his death still did not quench his thirst for revenge because he did not have the privilege of killing his father. And when hateful feelings fester, nothing good can come out of that. Enter Sticky Hines.

Since Jessie was a little kid, everybody in the hood talked about how Sticky Hines, who was Harlem's biggest drug supplier back in the days, got busted by the feds and snitched on the whole Harlem drug syndicate—even Pop Swayze—to save his own ass. In return for his cooperation, the feds made sure he did minimum jail time, kept most of his drug proceeds and received plastic surgery in order to fool all the people who wanted to kill him.

Sticky Hines' story was legendary in the hood.

* * *

People say you can fool some of the people some of the time but you cannot fool all of the people all of the time. In this particular case, Jessie fit in the latter part.

He once was blind but now he saw what had been staring in his face for far too long. Jessie thought back to the times he ate at Sylvia's, his favorite restaurant, and an old man would always stare at him. Then after eating, the man passed by his table on the way out and offered strange advice. Jessie never really quite understood why. One time the old guy was seated at the next table with a gorgeous young lady when the maitre d' and a waitresses brought a chocolate cake that had "Happy Birthday Mr. Leroy Jenkins" (Jessie knew now he was Sticky Hines) written on it with a bunch of candles. Remembering the old guy's name, Jessie immediately called the restaurant using a ploy about needing to know if they had his correct address in their registry. The person that answered the phone stupidly provided the address that they had listed for Leroy Jenkins. Jessie's heart pumped faster after retrieving the information needed to put his plan in motion.

In Jessie's twisted, drug-fueled frame of mind, killing Sticky Hines would be a justifiable payback for all the pain, drama and chaos that his father's messed-up snitch legacy had caused him. As Jessie headed to the door with a cache of weapons, he added a remix to his dead father's favorite *Super Fly* song, called "Freddie's Dead." "Sticky's dead doon-doon-dun, that's what I said, doon-doon-dun, Sticky's dead . . . "

65

On the Road to the Snitches

The last thing Jessie wanted to hear on his way to Sticky's house was the fool driving right beside him in a banged-up hooptie yelling, "It's on fire tonight!" to some rap song playing on his radio.

"I could just kill a man!" yelled Jessie talking to no one but himself as he slowly made his way to give Sticky Hines a welcome back to the game party accompanied by fireworks. His head ached like it was going to explode.

* * *

Sitting in his truck in the parking lot of a colony of big beautiful homes and meticulously manicured lawns, Jessie patiently awaited the arrival of Sticky Hines.

While parked beside Beemers, Lexuses, and Benzes, he decided to make a call on his cell phone.

The phone rang a few times and went straight to voice mail. "Hello, this is the King Don Master Ruler Wayne. Sorry I'm kinda busy right (*swoo, swoo*) now, but if you just (*swoo, swoo*) leave a message (*cah-cah*), I promise I'll get at ya, holla."

Jessie hung up and called repeatedly to listen to Wayne's voice and the sound of him inhaling and coughing, without saying a word.

His head pounding, Jessie called again and said, "Wwwwayne I d-didn't mean ta-ta to p-pull that trigger, it was a terrible accident. Even I don't know why I was doing the fucked up shit you caught me doing. I know you and C-c-crystal loved each other and my sick ass messed it up. Please f-faf-forgive m—" Jessie closed the cell phone before he could finish and threw it on the back leather seat of the Cadillac Escalade.

Tears rolled down his face as he reminisced. "Jessie, we gon' be like Shaq and Kobe when we make it to the NBA— we gon' be unstoppable," he remembered Wayne saying.

"Wayne, you and I both know I can't play no damn basketball."

"Well, then you gon' be my agent."

"Yo, Chauncey, ain't that little yellow nigga Lorenzo's son?"

"Yeah, that's his seed."

"Yo, shorty, come here—*slap, slap, slap*—now get your little begging ass outta my face and go get some money from your snitch-ass father in prison."

"I will kill a motherfucker, kill a motherfucker," whispered Jessie to the 9 mm automatic in his hand.

When Jessie looked up to the other end of the long parking lot he spotted a brand-new black Jaguar being parked and a brown-skinned bald headed man with an expensive gray suit, white shirt and red bow tie getting out of the car.

Jessie slowly got out of his truck, grabbed the bag of weapons and slid the strap on his shoulder. The shiny silver 9 mm automatic gripped tightly in his hand, he headed to the beautiful brick colonial house and hid behind a bushy apple tree as he waited for Sticky Hines.

Sticky Hines, walking with the grace of a president and not a care in the world, made it to the lacquered oak front door, then opened it. Before he even knew what was happening, Jessie bumrushed his cushy world by pointing the 9 mm automatic to his head.

"Nigga, get yo bitch-ass inside, this time I'm gonna be doing the talking," said Jessie.

Sticky, caught off guard, did as he was told and said nothing as he was led into the huge living room with expensive furnishings.

Then Jessie kicked him straight up the ass and watched him fall on the plush eggshell white carpet. While Sticky Hines lay there, both of their eyes briefly met and they stared at each other like two boxers getting ready to square off. Jessie KO'd the eyeball battle by pointing the gun at Sticky Hines and motioning him to get up. He did, while never uttering a word. As Jessie led him to the dining area connected to the living room, he grabbed a plush white and black velvet dinette chair and pushed Sticky Hines down on it. Then he reached inside the bag with the weapons and pulled out rope and tape to tightly tie up and put across Sticky Hines' mouth.

A neighbor, who from a house across the street had witnessed Jessie taking Sticky Hines hostage, had called the police.

"Yo, Sticky, did your heart start pumping Kool-Aid when you felt that cold steel on that big noggin of yours? You can't tell me you didn't think this was a put 'em up, stick 'em, ha ha, stick 'em," joked Jessie, using a line from a classic rap song.

At that point Sticky Hines realized the guy standing in front of him was a nut case, so he tread lightly.

"Listen here, asshole, I got some good news, and I got some bad news. I'll start with the good news. First of all, you snitch bastard, we're gonna start this off the same way your good friends, the feds, do. This is more like what is it they call it? Yeah, I got it, a 'debriefing' before we get down to business," said Jessie as he poked Sticky Hines in the face with the butt of the 9 mm automatic.

Jessie heard someone on a bullhorn outside the house say, "Jessie, let your hostage go and come out with your hands up."

From the window Jessie saw people and police outside.

He let off a few shots, shattering part of the window. Then he yelled, "If you come in here, there's plenty more where that came from."

He walked back to Sticky Hines, as if nothing had happened and continued his questions.

"Mr. Hines, you know how the feds say we can do this the easy way or we can do this the hard way, it's all up to you. Well the same rule applies here. If you want to make things easy on yourself, all you have to do is do what I say and everything is gonna be okay. That's the good news. Now the bad news is, Mr. Sticky Hines, slash feds' favorite informant, you got one chance and one chance only to lie to me when I ask you some important questions that I really need answered, and you're a dead man," said Jessie in a deadly serious tone. Then he slapped Sticky Hines across the side of his face with the gun.

"I'm truly sorry, Mr. Hines, for being so disrespectful, being that you were kind enough to invite me into your beautiful home without an invitation." Jessie laughed hysterically like the crazy man he had become. "By the way, I would like to express my sincere condolences for hitting you, but to tell you the truth, I can't mess up that new face of yours any worse than it already is. Man, you must have gotten your plastic surgery at the same place Michael Jackson went 'cause they messed up real bad. Y'all couldn't fool the kid 'cause I can spot a snitch's little beady eyes anywhere. Don't say nothing man, I know exactly what you're thinking. Man, won't this fool get to the questions so that we can get all this crap over with." Jessie laughed.

"Okay, here it goes. Why did you snitch on all your home boys? Damn, wait a minute. Oh, how stupid of me. I must be getting senile like you. A brother can't talk with his mouth taped up. My bad. Let me take that shit off."

In one quick move, Jessie pulled the tape off his mouth. Sticky Hines shrieked. This made Jessie laugh while imitating the same sound.

"Okay, Mr. Sticky Hines, let's get down to business. I got a few questions for your bourgeois ass and you betta think real hard 'cause the answers you give could mean life or death. Do you hear me, fool?" said Jessie, losing his cool.

Sticky stared at him real hard and said, "Yes, I hear you."

"Now that we got that shit out the way, tell me what type of person rats out his own friends?" said Jessie.

"A no-good slimy bastard who does not care about anybody but himself and hates being jailed, plus I am claustrophobic and I cannot stand being locked up," he said.

His blunt answer caught Jessie off guard because he expected to hear him cry the blues and cop a sorry plea.

"Nigga, you got some nerve. You mean to tell me you didn't even care about what harm your snitching would cause your wife, kids and family?" said Jessie, putting his finger on the trigger. "I want to know a snitch's mind-set, and who could be better to provide the answers than Sticky Hines, the king snitch of them all."

"Quiet as it's kept—nah, I was just trying to cover my own ass and besides I did not even have time to think about that. The feds was throwing football numbers at me. I would have sold my soul to the devil if it could have kept me from going to prison. Young'un, let me hip you to something. One of the first laws of nature is self-preservation. So ain't nothing sacred, and aint' nothing secret," said Sticky Hines.

"You see, that's why bitch niggas like you should be tortured and burned at the stake. Everything is all love, love, when you out there selling all the drugs, making the fast money, buying all the fly shit and fucking all the hoes. But the minute you get caught ya turn cold pussy and start yapping yo jaws and singing to po-po," said Jessie speaking the hateful words he wished he could have had the chance to tell his father.

Then Jessie's eyes started playing tricks on him and Sticky Hines's round face became blurred and the crazy voices inside his head told him to *bam-bam! Take that, you yap-*

ping bastard, as he smashed the butt of his gun into Sticky's mouth, knocking out a few teeth.

Sticky grimaced and spit out teeth and blood by Jessie's feet, making Jessie hit him again in the face, cracking the glass of his expensive Christian Dior eyeglasses.

Although Jessie could not see Sticky Hines's eyes he was still glaring in defiance.

"Oh, I'm so sorry for that, Mr. Sticky, please accept my sincere apologies. Okay, chump, here's where the fun begins and, like I said before, you better think hard about your answers. What was the point of all that crap you used to tell me in the restaurant?" said Jessie.

Sticky, finding it real hard to talk with a swollen mouth and busted jaw, tried his best. "Jess—" said Sticky.

"Don't say my name, chump," said Jessie.

"Whatever, from the moment, uh, I laid eyes on you in Sylvia's restaurant, uh, uh, I knew you were a drug dealer and, even though I'm not in the hood, I still know what goes on and people talk and, uh, uh, your name is in the atmosphere," said Sticky.

"Yeah, I know people talk," said Jessie, sarcastically.

Sticky spit out a glob of blood, which cleared his throat, and he continued. "My main reasoning for saying something to you was my way of trying to save your punk ass from the pitfalls of the drug game. And if you don't know by now, it's prison or death."

Sticky's "punk ass" comment enraged Jessie and without thinking he grabbed a Tech Nine automatic out of his bag of artillery and emptied the clip into Sticky.

Jessie yelled, "Damn, why did I do that? I killed my own damn hostage."

Luckily for Jessie, the Tech Nine automatic had a silencer on it so the police outside had no way of knowing what he just did.

But Jessie was still petrified.

66

Run, Jessie, Run

"Run, Jessie, run! Run, Jessie, run! Don't let them catch you like OJ," screamed the Shot 99 hip-hop station disc jockey.

"Yo, Bones, don't do that. Are you trying to get us in some more trouble with the FCC and those damn protesters," screamed his female sidekick, Destiny.

The Shot 99 disc jockeys and those on other stations said that Jessie's killing of a cop allegedly had something to do with police corruption and snitching. These are subjects that most people have strong feelings about. Listeners became vocal and supported Jessie.

All on the streets, places of business, and throughout the city, people yelled, "Run, Jessie, run!" Even when Pop Swayze heard on a drug den's radio, that there was a massive manhunt for Jessie. He yelled, "Run, Jessie, run, goddamit, run!"

Another dope fiend in the drug spot who had a box-head like Frankenstein, replied, "Shut the fuck up!"

"Go head wit' you self man, go head, 'cause if I hit you, I got to kill you and if I kill you, I got to cut you up into little pieces so the cops can't find your body. I'm dangerous maaaaaan. . . .," said Pop Swayze, looking like the bugged-eyed Chris Tucker.

"Prove it, nigga," said the dope fiend, swaying his head

back and forth.

Pop Swayze, looking to try out a new form of substance abuse therapy and defend his point of view, ran toward the guy. The cocaine in the guy's system gave him a boost of energy and he quickly moved out the way making Pop Swayze run face first into a brick wall.

The radio stations announced that the cop and Wayne had been killed and the police were on their way to apprehend Jessie at his hideaway in New Jersey. Then, after the cops heard from a witness that Jessie had arrived at Sticky Hines' house, everyone hurried there. A new millennium snitch posted that address on the Internet, so a lot of people, including Kathy, Crystal and Red headed there, too.

* * *

A huge crowd gathered. Crystal and Red stood by Jessie's Escalade, while Kathy paced back and forth. They tried to figure out how to stop the madness and prevent more casualties.

Crystal even thought that maybe if they made up a lie and told Jessie her water broke and she's about to have the babies, it might convince him to surrender. But, instead she hoped that her mother had the answer to their problems.

Kathy had had to overcome many adversities while raising her children. No matter what they did, it was clear that a mother's love has no boundaries and no limits when it comes to protecting and taking care of them—even if it meant lying, cheating or stealing. Kathy, like her daughter, had her own little something in mind that might help their situation. Was this the time to tell a deep dark secret about his father? But, how could she explain something to him that she herself had a hard time coming to grips with? Something so deep that she managed to trick herself into living a lie? Kathy understood that the truth was not going to set her son free, but maybe it would save his life.

"Red, I been thinking maybe if we tell Jessie the truth, we can end all of this before somebody else gets hurt or killed. We both know that most of his problems stem from Lorenzo's actions," said Kathy nervously.

Red immediately made the connection to what she was alluding and said, "Kathy, if we tell him it could possibly escalate the situation."

Crystal who stood by and was listening to their every word was totally dumbfounded to what they were talking about. "Tell Jessie what, ma?" she asked.

Kathy just looked at Red and paid her daughter no mind as she pondered his suggestion.

Knowing she had to do something, Kathy, at her wit's end, spotted a sharply dressed, blue pin-striped suited Mayor Robert Edwards at the end of the parking lot. He was standing by Chief of Police Patrick Miller and Pastor Lee who had a stupid tap-dancing grin on his face.

A few feet away, stood Fort Lee Mayor Gregory Perkins, New Jersey police officers, who were in charge of the crime scene because it was their jurisdiction. They welcomed help from the New Yorkers to apprehend the cop killer. Other bystanders hung around the parking lot and areas that were not cordoned off by the police. They speculated that Jessie might go out in a blaze of glory, or that he was a victim of his father's snitch legacy.

Kathy quickly made her way over there and poured her aching heart and soul out to the mayor, asking him to spare her son's life.

Mayor Robert Edwards, who always sided with the police, in this rare case happened to be receptive to Kathy's plight. The reason being he was receiving a lot of backlash from a police "driving-while-black" scandal that threatened to cause him a lot of the black vote in the next election.

Through no small feat, Kathy convinced Mayor Edwards to let Red, whom Jessie respected to the fullest, an opportunity to try and convince her son to surrender. New Jersey authorities agreed to the plan.

67

Yo, Son

When Red strode over to Sticky Hines's house, a sharp-shooting cop was waiting in the tree for a chance to put a bullet in Jessie's head. He pointed his Remington 700 high-powered rifle with mounted scope in Red's direction. He secretly wished he could also shoot the light-skinned nigga who, he suspected by the complexion of his skin, maybe was fathered by a white man. The thought alone made his palms sweat and his fingers get itchy.

As soon as Red got to Sticky Hines's door he slammed the gold knocker against it and yelled real loud, "Yo, Jessie, it's me. Red! Open up!"

After a few seconds the door opened slightly, and a shirtless Jessie, whose muscular physique had gotten like the rapper, 50 Cents, from years of weightlifting, motioned with the 9 mm automatic for Red to quickly come inside and he did. Then he told Red to go to the other side of the room and he complied. That's when Red spotted the dead Sticky Hines, slumped in a chair, with a slight smile on his face.

But something else caught Red's eye as he then stared at Jessie while making his way over there. What he saw confirmed what he already knew in his heart to be true, but for a long time had a hard time coming to grips with. A distinctive birthmark in the middle of Jessie's chest that looked like a black lima bean confirmed Red's suspicions. Red and his own deceased father had the same birthmark in the same place. His mother had told him that it ran in his father's side of the family. Now everything made sense. The first time Lorenzo told him Kathy was going to have a baby he secretly thought that there was a chance he could be a father. Red's suspicions were not farfetched due to the fact that he had sex with Kathy a month before she hooked up with his best friend.

When Jessie was born he looked just like his mother but as he grew up he acted like Lorenzo, who had some of the same personality traits as Red. They all were strong-minded, tough and sure of themselves. Their only differences were Lorenzo craved the spotlight and sometimes did things without thinking. Through the years, Red tried to use the same rationale that had him thinking Jessie was his son, to disprove he was not. *I only had sex with her once, so she can't be pregnant by me . . .* he used to think.

It did not sit well with his conscience then or now. Deep down, Red knew that the reason for all of Jessie's pain and misery that led to him killing people had a lot to do with being the son of a snitch. Red felt a strong urge to reveal to Jessie that he was his father, but he did not know how his son would take it, or if it would add fuel to the fire. So he proceeded with caution.

This was something that Kathy chose not to do. When Kathy found out she was pregnant by Red, they had already broken up and she had fallen in love with Lorenzo. So, she made a conscious decision to lie and deceive Lorenzo by telling him he was the father of her unborn child. Red's own words of not wanting to bring any kids into this messed up world also played a big part in Kathy's deception.

"Red, I'm really sorry for us to be meeting under these circumstances but this is my battle not yours" said Jessie, pacing back and forth.

"If something happens to me, I need for you to tell my

mother and Crystal that I love them and that none of this bullshit—I mean ain't none of this their fault. I take full responsibility for all the crazy things I've done in this world, including killing my best friend. He didn't deserve to die. The world don't need another sick bastard like me walking around."

The vision of Wayne laying dead passed before Jessie's eyes, making him reach in his pocket with the hand that was not holding a gun to retrieve a small bag of cocaine.

Jessie quickly took a few hits. When the high potency of the drug attacked his brain the little voices inside his head started. *Stop talking, a real nigga would go out in a blaze of glory—real niggas do real things. Ya-ya-ya, fuck the police, ya-ya-ya, fuck the police.*

Jessie screamed at the top of his lungs, "Shut the fuck up, goddammit! Shut the fuck up!"

Red picking up on the fact that Jessie was drifting in and out of reality slowly made his way across the room plotting to save a man from himself.

"Red, I'm sorry for all the pain I've caused the streets but killing all of these rats plus the king rat of them all Sticky Hines should be more than enough to squash my father's debt for breaking the code of the streets. My father, that snitch bastard, I'd kill him right now if he wasn't already dead."

Red decided to use reverse psychology by playing into everything Jessie had expressed to him.

Jessie, son, I agree with you one hundred percent. Everything is paid in full. The streets been watching and I'm here to tell you that everybody been giving you your props for the position you took. To them your killing snitches was justifiable homicides. But, Jess, you remember when you was a little snotty-nosed kid and I taught you how to play poker because you were so curious about the game?"

"Yeah, Red, I remember."

"Well, Jess, what was one of the most important things I

told you about the game?"

In unison they said, "You got to know when to fold."

"Well, my man, the same rule applies here. You got to know when to fold, and now is the time."

As Jessie fumbled with the 9 mm in his hand and the Tech Nine on the table right beside him, for a moment he seemed to really be giving some serious thought to what Red just said.

Then he countered, "I understand a little bit what you just said Red, but that's a card game, this shit is different."

"But, Jess, aren't we all just dealing with the cards that's dealt to us? There are those that get dealt a good hand in life, and others like us who get the shaft."

"Red, there you go, always getting philosophical, just like my daddy dearest. If it wasn't for his bitch-ass yapping his jaws, I wouldn't even be in this predicament."

"Yeah, ain't life a bitch, but, Jess, it's too late to dwell on that now—'cause the cops are outside waiting to blow you away, and you don't want your family to have to witness that, do you? So let's end the madness. Don't give the cops what they want," said Red.

Just when Jessie decided to listen to Red's insistence that he give himself up, a cluster of smoke bombs shattered the front window of the living room, knocking down the colorful plants on the ledge and clouding the whole room, as bloody mayhem began to unfold.

At the same time, two cops bashed through the front door letting off shots from automatic weaponry. Jessie, in one swift move grabbed the Tech Nine off the table and returned rapid fire from both of his weapons.

Although the cops' bulletproof armor gear protected one of them, Jessie's split-second rapid fire and the forceful pressure from the blast of the bullets knocked him out cold. While the other cop, maybe wishing he stayed home and watched Court TV, got his face blown off.

When the smoke cleared, Jessie wiped his burning eyes

and spotted the cops lying on the living room's eggshell white carpet, leaking blood.

On the other side of the blood-splattered room sat an already dead Sticky Hines, shot again by his cop friends.

Before Jessie could gather his thoughts, he spotted Red leaning against a wall in a twisted position with a nasty gaping hole in his stomach. Jessie with guns in hand, ran to Red. He kneeled beside him, and with tears in his eyes said, "You gonna be all right, Red. Just hold on. You gonna be all right."

Red, with a pained expression on his face struggled to say something, "Je-Je-Jess, I uh-uh, I'm You . . you're fa . . ." Before he could finish, he made a gurgling sound, gasped and died. While Jessie rolled down Red's eyelids, he said, "Damn, what was Red trying to tell me?" As Jessie rose up from the bloodied floor, he saw that Red scribbled in blood, 'I'm your father.'

"Ahh, ahh," he screamed. "Lies on top of lies. Mama lied. Pops lied. Everyone lied!"

Hearing the terrible scream, Crystal, and her mother, wept as they wondered what had just happened inside.

Jessie, dazed, stared blindly at Red, blaming himself for his death. Feelings of gloom and doom overtook his brain. In a moment of clarity he gathered his frayed emotions, sensing there was no time to be going off the deep end. But that had already happened a long time ago. When his eyes drifted over to the unconscious cop lying on the floor, he immediately swept into action. He snatched the cop off the floor by his bulletproof vest, then woke him up by sticking a gun in his face.

"Yeah, nigga, no more sweet dreams. If you don't want the same thing to happen to you like your partner over there, you better do as I say. Do you understand what I'm saying, asshole? Know what I'm saying? Know what I'm saying?" said Jessie.

The nervous cop, quickly realizing that Jessie was not

playing with a full deck, said, "Loud and clear."

Then Jessie pointed the Tech Nine at the cop's back and led him to the living room's wide front shattered window.

"Listen here, you jake bitches, I done already killed one of you assholes and I won't hesitate to kill another one. I ain't got nothing to lose—so if y'all try anything stupid, you can kiss this fool right here good-bye," yelled Jessie.

As Jessie ranted, a cop positioned in a bushy tree a few hundred feet away jockeyed to get a clear shot. But his partner was in the way and he did not want to risk missing his target. So he waited with his finger on the trigger of his Remington 700 high-powered rifle, comforted in the fact that he had never missed a target and killing a cop-killer could be the sweetest of them all.

68

Shut Up, Shutting Up

Still ranting and raving, Jessie walked over to a black and white marble, well-stocked mini-bar with matching velvet-covered stool seats. He grabbed a fifth of Jack Daniels and removed the cap. As he swigged the strong whiskey, he sniffed line after line of cocaine until he had a burst of false courage. He recited something he had once memorized:

When all the chips are down and there's no escaping from Alcatraz, and telling the police to have a helicopter on the roof is not an option because you have an extreme fear of flying, but you still faking like you "ain't never scared," who you gon' call?

I hope it's not the ghostbusters because that done played out a long time ago. Mama, Mama.

Yeah, she brought you in this world but you been doing your dirt all by your lonely for far too long. That's why through fault of your own, somebody else might have to take you outta here.

So let's get ready to rumble. Rumble, young man, rumble.

Then Jessie defiantly said to the cop tied up in a chair, "I ain't never scared."

As the cop stared at a person in the throes of madness, Jessie walked past the shattered window and narrowly escaped being hit by the sharpshooter across the street.

"Jessie, would you mind if I add my little two cents in concerning this here situation?" said the cop, who desperately wanted to make it home to his beautiful wife and kids.

"Man, what the fuck you wanna say, man?" said Jessie with bass in his voice and still nervously pacing around the living room.

"Jessie, before I came busting in here I had a chance to talk to your mother, Kathy, and your pregnant sister. They are all shaken up and they want you to give yourself up before anybody else gets hurt. Your sister does not look well at all and I suggested we call EMS but she refused. By all that's been going on she could possibly miscarry out there. It doesn't look good, Jessie. This whole thing just doesn't look good," said the cop.

"Listen here, chump, you don't give a rat's ass about me and my family, so don't even try to run some psychological babble you learned in the police academy," said Jessie.

"Jessie, you don't really believe that, do you? But if you do, the question then is, do you care about your family?"

"Nigga, don't call me Jessie. You don't even know me like that. The last person who tried to get familiar is laying dead over there by that table," said Jessie, heading in Sticky Hines's direction.

Jessie kicked an already-dead and crumpled-over-in-a-chair Sticky Hines in the face making him fall on the carpet.

The cop grimaced then regained some of his composure and continued, "Somebody calling your name is the least of your worries because in a few minutes some more of my buddies are gonna be busting in here. So you betta make up your mind real quick about what you're gonna do," said the cop shuffling a little in his chair, trying to loosen the tight rope.

Jessie yelled, "Shut up, shutting up! Just shut the fuck up!" talking more to the voices in his head, as he pointed his gun at the cop.

263

"Jessie, Jessie, we got the whole area surrounded so come out with your hands up, you have no chance of getting away. The mayor who stands beside me has made a vow to your mother that you will not be shot and you will receive a fair trial. Please, Jessie, just put down the guns, let go all the hostages and surrender peacefully," yelled the black, pot-bellied police chief on the bullhorn.

The police chief despised street thugs because he thought they were all stupid and ignorant bastards. He also felt they messed everything up for the decent, law-abiding citizens and he would like nothing better than to give the signal to the sharpshooter to blow Jessie's brains out. But the mayor called the shots and he was just trying to get a nut.

69

Tumbling Down

As Jessie looked at Sticky Hines's broken nose and bashed in face all of a sudden it turned into Lorenzo's face. Jessie realized that no matter how many people he killed, it would never satisfy the twisted obsession of a son hell bent on paying back a bitch-ass father whose snitch legacy had wreaked pure havoc on his life, as well as those caught in the crossfire, Crystal included. He rationalized that the mental toll of it all possibly caused a brother to seek sexual comfort from all the stress, pain and misery from one of the people closest to him. His sister.

Just as Jessie finally decided to put the guns down and end all of the madness, detectives Kennedy and O'Grady slowly inched up the stairs of the basement with guns drawn. Before Jessie could put down the 9 mm automatic and Tech Nine to untie the cop, bullets sprayed in his direction. As Jessie let off a few shots and ran towards the front door, he never spotted Detective Kennedy, who had headed him off at the path and stuck a foot out, making his whole world come tumbling down.

As the gun fell out of Jessie's hands, both detectives gave him the beating of his life. Jessie did not utter a sound as he received painful blow after blow at the hands of detectives who hated him with a passion. The tied-up cop smiled as his comrades in blue knew what to do.

After the vicious beating they placed handcuffs to the last latch on Jessie's swollen wrists. He was a bloody mess. When the smiling cops escorted him outside, his mother screamed like she had just seen the battered face of a dead Emmit Till.

Crystal fell flat on her stomach, screaming, "Help me! Help me! I think the babies are coming early!

Jessie, semiconscious was placed in an emergency squad van and whisked away. Paramedics signaled for a second ambulance to aid his sister.

* * *

Bernard Graham, the head of the FBI, placed a call to the 25th precinct. After talking to Sergeant Gilbride and Chief of Police Patrick Miller to congratulate them on a job well done, he asked to talk with the detectives who had arrested Jessie.

When Detective Kennedy came to the phone, the head of the FBI said, "Congratulations and how's it going Detective Kennedy? I heard about your big take down of the city's number one fugitive. I must say you and your partner gave that asshole Jessie a beautiful face lift."

Both detectives laughed their heads off.

"He's lucky. That prick deserved nothing less than death for killing two cops," said Detective Kennedy. Then not forgetting the NYPD and feds' ongoing rivalry, he slyly added, "And to top it off he even killed that snitch Sticky Hines who was responsible for you getting that big position of yours." Detective Kennedy nudged his smirking partner O'Grady, who stood by.

The backdoor snide remark caught Agent Graham off guard, but he faked a slight chuckle and said, "I will not even get into telling you city boys what we do to cop killers 'cause it goes without saying."

Detective Kennedy jokingly said, "Mr. Biggs, everything is gonna be taken care of." He was offended that the dick head he just hung up on had the audacity to question the NYPD capabilities of meting out the proper and unauthorized punishment for cop killers.

After picking up his coffee off the desk, and seeing that nobody was looking, he scratched his smelly balls, took two quick sniffs, smiled and headed to Jessie's cell, followed by Detective O'Grady.

* * *

While waiting for Crystal to wake up after the emergency cesarean to save the twins, Kathy placed a call to Pastor Lee. She desperately wanted to find out why, after six hours, a brutally battered Jessie still had not arrived at the hospital. After a bunch of shucking and jiving and beating around the bush, the poor excuse of a pastor promised to look into it.

Because of not being told about Jessie's whereabouts before at the church, Pastor Lee secretly did not care one bit about Kathy and her family's terrible predicament, which cost him fiddy big ones. He felt Jessie was getting his just desserts. But he gladly provided Kathy lip service with a smile, thinking being her sympathetic ear during a trying time could possibly lead to a little bump and grind down the road.

69

Dead on Arrival

Pop Swayze, hungover and wearing a dirty used-to-be white T-shirt and crumpled clothes to match sat on a urine-stained bench in Mount Morris Park. He spotted an old white man walking a little spit-slobbering bull dog. The man was holding a *New York Post.*

"Hey, mister, would you mind if I take a quick look at the front page of your paper?" said Pop Swayze.

Even though the old white man was a bit surprised that the bum could read, he said, "Sure, no problem." When the paper was passed to Pop Swayze, and he got a look at the front page headline: SNITCH KILLER FOUND HUNG IN CELL. Pop Swayze, crumpled over as he yelled out, "Those dirty bastards!"

Street Slang Glossary

Ace boon coon: Good friend, trusted friend
Benjamins: Money. (Benjamin Franklin's picture on bills)
Bling: Diamonds, sparkling jewelry
Blue coat: Cop
Blunt: Marijuana rolled in cigar paper
Boo: Female, or male term of endearment
Booty call: Late night call for sex
Buggin': Losing one's mind
Ceelo: A dice game
Cheddar: Money
Chicken head: Whore, fast female
Chocolate Thai: potent marijuana
Cipher: Rappers coming together, vibing
C-note: $100 bill
Crackhead: Free-basing cocaine addict
Crazy crossover: Incredible dribbling skills
Crib: House or apartment
Cristal: Expensive champagne
DAT: Desk appearance ticket
Diddy bop: Walking with a bop, showing off
Dick Dastardly: Conniving, untrustworthy
Dimepiece: Beautiful female (scale of ten)
Drop a dime: Tell the cops; inform
Duji: Heroin
Funny style: Conniving, untrustworthy

GHB: Date rape drug
Girlfriend: Gun
Giving brain: Blow job, oral sex
Giving props: Respect
Homeboy; homegirl: Friend
Homo thug: Has sexual relations with men and women
Ice grilled: Mean stare-down, menacing look
Jumbos: Crack
Jump off: Sex partner
Keys: Kilos of cocaine
Kicking: Talking, conversing
Knuckle game: Fighting skills
Laying smack down: Beating up
Macked: Conning, persuading, getting over
Monster: AIDS
My bad: Admitting one's mistake
OG: Original gangster
OT: Out of town
Peasy: Knotted, uncombed hair
Pedico: Cocaine
Playa hata: Jealous person
Po-po: Police
Punk City: Protective custody
Purple Haze: Potent marijuana
Rat: Snitch, informant
Real nigga: Tough, street smart
Ride or die: Down for anything
Ringing bells: Talk of the town
Shotgun: Blowing marijuana smoke mouth to mouth
Shorty: A person of small stature, a young guy or kid
Snitch: Informant
Spaz: Flip out, lose it, bug-out
SRO: Single room occupancy
Sweated: Admired
Thing-thing (or thang-thang): Drugs
Wick wick wack: Not good, corny

About the Author

Michael Evans grew up on the Midtown Manhattan streets from 1979 to 1986 among the con men, pimps, prostitutes and hustlers. He excelled as a three-card monte player before he turned his life around. His autobiography, *It Was All in the Cards: the Life and Times of Midtown Mik*e is his first book.